All For You

Sunny Brook Farms, Book Four

USA TODAY bestselling author
RENEE HARLESS

All rights reserved.

ISBN: 978-1-962459-04-4

Copyright ©2024 Renee Harless

This work is one of fiction. Any resemblance of characters to persons, living or deceased, is purely coincidental. Names, places, and characters are figments of the author's imagination. All trademarked items included in this novel have been recognized as so by the author. The author holds exclusive rights to this work. Unauthorized duplication is prohibited and this includes the use of artificial programs to mimic and reproduce like works.

All rights reserved

Cover design by Porcelain Paper Designs

Editor: Kayla Robichaux

Proofreader: Crystal Clear Author Services

Paperback edition

All For You

Sunny Brook Farms, Book Four

USA TODAY bestselling author
RENEE HARLESS

Taking over the family farm in our small town was the only future I knew. But the never ending work left me with no social life and my virginity intact. Until my childhood rival graced us with his presence and was convinced he could help me with my...problem.

Owen Ramsey was an elite professional baseball player that left Ashfield without a backward glance. But when he was left at the altar, he sought refuge back in our town. I hated how he could simultaneously make my heart race and my hands fist. And I really despised how good he looked in a pair of baseball pants.

He needed my help just as much as I needed his. If I agreed to fake date him, he would help me snag the man I had my eye on and I would help convince his ex that he wasn't heartbroken.

But with his return to baseball looming, we realized maybe the hate we felt was really something more like love.

The fear of disappointing my family was too great, even though I craved something different for the first time ever. Owen was used to hitting balls out of the park, but I wasn't sure I was meant to be his home run.

For a list of content warnings in All For You, please check the book's page at http://www.reneeharless.com/allforyou

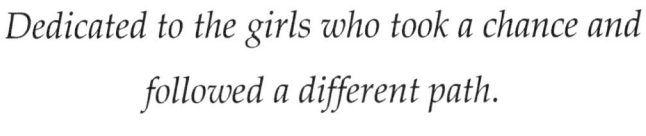

*Dedicated to the girls who took a chance and followed a different path.
And to the wallflowers… this one is for you.*

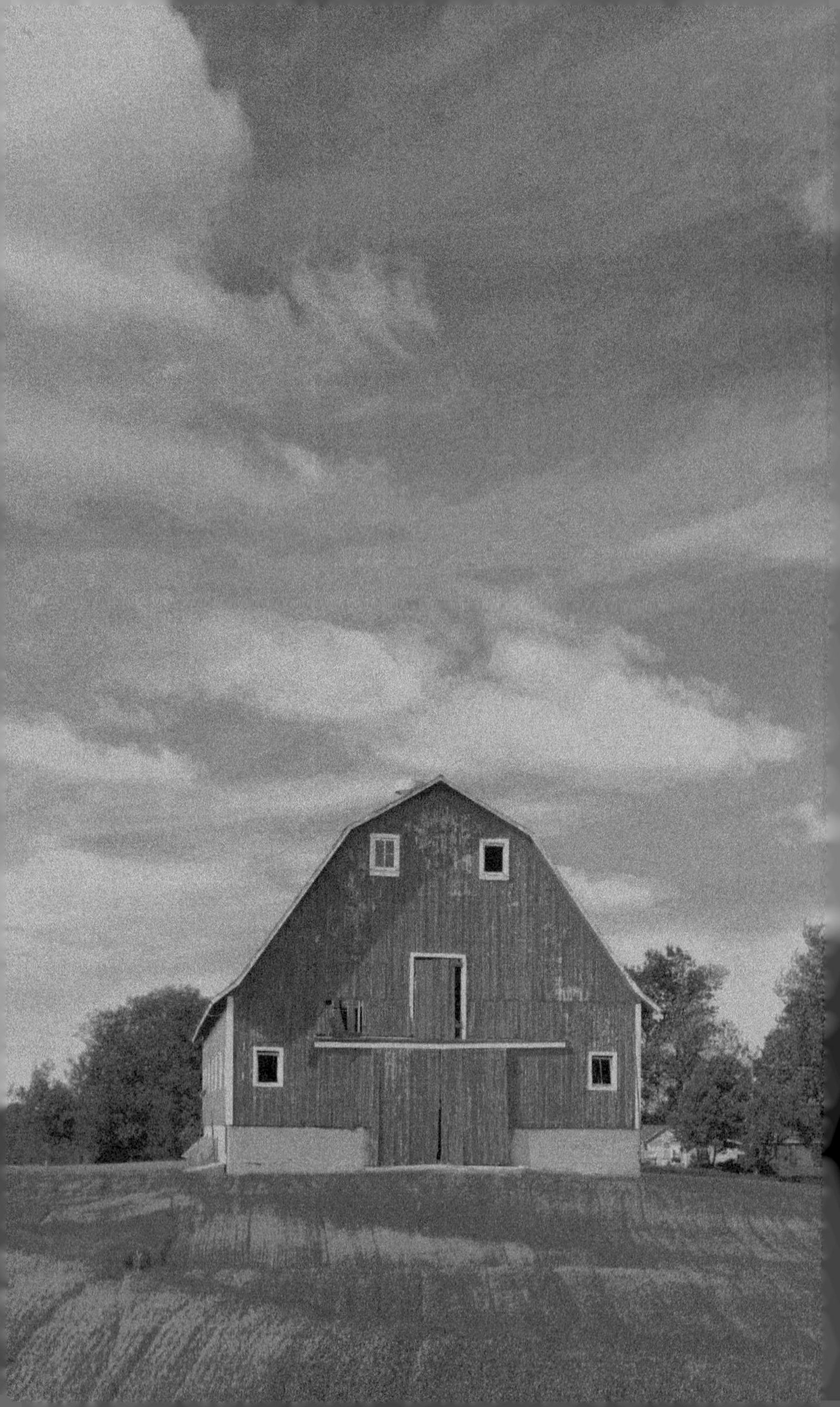

Chapter One

Aspen

Hefting another full crate from the back of my sister's truck, I twisted around to set it onto the wooden tabletop of our market booth, only to trip over a pair of suit-clad legs. I nearly topple over my friend, who was casually leaning against the table, his long legs stretched out and crossed at the ankles. But before I could, along with the container of asparagus no less, I felt a strong hand grip the back of my overalls, then hoist me into the air like a toddler.

"You know," I said, dropping the crate onto the table and readjusted my overalls and underwear, which had been wedged between my ass cheeks, "when you asked if you could come along, I assumed you were going to help, not get in the way."

I turned back around to grab another crate, when I'm halted by the same grip on my overalls once again. "I'm sorry, snowflake. What can I do to help?"

I look up, way up, at Dean's overly handsome face. It really was a shame he looked so damn gorgeous, with all his chiseled features, and my body felt nothing toward him. Not even the tiniest of sparks. Heaving an overly dramatic sigh, I replied, "Dean. First, you can stop calling me snowflake. I *hate* nicknames. I told you this."

"But it suits you. You're all dainty and have that white-blonde hair."

"I am not dainty," I grumbled as I lifted another crate from the back of the vintage red truck. "And just help me get these crates from the truck and onto the table so I can set it all up."

Together, Dean and I moved the produce from point A to point B. He was in town for the housewarming party for my sister, Aurora, and his best friend, Talon, who she was married to. They'd been married for about two years now, of which some of that time was a contract, an arrangement to get him access to his family hotel. The rest of the time, they were a lovey-dovey couple who thought each other hung the moon.

Gag.

My *entire* family—everyone was dropping like flies. Thankfully, my brother and I steered clear of Cupid.

"You work too hard," Dean said as he set the final crate at my feet. I was busy sorting through the fruits and vegetables, selecting the best to put on the front of the display. Summer was coming to a close, and I knew we'd have a busy weekend. School had been in session for a month already, but the heat and humidity of the summer still clung to the air.

Setting some figs along the front of the market table, I turned toward Dean, wiping my hands on the rag I kept tucked in my pocket, and said, "I'm just doing what needs to be done."

He cocked one of his thick eyebrows, and his tan skin wrinkled along his forehead. "But at what expense?"

I rolled my eyes at him just as the first marketgoers started to arrive. The sun had barely peaked over the trees, illuminating the sky in an orange haze. The customers appeared like little shadows across the expansive lot.

"I know what you need," Dean said as he popped open a chair and gracefully folded his big body into it, making it seem more like a throne than a camping seat.

In a hushed tone, I murmured, "If you say 'some dick,' I'm going to smack you."

He had the audacity to chuckle. "No, though you definitely could use that too. What I was going to say is that you need a vacation."

"Yeah, and who would take care of the farm if I took one? You know my dad is retiring, and everyone else if off doing their own things. I'm all Sunny Brook Farms has."

"And that's fair to you, how?"

I didn't offer a response, just rolled my eyes as my first customer arrived. A steady stream of people fell in line to purchase some of our locally grown fruits and vegetables. Sunny Brook Farms' main produce was corn. We sold it all over the country. But my three sisters and I kept up with my great-great-grandmother's garden. We sold those items weekly at the farmers market.

Dean didn't do much more than offer a suggestive wink to the women and mothers as they made their purchases. After an hour, there was a lull in the crowd.

"You know, I won that trip to Scotland. You should come with me," he suggested, and my eyebrows rose. Dean was aware I was as innocent as they came. I couldn't imagine letting an experienced man like Dean pop my cherry. "I didn't mean like that, snowflake."

"Sure," I added, chuckling to myself at the thought of Dean being interested in me at all. That was laughable. No one ever showed an interest in me. Growing up, I used to think it was due to my older brother's influence, but now that he lived an hour away from Ashfield, I was certain it was just me.

"Can you watch the booth while I run to the restroom?" I didn't bother asking him if he knew what do to. I had faith he paid enough attention earlier.

Thankfully, he nodded, and I slipped out from under the canopy, the sun's rays immediately causing me to wince. With each step I took across the market, I felt eyes on me. Did they all know I was a twenty-four-year-old virgin? Did they all look at me with wrinkled noses, as if they smelled something unpleasant.

What's wrong with me?

I relieved myself in the park's bathroom across the street. As far as public restrooms went, Ashfield prided itself on their cleanliness.

Just as I stepped free, I bumped into Magnolia Hayes. Ashfield's beauty queen and one of the many reasons I had always dreaded school. She and her clique always found a way to torment me. Not much changed in the past six years, since we graduated. Other than she and our high-school-quarterback husband were pregnant with their third baby. I actually hated how beautiful she still looked. It didn't seem that karma was on my side.

"Oh, I didn't see you there," the statuesque woman said as she gently rubbed her belly. I may have been small, but there was no way she couldn't have seen me opening the door.

"Magnolia. How are you?" I almost giggled at the shocked expression on her face. It was so tiring to stay mad at my old schoolmates all the time, so I optioned to be nice and polite instead. There was sweet satisfaction in watching their confused gazes dart around wildly, waiting for the other shoe to drop. They had every reason to be suspicious though. In high school, I was known to give it back just as good as I got it.

"I'm good, thanks. I… er… need to use the bathroom. Baby pressing on the bladder and all."

"Yes, I've heard stories about that. Enjoy your day." I left her lingering by the bathroom entrance as I made the trek back to my booth. I always did my best to keep a pleasant tone whenever I spoke with my old tormenters. I gave up trying to enact some sort of revenge. Instead, I saw them as potential buyers or customers. Or, at the very least, because it was the mature thing to do. There was only one person who still deserved all my wrath, and he had only shown his face once in this town since he went off to college and was drafted by the Los Angeles Coyotes. His random appearance at my sister's best friend Frannie's wedding had thrown the town into a spiral. He was Ashfield's golden child.

My steps morphed into stomps as I continued to think about the overly gorgeous man who made my life a living hell. Glancing up and across the park, I saw the large sign with his name on it above the baseball field before looking at the ground once again.

Owen Ramsey Played Here.

Even in his absence, I couldn't escape him. Grumbling, I crossed the street without raising my gaze until I was nearly clipped by a passing car. That's when, from a distance, I could see there was a crowd growing around the Sunny Brook Farms stand, so I rushed back over to relieve Dean. But I was surprised to find him throwing quips back and forth with Mrs. Hensen, our beloved and notoriously dirty-minded resident of Ashfield.

I hurried over, hoping to alleviate a situation before it escalated. Dean held up a fig that'd been sliced in half and explained to Mrs. Hensen how it was a little-known aphrodisiac.

"They also aid in a woman's fertility. The Greeks were the first to discover that fact. They're also incredibly sweet when they're ripe and plump." He leaned toward her, holding the fig between his thumb and forefinger, and lifted it closer to her gaze. The older woman looked interested, but as I got near, I could see there was also a gleam there that had me halting in place.

I'd seen that look before.

"Oh, what an interesting fact, young man. Now, if you're looking for a *really* salacious vegetable, look no further than celery," she said as she reached down and grabbed a stalk of the light-green vegetable. "Celery contains a chemical that acts like a natural Viagra. It worked for my dear Mr. Hensen for many years."

I choked back vomit at the thought of the widowed octogenarian and her late husband going crazy in the bedroom. He used to play the organ for our church, and I refused to believe he did anything sexual. Ever.

"Also, that same chemical ignites the female libido as well," Dean added, setting the fig back down with one of his sinister grins, as more customers gathered around the booth, enthralled by the back-and-forth between the two.

When he reached for the single pineapple—an item I grabbed from the store to cut up for myself as a snack later—I immediately stepped forward. I knew where he was headed with his next round of comments and information, and there were too many children listening in.

Reaching across the display, I snatched the pineapple from his grasp, wincing as the pointy edges dug into my palm, and set the pineapple back down behind the produce for sale. "I'll take back over. Thanks for covering for me, Dean. Mrs. Hensen, it's always a pleasure to see you. What can I get you this morning?"

Her nose wrinkled as she explored the display. The patrons who had gathered began dispersing, realizing the show was now over.

"I'll take ten figs and four celery stalks," she replied with a sigh.

"Of course. What sort of concoction are you making this time?" I asked, trying to distract her from the conversation with Dean, who was back in his camping chair with his feet propped up on the table.

"I was thinking of making some fig tarts for the local bake sale tomorrow, and the celery for a Bloody Mary, just because I like a little spice in my life."

I nearly choked on my tongue at her statement—not that what she said surprised me. Mrs. Hensen always knew how to keep us on our toes. She was quickly on her way after I packaged up her items and took her payment.

When the coast was clear, I spun around and chastised Dean, who sat behind me smugly. "You're incorrigible." He knew exactly what he was doing with the elderly woman.

"Ah, she likes it. Anyway, back to my previous statement. You should come with me to Scotland next month."

Sighing, I turned my attention away from him and leaned against the table, crossing my arms against my chest. I hadn't been on a vacation since my high school spring break trip with my friend Jenna. Our senior year, we took a very tame trip to Myrtle Beach, South Carolina. While the rest of our class traveled to Miami and caused all sorts of raucous, we were sitting poolside with a book and an iced tea as her parents watched over us.

Yep, I hadn't been on an actual vacation in six years. I couldn't have gotten any lamer if I tried.

Before I could respond, I felt Dean's large body press up next to mine as he draped his arm across my shoulders. "Look, kid, I just don't want you to work yourself into the ground. You'll wake up one day, and you'll be thirty, or even forty, wondering what all that work was for." His words hit me right in my chest. I glanced up at my friend and noticed the forlorn look in his eyes as he gazed across the market.

Uncrossing my arms, I wrapped one around his waist and leaned my head against his chest. "I can't take the trip with you, but I promise to cut back on the work just a little. Maybe even go out a bit more."

"That's my girl," Dean said, before releasing me and reaching for his phone tucked in his pants pocket.

While he chatted with whoever was on the other end of the call, I rang up the couple who let their kids pick out a bunch of fruit for their lunches the coming week, and there was a steady flow of customers for an hour more. When I looked up after the last person in line, I glanced around at the dwindling crowd. Noticing some of the other booths were already packing up, I started to do the same. Most of the produce was gone, so I packaged up what I had left into a single bag, which I planned to drop off at the church in town. They'd distribute it to local families in need and those in the surrounding counties.

Despite Ashfield flourishing over the last couple of decades, there were still families who struggled, especially as more and more developers moved close by and grocery stores stopped selling locally grown produce. My family and a lot of neighboring vendors did our part the best we could. Even though we lived in a small town, and everyone knew most things about everyone, there were still secrets that lingered. Sometimes, it was in everyone's best interest to keep quiet, usually to not embarrass someone.

"Are you heading back to the farm, or over to Talon's?" I asked, referring to my brother-in-law, who was Dean's best friend.

"Yeah, I have some work to do in Knoxville, then I'll be traveling. You probably won't get to see my handsome mug for a couple of weeks. I know that devastates you."

Pretending to be in shock, I slammed my hand against my chest, my mouth falling open. "Whatever shall I do while I wait for your return?" I asked in an over-the-top Southern accent, reminiscent of actresses in classic movies.

I began loading the back of the truck with the empty crates, stacking them in the way my mom preferred. Dean had to answer another call, so I hauled the last crate into the back and shut the tailgate.

Off in the distance, I vaguely heard the sound of a name being called, but I ignored it and continued to tear down the booth setup. Without Dean's help, I struggled with the canopy and unlatching the legs.

"Dammit!" I hissed as the metal button pinched my thumb.

The shouting continued across the lot, and I quickly realized the name they were calling was mine.

"Aspen!"

Turning around, I was nearly tackled by my best friend Jenna as she dashed over to me.

"Aspen, oh my gosh," she said as she leaned forward, hands on her knees, as she worked to catch her breath.

"Jenna, what's wrong? Is everything okay?"

At that moment, Dean must have ended his call, because he stepped up beside me with a puzzled look on his face.

"She having a heart attack?" he asked as she reached out for my arm while she huffed. Jenna had a naturally athletic-looking build but had never worked out a day in her life. I would've hated her if she hadn't been my closest friend since we were in preschool.

I didn't acknowledge his question but slapped him across the stomach, then took a step closer to Jenna.

"You okay?" I asked as I rested my hand on her back, gently sliding it up and down to comfort her.

"Yes," she finally responded, straightening, and that's when I noticed her hand tightly gripping her phone. "Aspen, have you seen the gossip channels this morning?"

"You know that's more your cup of tea. I stay away from all that stuff." Ever since my older sisters married people who were in the public eye, I steered clear of the tabloids. I didn't know how they dealt with it. Seeing nasty, fake headlines posted about someone I love would've been too much for me.

Out the corner of my eye, I watched as Dean slipped his phone out of his pocket and began scrolling. What he was looking for, I wasn't sure.

"Well, you need to read this." Jenna shoved her phone into my hand, ignoring the fact that I held my aching thumb in my opposite fist.

"What am I looking for?" I asked as I typed in her passcode.

"You'll know when you see it."

On her screen, I scrolled through the articles until one caught my attention, and my entire body lit up like grand-finale fireworks on the Fourth of July.

"No way. Is this real?" I asked, my giddiness bubbling up to the surface as I suppress a laugh.

"It is."

"Oh my gosh. This is the best thing I've read in weeks."

Beside me, Dean asked, "What is it?"

I read the headline aloud. "Baseball Star, Owen Ramsey, Left at the Altar During Tropical Destination Wedding."

"Oh damn." Dean winced.

"Don't you dare feel sorry for him. Believe me when I say he deserves *all* the worst kind of karma." Turning my attention back to the screen, I skimmed through the article, noting how the surprise nuptials had very few attendants, mostly *her* friends and family. I knew for a fact that his mother hadn't been there, since I saw her yesterday. "Oh, shit," I mumbled as I read the last line.

"What?" Jenna questioned as she ripped the phone out of my hand and read over the words on the screen. "Oh, shit."

"Will someone please fill me in?" Dean inquired as he crossed his arms over his chest.

Jenna replied immediately, her eyes darting over to me, "Owen's coming home."

Chewing my bottom lip, I let the words sink in. Owen never visited Ashfield. It was a fluke when he showed up for the wedding with his mom. Rumor was they were settling his father's estate that weekend and she convinced him to be her plus-one. He'd been invited to every festival, every town parade, every graduation… but he never accepted the requests. I didn't keep up with his life, unlike everyone else in town, but from what I knew, Owen was more than content to view Ashfield as nothing more than a memory. It was something I couldn't fathom. The man had the world at his fingertips but couldn't so much as take the time to call his old friends nor his family.

"Oh no," I whispered. "I wonder if Beverly knows."

Chapter Two

Owen

My eyes felt dry and crusty as I pried them open. I lifted my head off the table in the airport lounge as the boarding group of first-class passengers was called. I smacked my lips as the cotton feeling transferred to my taste buds. It felt like I was coming off a three-day bender, even though I hadn't touched a drop of alcohol since my wedding day. Well, what *would have been* my wedding day.

Being left at the altar should have been the most embarrassing moment of my life. Instead, that was eclipsed by finding my fiancée and her male best friend doing their own horizontal tango in the reception hall right next to the ten-thousand dollar cake she *had* to have. What made it worse was that the small gathering of wedding guests witnessed it along with me.

I stood there dumbfounded for a solid minute before I realized what was happening. My best friend, Marc, tried to shield me from the chaos erupting before my eyes, but I shoved him away as I made my way toward the couple.

Vanessa and I locked eyes, but her pal, Francisco, didn't relent from his pounding into her. I wasn't sure if he even knew anyone was there, or if he just didn't care. As I moved toward them, her eyes grew wider with my every step, and then I watched her mouth fall open as she screamed out her orgasm—something I had seen her do hundreds of times—as I cut into our wedding cake and plated a slice. The more I thought about it, the more I wondered if she screamed from pleasure, or anger at the fact that I ruined the dessert.

"Help yourself, everyone!" I shouted to the crowd as my ex-fiancée tried to scurry away from Francisco. I left the room without a backward glance, Marc and Brent hot on my heels.

Now, beside my arm on the table, I watched my phone light up again for the thousandth time over the last three days. Vanessa's name flashed, and I flipped it over so I didn't have to look at her face again. I gave my lawyer strict instructions for getting Vanessa out of my house by the time I returned. I knew he'd get it taken care of.

In the meantime, I was more distraught about where I was headed, not so much about the events that occurred recently. It was a place I vowed to never return to unless it was necessary. I never understood why my mom didn't leave at the first chance she got.

As I left the lounge and headed toward the boarding area, I tugged my ball cap farther down in an attempt to mask my face. The prying eyes were like lasers searing my skin.

"Sir, can I help you with your bag?" the flight attendant asked, as I left my hard case of bats at the gate check and proceeded into the plane with my carry-on.

"I've got it, thanks," I grumbled as I stored the small piece of luggage in the cubby above me, then settled into my seat. I booked the three seats in my row, because I needed both the leg room and the privacy.

In my pocket, my phone buzzed again, and I worried it was another incessant call from Vanessa, but I was waiting for a call from both my coach and agent, so I couldn't just ignore it. Glancing at the device, I winced as

I realized it was none of those options. My mom's name was flashing on the screen. I thought about ignoring it, like I had over the years. We talked, but not nearly as much as some of my teammates and their parents. With us, it was all forced. Nothing personal, ever.

I begrudgingly pressed the green button and held the phone up to my ear. "Hi, Mom."

"Owen, is it true? Are you coming home?" she asked, elation weaving through her voice.

Squirming in my chair, I wondered if the relentless messages from Vanessa had to do with our lack of marital bliss hitting the gossip rags. I knew it was only a matter of time before the story would leak. I'd already met with the team's PR group, which was why I was headed to the last place I wanted to be. This morning must have been the day of the drop. Tabloids were probably running wild with the story. I could see it now: **One of the Country's Hottest and Highest-Paid Baseball Players Now a Jilted Groom.**

"When did you find out?" I asked.

"Well, I overheard Aspen speaking to her mom and sisters at the bed-and-breakfast this morning."

My back straightened at the sound of the youngest Easterly's name. She'd been a thorn in my side from the day I stepped into our first-grade class, her always having to be better than everyone else, always having to be first at everything. Her family alone pretty much ran the town. It was a shame, since I liked most of them. Hell, I idolized her older brother when I was a kid. But Aspen… she made me act in ways I wasn't proud of. Mostly at her expense.

I'd seen her only once since I left, when I went home for a wedding, and I got a smug sense of pleasure at watching her eyes rake over me in my fitted suit. It was too bad her face appeared as if I were a dead mouse dragged in by a cat.

I remembered vividly the words she spoke, low and raspy, as if she'd been fighting off a cold. "You aren't welcome here." Her father joined us at the same moment, and he quickly steered her away before coming back to catch up with me.

Like I said, I'd always been a fan of her family, her father especially. Our property butted up to the backside of theirs, and on one too many occasions, he would catch me camping along the stream that separated our properties.

At my silence, my mother pressed me again. "So, is it?"

"Is what?"

"Is it true? Are you coming home?"

Lifting my hat, I ran my hand through the brown strands, tugging the ends a bit at my frustration. "Yes, but it's only temporary."

Her joyful scream rang in my ear, and I had to pull my phone away. I knew I needed to squash this real fast, or she'd start asking questions I didn't want to answer.

"Look, Mom, we're boarding the plane. I need to get off the phone. I've rented a car, and I'll see you at the house this evening."

"Oh... but, Owen, rememb—"

I cut her off by ending the call. It was rude as hell, but I didn't want to think about staying at the house I grew up in. I never understood why she didn't want to sell it, take the money, and run. I sent her a hefty part of my contract payouts every year, but she still stayed in the house that was our own personal nightmare.

Slouching down in my seat, I gripped the phone in my hand as if I could inflict the same pain on the inanimate object that I felt as a child. But unlike my asshole of a father, I had never been violent. My vision was turning red, but I knew not to let the anger overpower me.

Suddenly, the plane's movements jarred me upright. It was taxiing down the runway, and I was too lost in my own thoughts to notice.

One flight attendant, an attractive woman with her dark hair pinned in a twist at the back of her head, stopped at my row.

"Sir, please buckle your safety belt before takeoff," she said with a wink, then she continued down the row.

As I blindly clicked the ends of the belt together, I wondered what she'd look like with mussed hair after being fucked senseless.

Shifting in my seat, I pulled my cap lower over my face, shielding my eyes, and tilted my head as far back as I could with the seats upright. I'd never been one to hide… until now.

By the time the plane jostled as it touched down, I realized I slept through the entire flight. I must have been more tired than I thought. Glancing down at my hand, I noticed I was still gripping my phone tightly. Tilting my head from side to side, the ache radiated down my arms. Sitting in one position for six hours was never good for my muscles. I usually needed to meet with the team's physical therapist after a long flight whenever we traveled for games.

"Sir, do you need any assistance?" the same brunette from before asked. This time, I pulled my hat into its right position and pinned her with my eyes. The steely-blue color usually worked their magic with very little effort from me. And by the way her cheeks reddened, it seemed they hadn't lost their touch. Even after two years and a six-month engagement with Vanessa, I knew I still held some physical appeal to women.

I'd never been much of a playboy prior to meeting Vanessa, but maybe this was my chance to explore that life. Though I always pictured myself settled down with a family at a young age. I envisioned my own brood traveling with me to games and cheering for me in the stands.

As I continued to stare at the flight attendant, she leaned in and, without missing a beat, unlatched my belt for me, letting her fingers linger around my crotch area for a beat.

"I have a two-day layover in Nashville," she whispered.

Just as I was about to respond, because I was definitely interested in what she was offering, the little boy seated diagonally from me enthusiastically peered over the top of his seat. His finger pointed in my direction as he turned toward a woman in the seat next to him.

"Mom!" I heard him say not so subtly, "That *is* Owen Ramsey, the shortstop for the Coyotes. I told you!"

"Oh," the flight attendant leaning toward me purred, and I watched as dollar signs appeared in her eyes and her entire demeanor change. I assumed when I checked in that they knew I was on this flight, but I supposed my name was fairly common. It was when a baseball fan recognized me that everyone changed.

"Sorry," I said as I stood up and brushed past her, already gripping the handle of my carry-on from the upper storage area. "I have somewhere to be. Appreciate the offer." I brushed past her, using my free hand to reach into my pocket.

The dense cardstock felt like a million tons when I placed it in my palm. It wasn't the kid's fault that he recognized me, but I enjoyed the solitude for the last six hours.

"Here, kid." Holding out the signed baseball card from the stack I always kept in my pocket for young fans, I smiled warmly. He was awestruck as he took the card with a shaking hand and whispered his thanks. Continuing down the aisle, my mood sullied further as I rented a car and stored my luggage and bats inside the trunk.

Ashfield was not a place I desired to go, but I knew it was time. I'd been avoiding some things for too long, and my therapist thought, after the implosion of my engagement, that this was a good time to get closure on my past.

I wasn't sure I was ready for the closure yet, because it was far too easy to just stay angry.

An hour later, the green sign posted alongside the highway directed me toward the small town of Ashfield, an idyllic small town nestled in the valley of the Smoky Mountains of Tennessee. I'd been excited when my father moved us here when I was six, buying a huge plot of land he intended on farming. It wasn't until I learned his goal had been to hide us away that the town started to feel more like a jail cell than a wide-open space.

Just like the last time I'd been home, my pulse raced, and my fingers tightened around the steering wheel. The car crested the hill, giving the perfect view of the picturesque town below. Despite the misgivings of small-town living, the town was bustling. More people had moved to town, and businesses were flourishing. At least, that's what my mom told me whenever I let her ramble about the town during our brief chats.

I hesitated at the top of the hill. Did I want to subject myself to the townspeople? These were men and women who watched me grow up, watched my life upend, and watched me leave at the first chance I got. But they also cheered me on at every game and chipped in at the farm whenever my dad's wild ideas failed. And I had friends here at one point. Guys I used to play ball with. Girls I dated and kissed under the bleachers.

I hoped they'd forgotten me.

It was easy enough to slip in and out when I was here for the wedding. I barely stayed for an hour, before I high-tailed it out of town when Mom and I received the news we'd been waiting for. The news that finally closed an open circuit in my life that kept buzzing in the back of my head.

The longer I sat here looking down into the valley, the smaller I felt. My breaths came in short pants until I felt like I was having a full-blown panic attack. Something I hadn't experienced since I was in high school. Prom night, to be exact. Not even a cheating fiancée could trigger that reaction in me.

I wasn't sure how long I sat in the idling car, allowing the blackness to creep in, but a screeching noise from off in the distance brought my gaze up to the rearview mirror. Behind me, a tractor that spanned the entire width of the road was slowly approaching. It was a common scenario living in a farming town.

Somehow, it made me chuckle out of my panic, as I recalled the time my buddies and I stole a tractor from the old Marshall dairy farm and rode it through town. Finally, I put my foot on the gas and proceeded toward Ashfield.

Everything glistened before me, the sunrays ricocheting off the windows, making the road light up with little prisms of color from some of the stained glass. If there was one thing Ashfield did well, it was taking the nature around it and highlighting it.

As the front bumper of the rental car passed the first street sign decorated with flowers and a flag, I released a breath I'd been unconsciously holding. The brick buildings were all familiar but foreign at the same time. The signs had been changed since I left after high school. I paid little attention when I was here for the wedding. Red-eye flights had a way of doing that. The awnings changed. The businesses updated. But all of it felt the same. The same places that kicked me out at closing. The same places that told me they were calling the sheriff if I didn't stop hanging out in the alleyways.

The same places that called me whenever my father was too far gone and needed a ride home, even though I had a test at school the next day.

It's all the same.

But a flash of pale-blonde hair crossing the street brought me back into the now. And my entire demeanor changed. Now, I was on the hunt for her. For a second, my guard dropped, and I watched the lithe female dart across the road into the grocery store—Chuck's. It had been there forever.

I made an impromptu stop and pulled up beside her beat-up sedan in the store parking lot. The clock on the generic dashboard of my rental showed 4:30 p.m. Without hesitation, I turned off the engine, stepped out of the car, and made my way toward the entrance.

Casually, I started in the bakery area, grabbing a box of my mom's favorite cookies along the way. Figured I wouldn't show up at the house empty-handed.

Continuing around the store, I peered down each aisle, tugging the brim of my baseball cap lower to shield my face whenever I caught someone's attention.

By the time I reached the other end of the store, I started to believe I must have been seeing things. My little nemesis was nowhere to be found.

About ready to give up, I stepped toward the registers, only to collide with someone. I knew her scent immediately, the same combination it had always been. A mix of vanilla and hay.

Gripping her biceps, I helped steady her. She barely hung on to the loaf of bread in her hands as she looked up at me, and her brown eyes widened as she realized who she bumped into.

"Well, hello there, cricket. Happy to see me?"

Chapter Three

Aspen

Damn, why did he have to look so good? Even better than the last time I came face-to-face with him. I'd given up hope that he peaked in high school. No, Owen Ramsey only got better with age. I was almost—*almost*—happy to see him. Because, let's be honest, most people who left town rarely returned. Just like with my eldest sister, the townspeople of Ashfield never expected him to step foot back in our town, especially once rumors began swirling about his father. His mother, Beverly, shouldered enough embarrassment for the both of them.

The use of the atrocious nickname quickly exterminated that twinge of happiness for me though. One I hadn't heard since I crossed the auditorium stage and received my high school diploma. I'd hoped to never hear it again, but lo and behold, Owen couldn't let that childish nickname drop.

"Don't call me that," I snarled as I twisted out of his hold.

I tried to brush past him but made the mistake of looking up into those gray eyes that captivated everyone he laid them on. It was like he dipped his irises in liquid mercury. They were the most startling shade.

"Aw, I didn't mean anything by it," he explained, as I moved toward the register, rolling my eyes as he followed like a lost puppy.

"Doubtful," I said over my shoulder, snagging one last glimpse of him. My entire goal while he was here was to avoid him as much as possible. But even I knew that was going to be hard, knowing exactly where he was going to be staying.

Just as I had that passing thought, Owen asked, "Know where I can find my mom?"

He set the box in his hand behind my bread on the conveyor belt.

"I don't," I lied. I knew exactly where she was.

"Shame. Though I can't say I'm unhappy with the company I've run into."

Turning around fully, I squint in his direction, my eyes searching his. "Since when have you ever been happy to see me, Owen?"

Instead of answering, Owen chuckled and threw a candy bar next to his cookies. A Butterfinger, which happened to be the one I always picked. "For you."

"How'd you know that's my favorite?" I asked him suspiciously as the teenager at the register scanned my lone item.

With the kind of grin that brought girls to their knees—*other* girls, not me—he replied, "I didn't."

The worker interrupted our back-and-forth with my total, and I handed him the two dollars for the bread, quickly gathered my bag, and made my way to the automatic doors.

I hurried out of the store toward my barely drivable sedan, leaving Owen without a backward glance. Just knowing he returned to Ashfield was enough to keep me from wanting to travel into town until I knew full well that he was gone. I could only hope his stay wasn't prolonged. Though, I had a feeling that once he knew what was going on with his family's property, he would be here until he absolutely had to return to his baseball team.

But none of that mattered to me. What Owen Ramsey did with his life was none of my business. I had enough on my plate with the farm and my fledgling social life.

As I got in my car, I looked up and watched as he strolled casually through the exit, heading in my direction. Panicked, I fumbled with my keys, jamming the right one into the side of the ignition repeatedly until I finally rung the hole and it slipped in. I turned the key quickly, praying the car started on the first go. Unfortunately, as Owen got closer, it refused to turn over.

"Come on. Come on. Come on," I pleaded with the vehicle.

A knock on my window sounded, and I sighed before I begrudgingly manually rolled down the window. My car was so old enough it didn't have power windows, so I actually understood the rolling the window down gesture most people my age didn't get.

"Yes?" I asked, annoyed.

He leaned one of his muscular arms on the side of my car, all sexy-like. I couldn't help but think he must've done this move hundreds of times with how effortless he appeared. Owen tilted his head down so he could peer through my open window, piercing me with those eyes.

"Having trouble?"

"No," I growled, again trying to start the car to no avail.

"You sure?"

"Is there something you need?"

"No, just thought I'd offer to help you out or give you a ride home, since you're on my way."

"You want to help me?" I asked cynically.

"Yeah. I mean, sure, why not?"

Leaning toward the window, I searched around the parking lot, looking for anything suspicious, but all I saw were a few of my mom's friends and a couple of women I went to high school with. They were all looking at Owen as if he simultaneously hung the moon and committed a crime.

"Am I being pranked right now? Is someone going to jump out from behind a vehicle and tell me this is all a joke?" I questioned, returning to the task of starting my car, which seemed as unwilling as ever.

"No prank, cricket."

Immediately, I sneered in his direction, my eyes narrowing as if I were formulating his slow and painful death.

"Come on, Aspen. I'm just trying to help. I also have your candy bar."

Sighing loudly, I squinted even more at him, like he'd grown two heads. "I realize you may have forgotten everything about our rivalry when you left town, but the last time I was in any moving vehicle with you, my jeans ended up super-glued to the vinyl seats of our school bus."

That day had been awful. Thankfully, my angel of a mother came to get me off the bus—once the driver returned to school at the end of the route—with an extra pair of pants, because I refused to try to stand up again while there were other passengers.

"We were kids. It was funny."

"Funny for you, maybe."

"Pretty sure you got your payback. Even though I think, in the long run, those sheer baseball pants you swapped in my bag before the championship game probably helped me land that underwear campaign I starred in last year."

Ignoring his chuckles, I attempted to turn on the car for the third time, and the answering click let me know my car wouldn't be going anywhere anytime soon.

Suddenly, the door swung open, and Owen stood there with one of those sexy trademark smirks of his. He stayed on the other side of it, probably to protect himself, waiting patiently for me to exit.

Eyes downcast, because I didn't have any other choice besides call one of my family members, I grabbed the loaf of bread and my bag before stepping out of the car. Without looking up at him, I shoved my keys into my bag, then rolled up the window, giving him my own smirk when he barely moved his fingers in time to not be pinched. With as much haughtiness as I could muster, I yanked the door from his hold, then shut and locked it.

Before submitting to his offer, I looked across the way, noticing our old science teacher from high school. Ms. Glenvar had the unfortunate luck of having both me and Owen in her eleventh-grade chemistry class during the same period. After one disastrous lab session, where Owen and I had to partner up, and our assignment caught the table on fire, Ms. Glenvar took a leave of absence for the rest of the year.

I still didn't believe it was our fault. It wasn't us who placed ourselves in a class together, and everyone in Ashfield knew the chaos we tended to cause when we were in close proximity. So whose bright idea was it to put us together in, of all things, *Chemistry*? They were just asking for it.

Ms. Glenvar must have felt my stare. Her beady eyes met mine, and her steps faltered as she took in the large body behind my much, *much* smaller one. As if witnessing a crime in action, she took a slow step backward, then another, until she was running to her car parked at the far end of the lot.

"What was that about?" Owen asked as he opened the door of a plain-looking sedan parked directly beside mine. I would have expected to see him driving an exotic car like one of my brothers-in-law owned, since the news made it well known how much Owen's recently signed contract was for.

With wide eyes, I spun around and looked at him in bewilderment. "Seriously?"

Owen gestured with an outstretched hand for me to enter the vehicle. I was still apprehensive, but I noticed the receipt from the rental company was resting on the center console, so I figured my pants were fairly safe.

"Thanks," I mumbled as I settled into the seat, grabbing my cell to text my family about my car. Of course, my phone's battery was hanging on for dear life, with only three percent left. Before it died completely, I shot off a message letting them know I was on my way home, then powered off the device.

"You're welcome."

I watched him close my door, then jog around the front of the sedan toward the driver side. Even compared to last year, when I saw him for only a quick moment, he seemed to fill out even more. He was both lean and muscular, the cotton of his T-shirt stretched around his bicep as if it would give way at any moment. I didn't recall his arms looking like that in high school. He also didn't have any of the ink that now swirled in bright colors and shades of black and gray.

My eyes focused on the intricate design as he settled into his own seat. They appeared to be landscapes and words, nothing I could determine without a closer look. And getting any closer to Owen wouldn't ever be a safe bet I'd take.

As he started the car and began pulling out of the parking spot, the people milling in and out of the store peered through our windows. The alarm was palpable as they darted away.

"Why is everyone running like the apocalypse is coming?"

Giggling, I said, "Because they probably think it is."

Owen glanced over at me as he pulled onto Main Street. The skin between his eyebrows wrinkled. When our eyes met, there was electricity there that forced me to turn my head away and stare out the window. I didn't have the time or energy to figure out what was going on.

"I don't understand," he mumbled.

"Really, Owen?" I didn't elaborate further, not only because he couldn't recall our tumultuous childhood with each other, but because I didn't have the energy.

We made it ten minutes into the drive before another word was spoken. During that time, I wondered what kind of posts were being made in the town's Facebook group. Not that I cared what was said about me, but I'd never been the topic of discussion before. At least not in this capacity.

Glancing at the clock, I noticed it was nearing four o'clock, and I knew my sister, Autumn, would be set to start dinner at the bed-and-breakfast soon. She roped me into the grocery store errand when she found me in our parents' barn. Normally, I'd have declined, but right now, she was so pregnant that she looked as if she swallowed a watermelon.

"So... what's new with you?" Owen asked, flexing his fingers along the steering wheel.

"Um... nothing really."

"Did you... uh... go away to college or anything?"

I faced him again. Cocking my head to the side, I wondered if he truly didn't keep up with anyone from town. I figured his mom would have at least kept him up-to-date on their land and our farm, since we signed the paperwork for the purchase last week.

"Are you joking right now?"

"What?"

"Your head is so far up your own ass that you have no idea whether or not I went to college? Pretty sure there was a listing at our graduation of where people were going, and my name was not on it."

"Oh. Sorry," he said with an unapologetic shrug. "My mind was elsewhere at graduation. Actually, it was elsewhere our entire senior year."

With a resounding huff, I mumbled, "It's fine. I took online classes to get an Associate's in Business, but the farm dictates most of my time."

"You're still working for your fami—"

I interrupted him and pointed toward the road leading to the Crawfords' bed-and-breakfast, where I was headed. "My sister, Autumn, and her husband, Colton, fixed up the old, worn-down farmhouse at the top of the hill and turned it into a B&B."

"Yeah? Didn't she move to New York or something like that?"

I was surprised he remembered that much but didn't know whether I went to college or not. But then again, the majority of my male classmates and a few females had a major crush on my older sisters, even memorizing their school and work schedules. So, him knowing what they did after graduation shouldn't have surprised me. But it did nonetheless.

"She did. She married someone you might recognize. Colton Crawford? He played professional hockey."

"I think I remember hearing that. I don't get a lot of downtime. Usually in the offseason, I'm training from sunup to sundown. So, unless it directly affects me or the team, I don't really know what's going on."

Knowing I only had a few seconds before we crested the hill, I wanted to ask about the gossip burning in the back of my mind. "What happened with the fiancée?"

"Ex-fiancée."

"Yeah. But if you don't want to talk about it, that's fine. I get it. I don't like to share my personal life either."

"It's fine. I haven't really talked to anyone about it. I left LA with only a message for my coach and suggestions from my PR team. Long story short, Vanessa decided she wanted to spend our wedding day screwing her best friend in the middle of our reception hall before we marched down the aisle."

"Wow. That's…. Wow." Shaking my head gently, I added, "I'm sorry. You probably expected me to say something more comforting."

With a chuckle, Owen replied, "No. Actually, I imagined you flipping this around on me and saying it was my fault, or confessing it was you who caused it. Maybe you paid off my fiancée, you know?"

My chest pinched. The sting reached low down in my spine and crackled upward toward my tear ducts. I blinked quickly to rid myself of the tears.

"I deserve that."

While I'd been speaking, he had pulled the car up in front of the large, restored farmhouse. As the vehicle came to a stop, Owen rested his hand on my exposed thigh. My eyes immediately darted down to the placement. It was the first time I could recall Owen ever touching me.

The spot sizzled.

He pulled his hand away just as quickly as it had landed there, as if it burned him in the process as well.

"Um... sorry. But no, Aspen, you didn't deserve that." After a long pause, Owen utters, "Tell your mom I said hello."

The chrome of the handle warmed under my touch as I opened the door. Just as I stepped out of the car with my bags in hand, I turned back to him. "You may want to come inside."

Leaning over the center console, Owen murmured, "Huh?"

"It's where you'll find your mother."

I didn't turn back to see if he'd follow after I closed the car door, but the sound of a second one shutting gave him away.

"What do you mean?" he hollered at me as I reach the porch steps.

I'd never admit it to my sister, but I was jealous about this entire house. It was gorgeous, and I dreamed of the double porches being on my fantasy home. Unfortunately, I would be stuck on the Sunny Brook Farms property for the unforeseeable future.

I knew from conversations with his mother that the two of them didn't speak often, not that it was on her end. She missed her son, but she also understood why he didn't want to return to town.

We all did. *Now*. His secrets were no longer his own. I wasn't even sure Owen Ramsey was aware of that fact.

"You'll see," I said, turning around as I reached the porch to face him. He was standing three steps below me, which brought us eye-to-eye. "Look, you haven't been back in a long time. Ignore last year, when you were here for a split second and left at the first chance you got. But things have changed. People and lives have changed. I don't want you thinking you played a part in any of it—good or bad. There were decisions made to better all parties involved. Please, keep that in mind, Owen. I'm begging you."

I ignored the way his eyes flared at my last statement, turned back around to take the three strides to the front door, and opened it without knocking, leaving him speechless still on the steps.

"Aspen!" he whisper-yelled. I almost cracked a smile, but I knew what he was going to walk in to. Something I figured out during the ride that he absolutely wasn't prepared for.

Following the hallway past the open foyer, I found my sister and her husband in the kitchen, prepping the dinner with their live-in chef. My other sister, Alex, used to cook the meals here, but now that her cake shop was inundated with orders, Autumn hired someone else. Tara, a guest chef on a cooking show Colton hosted, took the job.

"I'm here with the bread. Sorry it took so long. I had car trouble. Again." I handed the bread to Tara, who look relieved, as Colton thanked me profusely. Autumn sat on a barstool in the corner, looking a little green. She'd had morning sickness through her entire pregnancy. Normally, she ran the event venue on the far side of Sunny Brook Farms, but she handed off most tasks to her assistants.

"Aspen!" Owen shouted this time as he found his way to the kitchen and noticed the trio of other people. "Oh. Apologies for yelling. I was looking for Aspen."

"How interesting," Autumn whispered as she cocked her head. "I don't know if you remember me, but I'm Aspen's sister, Autumn." She pushed herself off the stool and moved toward the unexpected guest with her hand outstretched.

I rolled my eyes hard enough I saw stars as Owen blushed. The man had been engaged to a supermodel for cripes' sake, but my sister had him acting like a lovesick teen with a lifelong crush.

"This is Colton, my husband. He plays hockey and hosts a few television shows."

Shaking both their hands, Owen mentioned how he may have met Colton before at a sports network award show, and the two chat for a few minutes. Autumn winked in my direction, and I shot her a look of disgust.

"Owen?" she called for his attention, breaking up the impending bromance. "Are you staying for dinner? Our chef, Tara, is making manicotti."

"Oh, that's okay. Thank you for the offer, but—"

From off in the distance, the sound of fast-paced footsteps grew closer.

"Owen? You're here?"

I recognized Beverly's voice immediately. Of course, Owen had as well, and I didn't miss his subtle wince when his name echoed through the house.

His mother turned the corner, still wearing her Crawford Bed-and-Breakfast polo shirt, and dashed over to her son. Feeling like I would witness a private moment, I shuffled out of the kitchen toward the library.

Thankfully, Autumn and Colton had the same idea, and we found ourselves hiding out amongst the stacks of novels.

"Well, this is awkward," Autumn murmured as she rested against one of the bookshelves. "Owen didn't look too happy to see his mom."

"I'm not so sure he has the best relationship with her... and most definitely not the town," I replied.

Colton chimed in, "So, it's likely he has no idea his mom sold you their land."

"From what I gathered, he doesn't even know she works here," I pointed out.

Autumn's mouth transformed into a guileful grin as her arms crossed against her chest. "So... Owen drove you over here?"

"Don't," I pleaded. "It was nothing."

"Oh, I beg to differ. You and Owen being civil to one another for longer than five minutes is not *nothing*."

"Autumn, don't read into it."

"Hm. Colton, make sure we have bags packed somewhere."

He looked alarmed, eyes darting up and down between Autumn's face and belly. "Is it the baby?"

She laughed loudly. "No, silly. It's worse. The end of the world may happen sometime soon." Colton's face scrunched, and Autumn explained, "Because Aspen and Owen have been hating on each other since they were in elementary school. We've never had a single moment where they could be in a room together without something going awry."

My eyes rolled at her description, though she wasn't too far off. Of course, she left out the fact that Owen started our rivalry with that stupid nickname. But I couldn't expect anyone in my family to remember small details like that. I was merely the little shadow who tagged along everywhere. The afterthought.

Glancing over at my sister, I saw her husband was gently rubbing circles on her lower back as she turned toward him. They were in their own little world.

Feeling like a voyeur, I ducked out of the library, slinking along the hallway wall as to not disrupt whatever was going on with Owen and Beverly.

I caught sight of a couple of the guests milling around the living room area just as Owen stomped out of the kitchen toward me, but it was clear he had tunnel vision. I wasn't sure if I should follow him, but I did anyway.

"Owen!" I shouted as we made it outside.

"I… I can't talk to you right now," he said as he yanked open the driver-side door of his car.

I wasn't privy to the discussion he and Beverly had, but it was clear he was upset about something. I could only imagine some of the things that had come to light. And not that I *wanted* to blame him for ignoring calls from his mother, since I learned about his childhood, but all fingers pointed in his direction as the reason he was uninformed.

"Not that I care, but maybe you should let your mom explain."

Leaning against the car, resting his folded arms on the roof, he chastised me. "Look, cricket, in all the years I've known you, I've never asked for your advice. Why would I follow it, especially unsolicited, now?"

"You don't have to be an asshole to me just because you're angry."

"Go home to your perfect life, cricket. Don't worry about me."

Without another word, he slunk down onto his seat and started the car. Within seconds, he was kicking up dust and dirt as he left the B&B.

From behind me, I felt a presence and turned to find Beverly standing just behind the threshold of the door, her face crestfallen.

"Well, that didn't quite go as expected."

"What did you tell him exactly?" I asked.

"That I've been working here for the last year and the house was condemned."

"So, he doesn't even know yet that you sold the land?"

"We… um… didn't get that far. I'll see if I can book a room for him here while he's home. Or maybe there's a rental in town I can set up." She paused, and I noticed the glassiness of her eyes. "I was just so happy he was coming home, and now I'm afraid I ruined it."

"Can I ask why you didn't tell him anything before now? From what I've heard, I realize Owen isn't the easiest person to get ahold of, but it might not have been such a shock if you'd been able to tell him *something*."

"I tried, but he's so stubborn and refused to listen when I brought up anything not related to baseball. I stopped trying. I should have insisted, I guess."

Taking her shaking hand, I squeezed it gently between mine. "He'll come around."

She shakes her head but smiles at me at the same time. "You're a sweet girl. Are you headed back to the farm?"

"Yeah, I'll take one of the UTVs. I need to go over the books with my dad."

"You work too hard," she said like a scolding mother.

"You sound like Dean." He had become friends with most of the town, including Owen's mom. "I'll see you later, Miss Beverly. If there's anything we can do, just let me know."

I hurried around the side of the house, where we stored the UTVs. There was a path that connected the bed-and-breakfast to Sunny Brook Farms, which made it easier for us to travel back and forth.

While most people were ending their day, mine was still going strong. The workload of a farmer was never-ending.

But even after arriving back at my family's house and going through the financials with my father—something I was struggling to comprehend—I couldn't help thinking about how Owen's world was just flipped upside down.

I was so distracted that, instead of making up an excuse like I usually did, I agreed to join Jenna out for drinks tonight. Something I'd only ever done once since I turned twenty-one three years ago.

Chapter Four

Owen

"Another?"

The bartender stood before me as I sipped at the beer he handed me over an hour ago. I wasn't much of a drinker to begin with, but my mind was still spinning from the secrets my mother spilled this afternoon.

I stormed out after learning she lost the house I grew up in and had been working for the Easterlys for the past year, before which she'd held a few serving jobs after my high school graduation. I'd been sending her money for years, but she refused to touch any of it.

Driving around earlier, I thought about going to the bank to try to salvage the house, but a quick drive past the property showed me how in disarray it was. The roof had caved in from the large oak tree in the front falling over. The same tree I'd fallen from while climbing it when I was ten and broke my collarbone.

Just thinking of that accident left my shoulder twinging. That was another tribulation I was going to need to deal with soon. I'd scheduled time with one of the team's new sports medicine therapists to work on my shoulder for the upcoming season. I kept the prolonged aches and pains from my coach as long as I could, but he pulled me aside at the end of last season and requested I take care of it. Looking back, it wasn't so much a request as it was a demand. The team had a lot of money invested in me.

"Yeah."

Spinning around on my stool, I took in the crowd, noticing that the old bar filled up quickly. In my mental solitude, I'd ignored all the noise. It was a trick I learned on the field, a way to help me focus.

A group of women stood at a high-top table, and the second my eyes skimmed past them, they immediately started preening. One fluffed her hair, and another adjusted her top. The other three had their backs to me.

Running a hand through my own hair, I continued to take in the crowd, ignoring the women's come-hither stares. I instantly regretted not wearing my ball cap. Though, most of the townspeople I grew up with knew me better with it on than off. But to this new crop of Ashfield dwellers, I was fresh blood… and a celebrity. Seemed Colton's appeal had worn off.

"Shit," I mumbled as a group of guys started approaching. I didn't recognize any of them, but by the suits they wore, my guess was they worked for the bank or a law firm in town.

Unfortunately for them, I was not up for making new friends today—or, well, ever.

"Hey, man."

"Hey," I replied kindly, because the last thing I wanted to do was cause a PR nightmare. Thankfully, the bartender set the refreshed beer in front of me, giving me something to do with my hands and my mouth.

"You're Owen Ramsey, right?" the shortest of the trio asked, his eyes lighting up in the process. As nice as it was to be amidst a fan, I was not in the right headspace to make a lot of conversation.

"I am," I said, lifting the new glass and taking a sip of the amber lager.

"Wow. I knew you grew up here, but I never expected to see you in person. I'm a big fan." He continued to list off some plays and data like he was reading directly from my stats sheet.

One of the other two men seemed interested as well, while the other looked off and winked at the women who had been vying for my attention not a full minute before. Out of the three, he was what most women would call handsome. He resembled someone from a cologne advertisement I'd seen in a magazine at the airport. His blond hair was slicked back, and he had an end-of-the-day shadow along his jawline.

While I'd been busy eyeing his friend, the man who'd been chatting my ear off asked a question that I missed. Thankfully, he let it slide when I apologized, and he repeated himself.

"Want to join us for a game of pool?"

The hope in his eyes almost had me caving, but I held strong. Sipping my drink again, I shook my head slowly.

"Sorry. I'm… uh… waiting for a friend," I lied. For a split second, I thought about calling my old high-school buddy Chris, but I hadn't spoken a word to him since graduation.

Truthfully, I hadn't spoken a word to anyone since that day. I hadn't been close enough to anyone in school to want to keep in contact. The one time I'd been home as my mom's plus-one for a wedding I'd kept a low profile. It was easier. Safer.

"But maybe next time?" I added as the man's eyebrows tilted downward in disappointment. His demeanor instantly changed, and the three of them made their way to the side room where some pool tables were set up.

With my admirer's retreat, I spun to face the bar, turning my back to the crowd. I watched as the droplets of condensation raced down the side of the chilled beer glass. Two of them sped up, and I internally chose a winner, grinning when it reached the epoxy-coated bar top first.

From the corner of my eye, I watched as someone planted themselves on the barstool next to me. I really hoped it wasn't another fan. As much as I appreciated them, I just wanted to sit in peace and have a drink or five. I'd figure out later how I was getting home.

A home that no longer existed.

The thought of sleeping in my car left me gulping the rest of my beer in one fell swoop.

"Never thought I'd see the day," a rough but familiar voice said beside me, with a chuckle that wrapped around me like a tight embrace. I closed my eyes forcefully, relishing the sound.

Opening them in a flash, I spun on my stool, facing my guest with a grin that I usually reserved for myself. One of true happiness. "Coach Rudicell."

That man had been my savior when I was growing up. Because of our small town, he was the coach for the recreational T-ball and baseball teams I was on, as well as the high school baseball coach. But not only had he been my mentor, he'd been the closest thing I had to a real father. The kind who cared about you and made sure you were doing all the right things.

I feared he knew what my home life was like and did so out of pity, but I wouldn't have changed a second of the time I got to spend with him. Some days, I even lied to my mom about what time practice was ending, just so I could spend more time with him. Our one-on-one sessions were my lifeline.

"How you doing, kid?" The lines around his eyes deepened as he grinned. His face was leatherier than I remembered. Years of being out in the sun and having a hard life. His wife of thirty years had passed away when I was a junior in high school. That was the first time I'd ever witnessed an adult male crying.

"I'm… okay."

"Surprised to see you home. Heard about the wedding. Sorry about that."

"Yeah. It happens." I wasn't even heartbroken over it. Just hated I didn't find out until the day of our I-dos. "Coming home was the only way I could escape my ex and the paps."

He chuckled again before taking a sip of his own beer. I mimicked his movements and enjoyed the cool liquid sliding down my throat. "I can't imagine what that's like, but you know you can't avoid them forever. They'll find you if they look hard enough."

I recalled him saying something similar when I was packing up to leave town without a backward glance for the first time. That was an instance no one knew about. No one but Coach Rudicell. It was after my dad left a boot-sized bruise on the side of my ribs and I could barely catch my breath. I tried to fight back that day, but my father was a massive beast and took me down without much of a hassle. Rudicell caught me in the locker room after practice with my backpack filled with clothes. He was smart enough to put the pieces together and let me stay with him that night.

"I know. Come here often?"

"Nah. I heard you were in town, and your mom called and asked me to check up on you. I scoped the school and baseball fields first. This was my last stop."

Grumbling, I uttered, "I'm not a child."

Coach must have heard, because he replied, "We know that. She just cares. Your mom has missed you all these years, but she never complains. Anytime she gets the chance, she goes on and on about how proud she is of you."

Well, if hearing that didn't sting like a thousand porcupine quills. I knew her heart was in the right place, but I'd sent her all that money to help her move on from the lies and the heartbreak my dad caused. Not for her to stuff it away in an account that only I was able to access. The condemned house had been bad enough, but to hear she was working off the double mortgage and personal loans my father had taken out under her name and squandered had been overwhelming. If the man hadn't died, I would have killed him myself.

"I know she is. I'm not mad at her. Just upset that she kept me in the dark all these years."

"Hard to bring you to the light when you chain yourself to the shadows."

Tipping the glass back, I swallowed the rest of the liquid as I turned to face the mirror over the bar across from me.

"You're welcome to stay with me if you need to, but I think you need to have a sit-down with your mom. Let her explain."

"Since when have you and Beverly been so close?" I asked cynically.

"Since I was the only one who *really* listened." Coach quieted, letting his words sink in. It was confirmation that he'd known what had been going on all along.

Fucking embarrassing to realize my coach absolutely knew what was happening behind closed doors. About the torment my mother and I suffered. At any other time, I'd be angry as hell that he didn't help, but I remembered my attitude as a teen. I was a pompous asshole who acted out as a way to keep the attention there and away from the agony.

"Thanks for the offer," I said as I gestured to the bartender again, offering to refill Coach's as well. The burly man shook his head and slipped off the stool.

"I'll be seeing you around, kid. Would love to have you stop by the school and meet some of the players. Would mean a lot to them."

"You're still coaching?"

"They'll have to kill me before I stop," he joked as he set a twenty on the bar. His drink was only a quarter of that amount. "Don't be a stranger."

Our ten-minute conversation felt like it lasted years. I was worn out, as if dragged through the mud in the rain and left outside to weather the storm.

"Maybe something stronger with this too? Shot of gin?"

The bartender went to work on the shot after setting my frothy refill in front of me in a new frosty mug. A second later, he set the one-ounce glass in front of me and moved to the other end of the bar, lifting a hinged portion of it to leave it unmanned.

Splaying my hands on the sticky bar top, I watched as the expanse of my fingers nearly reached the opposite edge. Having large hands made my job much easier, even with a mitt. Grabbing the shot glass, two of my fingers wrapped around the drink. It reminded me of one of the thimbles my mom wore on her finger when she used to have to patch my clothes, since we couldn't afford new pairs of jeans and all mine had holes in them.

Fuck.

Thinking of my mom only depressed me more.

Tossing back the shot, I let the gin, which tasted awful, slip down my throat before chasing it with my beer.

I fucking hated liquor, but I needed something to take the edge off, and the beer wasn't cutting it.

An obnoxious scent clouded around me, and I nearly coughed when the brunette who had fluffed her hair earlier sidled up beside me. She didn't bother with the stool, instead wrapping her pink-tipped fingers around my forearm and pressing her breasts against my bicep. She was pretty. Even beneath all that makeup, she was probably still a knockout. But without even her making a suggestion, I knew my cock wasn't interested. Which was a shame, because at least if I went home with her, I'd have a place to sleep tonight.

My mind started playing out different scenarios as she fluttered her lashes and pursed her lips. I could get her off and hope that my dick would come around. That was the best-case situation.

"Hi," she finally said, licking her lips in invitation.

"Hey."

"I'm Kasey. I've been waiting for my chance to come over here. You're quite the popular fellow."

"Owen, and I'm sorry about that. Just a few people wanting to catch up." I smirked at her, but it felt off. Thankfully, she didn't seem to notice.

Deciding she was my shot at a bed instead of sleeping in my car or at my old coach's house, I played the part of the playboy. The part I perfected when I was drafted by the Coyotes. The part that got me the supermodel fiancée.

Ex-fiancée.

"Would you want to buy me a drink, Owen?"

I held back my sigh, not wanting her to notice how uninterested I was. Instead, I nodded just as the bartender returned and ordered her another dirty martini.

For a while, she droned on about her work—a teller at the bank, and her hobbies—watching reality television, specifically a show about marrying someone they just met. I did my best to feign interest, but I wouldn't recall a single detail if she quizzed me later. But she continued to inch closer, something I wasn't sure was possible, since her body was already pressed against mine.

The air shifted as the song on the jukebox changed, and I glanced up in the mirror to find my little nightmare stroll in. She was wearing the same pair of cutoff jeans that forced your eyes to gaze at her toned, tan legs. Even at her miniscule height, her legs looked like they went on for days. Tucked into the waistband was a loose white T-shirt, the neckline hanging off a bare shoulder. A pair of clean cowboy boots, these in much better condition than the ones she had on earlier, finished her ensemble.

Though it was a local pub, Aspen wasn't dressed like the rest of the women in the bar. She was all casual, where the rest were dressed for finding a husband, or a night of fun. But even without trying, she was the most beautiful woman in the place.

Definitely couldn't let that secret out. She'd hold it against me for all eternity.

I continued watching her in the mirror, chiming into my conversation with Kasey when necessary, but my mind was focused elsewhere. Specifically on the blonde sitting at a table in the corner with a friend who was staring at the group of suits near the pool tables.

They ordered drinks, and I was surprised when Aspen wanted a beer. She was the only female in the place that I could see without a cocktail of some sort.

Kasey must have noticed my wavering attention. Her nails sank into my skin, and my fist flexed out of reflex. Jerking my face in her direction, away from the mirror, I narrowed my gaze.

"Don't," I snapped harshly. It was my first reaction to the pain. Triggering a memory of someone gripping my arm, inflicting their strength over mine. I could only mask the fear with irritation.

Thankfully, Kasey was either too buzzed from the alcohol or too unobservant to notice. She perched her chin on my shoulder and whispered in my ear. I couldn't make out a lot of what she was saying, but I picked up on a phrase or two, like "have fun in the bathroom."

I was well past the college days of hooking up in a public bathroom.

From the corner of my eye, I noticed Aspen's friend stand up from the table and move down a hallway.

"Excuse me," I mumbled to Kasey. "I see my friend. Enjoy your drink."

I left her gaping like a catfish as I pushed away from the bar, and her hooks, making my way to my favorite person who hated me with a vengeance. I left her on a bad note earlier, lashing out when I'd been angry at myself and my mother.

Should I go over and apologize?

Yes.

Will I?

Absolutely not.

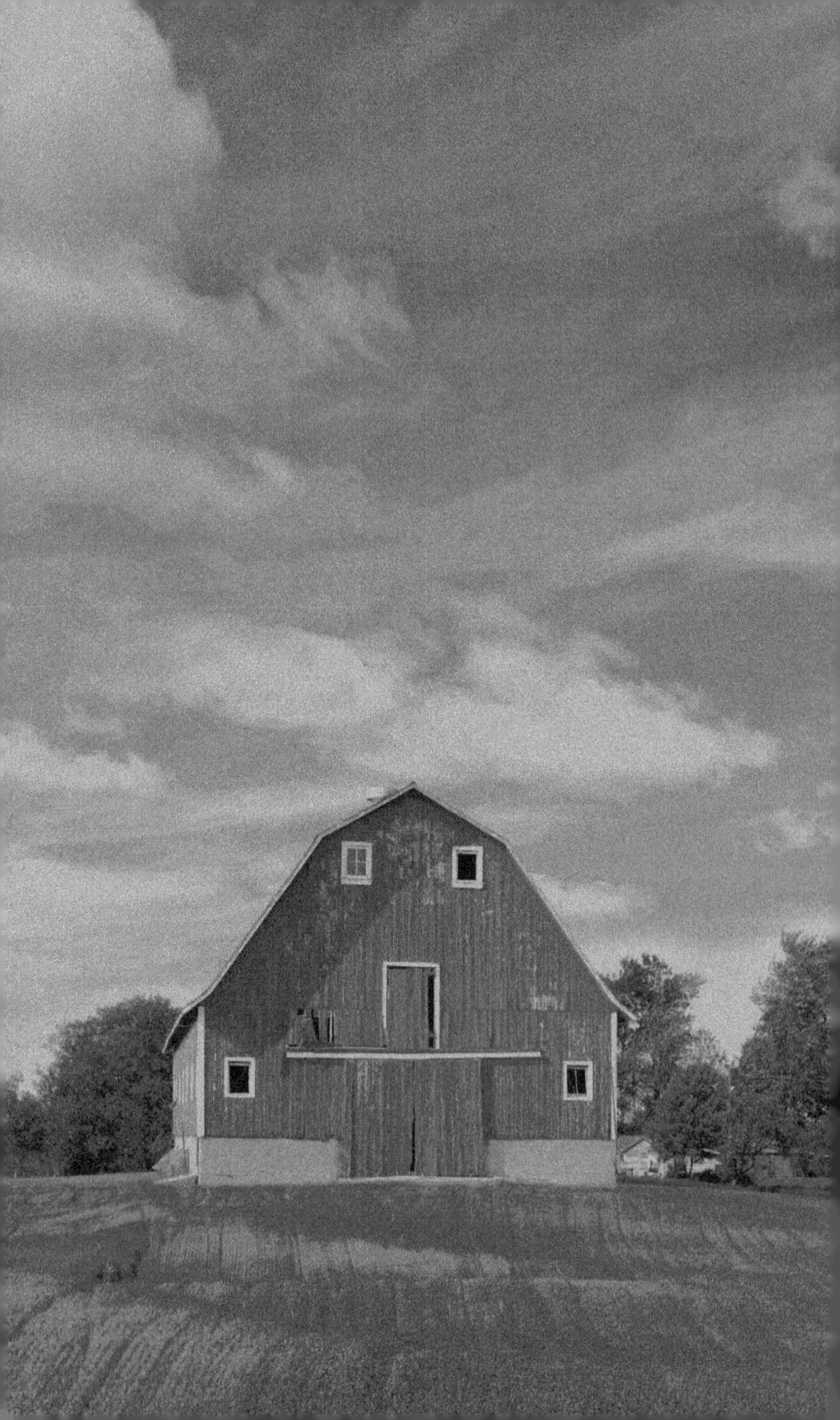

Chapter Five

Aspen

I felt like an anomaly, sitting in here. Not only was I severely underdressed compared to the other women in the bar, but I'd only been here once before to socialize.

My sister, Alex, used to manage the bar, so there were many nights when I would come to keep her company when it was slow, or I'd hide here when I wanted to get away from my parents. But for a night out with friends? This made twice.

Because this was not my natural habitat, and I felt like I stuck out like a sore thumb. I felt the eyes of both men and women as I walked into the space. Instantly, I felt like tugging down the hem of my shorts. I was a gazelle waltzing through a pride of lions. It was terrifying.

Thankfully, Jenna found a table right away, far in the corner, where I could observe but not be seen. Though, I still felt the wondering gazes and stares from the people close by.

Jenna ordered herself a Dirty Shirley. I knew nothing about cocktails, but I ordered a local beer on tap. She sneered but didn't say a word about my selection.

"I'm glad you finally joined me," she said the minute the server stepped away.

"You didn't leave me much choice." I promised her a few times over the summer I would make it out, but I failed every attempt. Not only did my anxiety skyrocket at the thought of being out in public, but I did not know how to act around people. Engaging in conversation with others was not my forte. I'd take hanging out with cattle or goats instead any day.

But today, when she messaged me to go out with her, like she did every weekend, I actually accepted. The interaction with Owen this afternoon left me frazzled. A stark reminder of why I stayed away from social settings, aside from the market when it was my turn to sell.

"Yes, but it didn't take much convincing. Tryston is over by the pool tables."

My eyes immediately darted in that direction over her shoulder. He was there, towering over his friends. He was still dressed in a suit, which I didn't understand, but Jenna tried explaining to me before that lawyers didn't take days off. I thought maybe he was just trying to appeal to the women in town.

For whatever reason, he was gorgeous to me, when not many men registered that way in my mind. He was taller than his two friends, but no more than six feet at best.

He moved to town a year ago, and I bumped into him at Chuck's Grocery. We reached for the Boston Crème Pie at the same time, and I'd been infatuated ever since. His New England accent pulled me in. I was so used to a Southern drawl that his seemed exotic.

I knew through the grapevine—aka Jenna—that he worked at the law office in town and was single. It was perfect for someone like me, who grew up with most of the eligible men in town. Most were either married already, or they were on the prowl for Susie Homemaker.

I was the complete opposite of that. I had my own farm to manage—or at least I would soon.

Sipping my beer, I let Jenna chatter on while I watched Tryston with rapt attention. He tossed his head back in laughter at something his friend said, and my own grin emerged.

Lost in my own thoughts, I almost missed her asking, "Is that Owen Ramsey at the bar?"

I glanced up to look at the crowd formed around the man seated at the bar. Owen was wearing his same shirt from earlier. But even without those clothes, I'd recognize him anywhere. Years of witnessing his retreating back as I glared at him and his clique cemented his body shape in my mind.

"Appears to be," I said nonchalantly as I took a drink. "Kasey already claimed him, it seems," I added.

Kasey Sinclair was a recently divorced bank teller. Despite how she appeared, with her hand wrapped possessively around Owen's arm, she was extremely nice. Last year, she went through a nasty divorce with the sous chef at world-renowned chef Roland McEntire's restaurant in town.

Like me, she was joining the dating pool again. Unlike me, she actually knew how to converse with men.

Chiming in after taking a deep sip of her drink, she said, "I don't think he's interested."

My brows pinched together as I asked, "What makes you say that?"

"Because in the mirror, he's staring at you. Only I can't decide if he's plotting your demise, like always, or if he's appreciating you."

Giggling, I set my beer down and replied, "Definitely plotting my demise. It's our MO, after all."

"Things change." She shrugged, one strap of her sundress slipping down her shoulder, and she pushed it up as she stood. "I need to use the restroom. Order me another?"

"Sure."

Failing in my attempt to *not* watch Tryston play pool with his friends, I locked eyes with him once, then I immediately glanced away. Just in time for Owen to slip into my line of sight.

My eyes rolled automatically. It was a reaction I conditioned myself to have in his presence many, many years ago.

"Hi, cricket," he said despondently. It was a tone I'd never heard from him before, and it made me curious. We didn't part on good terms earlier, but I assumed by now that he would be back to his cocky old self.

Despite that change, I sneered at him. "Don't call me that."

"What else should I call you?" he asked as he took the vacant seat.

"I don't know, Owen. Maybe my actual name?"

He pursed his lips, and I assumed he was considering my request. "Nah. I think I'll keep calling you cricket."

"Whatever," I mumbled as I took a sip of my beer and turned my gaze back up to the bar. Kasey leaned her lithe frame against the bar top, narrowing her eyes in my direction. I was fairly certain if I walked outside right now, she'd follow me and have me shanked. Nervous from that thought, I begrudgingly turned my attention back to Owen, whose eyes were glued to me.

I shifted in my seat. "You know, my friend will be back soon."

Leaning back in the chair, Owen replied, "I know. I don't think she'll mind if I'm here. We can always drag over another chair."

I almost spit out my beer at his arrogance. "Owen, you want to sit here, in the bar, with me and Jenna?"

"Jenna Tipson? I knew she looked familiar. I played ball with her older brother."

"Yes, I remember. Now, why do you want to sit with us?"

"Well…," he began, just as a woman sauntered over and slipped him her number.

My jaw unhinged as I watched her casually slink her fingers across his shoulder in her retreat.

She was the first but not the last.

In the time we sat waiting for Jenna's return, women vying for his attention approached him four more times. And, as usual, I was completely invisible to them all.

Thankfully, Jenna appeared from the hallway, chatting with a guy. That would explain what took her so long, while I had the "pleasure" of watching Owen's own dating show unfold before me.

"Does that get tiring?" I asked him after the fifth woman left.

"Until recently, it wasn't really a problem. My fiancée… well, ex-fiancée, always booked us private booths. Sometimes at games we get approached, but… yeah… I mean…." Owen's usually confident demeanor slipped, and I noticed the redness growing on his tan cheeks.

"Anyway, is there something you needed?" I asked, trying to get him to leave the table. The whispers were growing louder with each passing second, and there was already a group forming near the entrance to catch a glimpse of *the* Owen Ramsey. I almost wished the town wasn't growing like weeds. If we were in the bar with the people we grew up with, no one here would care much that Owen was back in Ashfield. They'd be more concerned that we were seated together.

Just that thought left me snickering. I covered my mouth with my hand but didn't miss the way Owen's eyes followed the movement.

"Maybe. Can I ask you something?"

"Uh, sure?" I cocked my head in intrigue.

"I watched you walk in—"

"Stalker much?"

Owen mimicked my head tilt, and continued, "I watched you walk in, and you seemed like you wanted to be anywhere else. Why is that?"

Pausing, I looked over at Jenna to find her even deeper in conversation with the man.

I leaned forward and rested my arms on the table, clasping both hands around my cold glass. "This isn't really my scene. Not that there's anything wrong with socializing at the local watering hole, but for me, I'm usually in bed in about an hour. Ugh. Just thinking about how tired I'm going to be tomorrow makes my eyes hurt."

Swigging his drink, Owen then mirrored my stance, his own glass wrapped between his large hands. "First off, no one uses the term 'watering hole.' We're not in a Western film. Second, you should take some time to get out every once in a while. I'm sure the farm will survive without you for a day or two."

He was making the same observation as Dean, yet it irked me to hear it from Owen. Especially since he had no clue about the plans I was drawing up for his family's property.

"We have some workers that live in town, but my dad and I are still very hands-on. And I wouldn't change anything. I love it."

"Do you though? Seems really lonely, if you ask me."

Well, shit. I didn't know how to respond to that, because Owen was absolutely right. Besides Jenna, I had no real friends, no actual relationships. My life had always been set to take over the farm. Everything else was unnecessary. Until Owen pointed it out, I hadn't realized how lonely I truly was.

But I could fix that. It was what drove me to meet up with Jenna in the first place. Did I need a relationship? No. Would it be nice? Sure. But what I sought was intimacy. I was a twenty-four-year-old virgin who had barely done more than kiss, aside from the single blowjob I'd given. There were teens who saw more action than I have. I knew for a fact that Jenna lost her virginity to Carl Southland at sixteen. I hadn't been jealous then, but I was now.

As a distraction, I gazed over at Tryston, who was bent over the pool table, his backside in my direction. Of course, he was showing a woman—one who'd propositioned Owen—how to line up a shot. She was pressed against him, and I instantly felt envious. Not of her flirting with Tryston, but of her confidence. I lacked that in spades.

I was too lost in my own world that I missed Owen following my stare, until he asked, "Who are we looking at?"

"We're not," I immediately corrected.

"My guess is the taller one. He seems like your type."

My gaze shooting to Owen, I asked, "What makes you say that?"

"Just taking a guess. Since you work outside most of the day, I assumed you probably want someone stable enough in their own career. The suit looks that way. Of course, I don't know who wears a suit to a bar on the weekend."

"He's a lawyer, and their practice is open seven days a week. Farmers aren't the only ones who have crazy schedules."

The corner of Owen's mouth tips upward, and he leans back in victory. "Yet he seems to make time to go out and pick up a woman or two."

"Touché."

"So, why aren't you over there talking to him?"

Sighing, I swirl my fingers through the condensation on the glass. "I don't know. I just…. I'm not that kind of girl."

"What do you mean?"

My fingers continue their wet path along the glass, creating images in the moisture. "I just…."

Suddenly, my fingers are pulled from their doodling, and they rest in Owen's warm grasp. "You just what?" he requested, but all I could focus on was the feel of his thumb rubbing small circles against my palm.

Without thinking, I said, "You know, people are going to wonder why you're holding my hand right now."

Immediately, he replied, "Let them wonder. Now, explain why you aren't over there talking to the guy you're attracted to?"

"Owen…," I whined.

He copycatted, "Aspen."

"Ugh, I can't believe I'm telling you this," I mumbled before slipping my hand free from his. I'd never admit how much I immediately missed the feeling. "I just don't know how, okay? I don't know how to flirt or appear interested. I barely know how to strike up a conversation with a stranger unless it's something work-related."

"That's not true. You're talking to me right now."

My head fell back in a haunted laugh. The kind that forces everyone to think you've gone crazy. "Owen, I'm only talking to you because I've known you since we were six. You know, when you made it your life's mission to see how much you could torment me?"

"Aw… cricket, that hurts. I thought you actually liked me."

"Why would I like you? When have we ever gotten along?"

"We're getting along now," he pointed out, and I paused because he was right. In the last ten minutes, we had been getting along. The world didn't implode, and the sun didn't detonate.

Now, I secretly wondered if someone was filming me for a prank show. Sitting up in my chair, I glanced around quickly, searching for any hidden cameras. I locked eyes with Jenna in my exploration, and she held up a hand to her newly acquired date, then made her way over to me.

"Owen Ramsey, what a surprise to see you here."

"It's nice to see you too, Jenna. It's been a while." She rested a hand on the back of his chair and tilted forward. But unlike the women who slipped Owen their numbers, nothing about her stance was sexual. It was friendly and open, yet I still felt a pang of jealousy, and I had no idea why.

I chalked it up to being envious of her ability to speak to everyone like a lifelong friend. It was a talent Jenna possessed since we were kids.

"It has," she added. "So, what are you two talking about over here?"

Chiming in quickly, I replied, "Nothing."

Both of them swiveled their heads in my direction at my outburst.

"Actually, we were just discussing Aspen's love life."

"Oh."

"I don't have a love life," I added. "And Owen was just leaving, now that you've returned."

Jenna's face pinched. "Actually, Derek and I are going to head out and go back to his place for a bit."

"Oh, well, I can close our tabs really quick." I'd driven separately, since my dad drove me to my car at Chuck's and gave it a jump before I came here, but I didn't want to hang out at the bar by myself if she was leaving. And I wasn't going to complain she was ditching me when I didn't want to be here in the first place.

As I went to stand, Jenna forcefully pushed at my shoulder for me to remain seated. "No, you stay."

I tried to argue with her that I had no reason to stay, but Owen inserted himself into the quarrel and said, "Actually, cricket, I have something I want to discuss with you. Please stay."

And shit, I was a goner. Even with him saying the nickname I despised, hearing Owen ask me so nicely to stay melted me faster than the frost on my beer glass.

"Fine," I grumbled, and I didn't miss the way his eyes lit up in triumph.

Jenna flagged down the server and paid her bill, then she said goodbye, leaving with Derek in tow. I watched them leave with a sense of longing. I'd never left anywhere with a guy before. Never taken a guy back to my place or gone back to theirs. I felt even smaller than a wallflower. I was the tiny seed that got no sun or rain. I had no way to grow.

"Earth to Aspen."

At the sound of my name, I jerked my head around to where Owen waited with a patient smile. It was a look I'd never witnessed on his face before.

"Sorry. You don't have to sit with me, you know. I'm a big girl."

"I know, but I wasn't lying. I actually have something to discuss with you. Something that may benefit both of us."

Just as he finished his statement, a gorgeous blonde I'd never seen in town before pranced over and fawned over Owen. It was like the world found out he was newly single, and the women were out for blood.

I watched, fascinated, as he gently pried her arms from around his shoulders and explained he was busy. The woman never even turned her head to look in my direction. Instead, she retrieved a marker from her purse, then quickly started jotting down a series of numbers across some of his tattoos on his forearm. She'd clearly done this before, the way she didn't even hesitate.

When he realized what she was doing, he jerked his arm away, the marker leaving a long streak in its wake.

Despite her actions, Owen scolded her tenderly as he stood. I realized for the first time that Owen rarely ever lost his cool. Even through all the antics I performed at his and his clique's expense during school, he never shouted or seemed angry. It was a shocking revelation after knowing what I did about his father.

The woman fled through the exit as quickly as she'd come.

"Look, I was being sincere when I said I wanted to talk to you about something, but I'm drawing a crowd. Is there anywhere else we could talk?"

"Talk?"

"Yes, form words with our tongues and create sentences. Just like that."

"Asshole. I know what you meant, but you *actually* want to talk to me about something?"

"I do. I want to help you, and I think you can help me."

I pondered his request, then stood, pulled a twenty out of my back pocket, and set it on the table, then gestured for him to follow me. "I suppose we're both in luck."

"What makes you say that?" he asked as he stood and moved around the table until he was barely an arm's length away.

"Because I may be able to help you out with something else too."

"Truce?" he prompted, holding out his hand, and I rolled my eyes, ignoring his gesture.

"Come on, baseball star. Follow me."

I turned to the door as Owen broke out in a grin, his hand still extended in the air. I ignored the curious looks and made my way to the exit, only to feel his arm drape over my shoulders when I reached the halfway mark.

I hated the attention the move caused, but at the same time, I tucked my chin toward my chest and hid my smile.

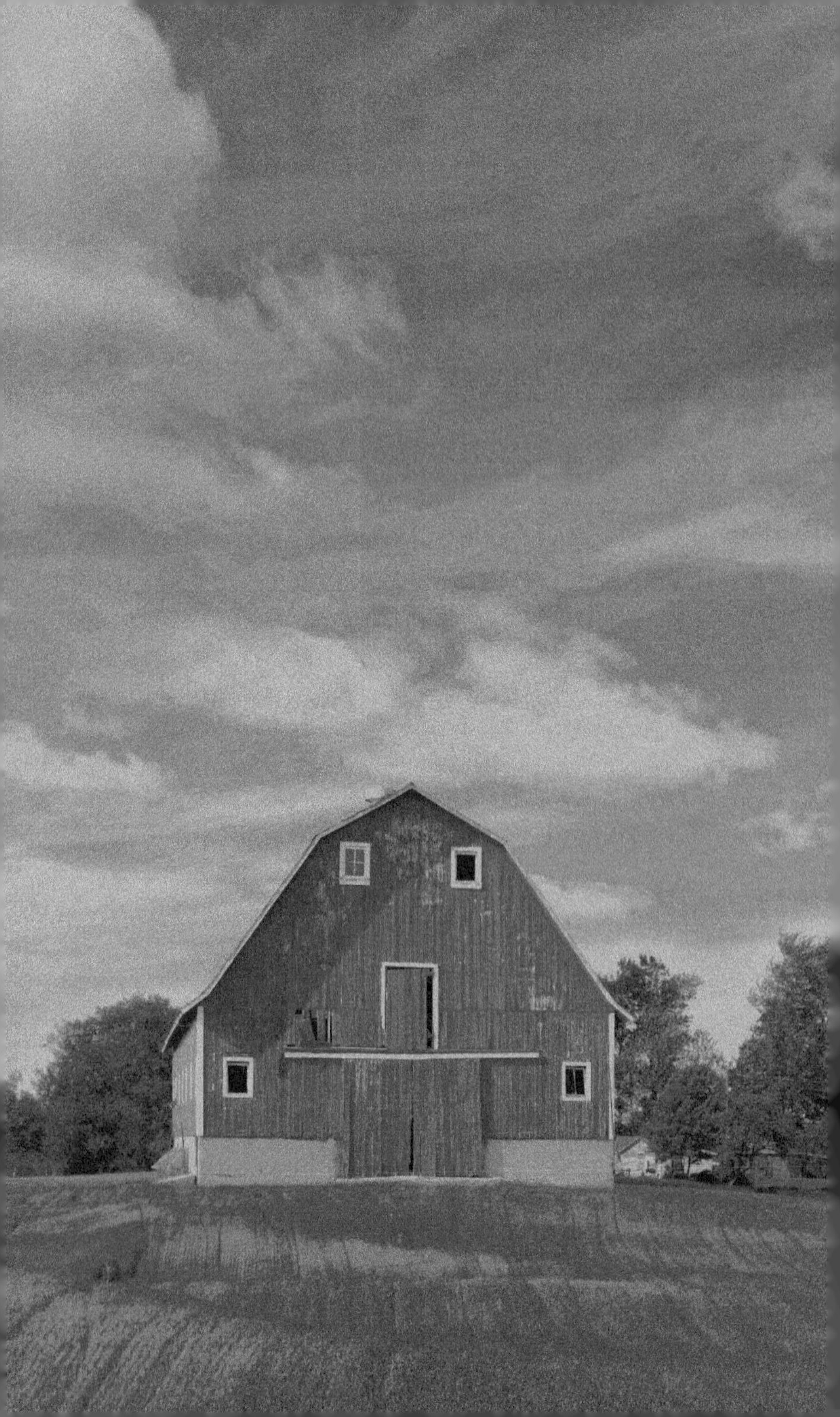

Chapter Six

Owen

Walking out of the bar, I felt like a zoo animal, everyone's eyes on us as they tried to catch a glimpse of something amazing. The spectacle was that Aspen and I were walking together. Something had possessed me to wrap my arm around her narrow shoulders and pull her closer. Maybe, deep inside, I wanted to see how shocked I could leave everyone.

Should I have been worried about pictures? Definitely. But with her, I didn't care. In the end, all of it would play into the ploy I was going to present her.

As we exited, I caught a quick peek of Aspen's face in the glass of the door. Her reflection showed a slight smile.

Once we escaped into the darkness of night, which was illuminated by twinkling lights strung across the road and sidewalk of downtown Ashfield, Aspen slipped out from under my arm.

An apology for the gesture sat at the edge of my lips, but I couldn't find it in myself to start the sentence. Instead, I followed her to her beat-up sedan. My own car was parked close by.

She spun on her heels and faced me, the sound of the loose gravel crunching surrounding us. "How intoxicated are you right now?"

Catching me off guard, I paused. "What?"

"How much have you had to drink?"

"I couple beers and a shot. Why?"

"Get in." Aspen gestured to her small car, and I sneered at the thought of contorting my body into the compact vehicle.

"Look, cricket—" I began, but she immediately cut me off as she added, "Owen, I will not let you drive if you've had more than two drinks. Got it?"

She even stomped her cute little foot, and I had to hold back my laughter.

"Look," I started, holding my hands up in surrender. "I understand. I'm just saying I don't think I'll fit in your car. Maybe we can take mine. I'll make sure you get home."

"Oh." Aspen glanced down at her car and then up at me, her eyes wide and sparkling from the lights. "You're probably right."

Chuckling, I asked her to repeat what she said, and she responded with a strangely powerful shove before walking over to my vehicle. By the time I arrived, her hand was outstretched for the keys, but she hesitated before getting inside.

"You didn't do anything to the car, did you? Like, cut the brake line or something like that?"

"Why would I do that, cricket?"

"So I'm framed for your murder. The ultimate prank."

"Wow, you are paranoid. Just get in the car and find a place for us to talk."

"I don't fully trust you."

"Well, I'm trusting you to drive me somewhere safely…"

I let my confession linger, opening the door for her, and I smiled as she nodded subtly and slunk down into the driver seat. After shutting her inside, I moved around the car and got into the passenger seat. Without a word, she turned on the car and pulled us out onto Main Street. Soon, we were headed toward a path I was very familiar with.

As if she could read my mind, Aspen informed me that we were going to Sunny Book Farms.

"You're welcome to stay at the bed-and-breakfast with your mom, if you'd like, but I figured you could stay at one of the ranch houses. We have a few vacant."

"Thanks, that's really nice of you."

"Don't get too excited. It's not long-term, but I may be able to get a place for you while you're home. I just need to ask my sister, Rory."

"You don't have to do any of this, Aspen."

"I know."

It was refreshing that she didn't offer an explanation or use it as a one-up on me. Maybe she felt a bit bad about everything that transpired earlier today with my mother and my childhood home, but none of that was her fault.

"I owe you."

Chuckling, she added, "You definitely don't." There was a pregnant pause before she said, "So…," then glanced over at me. Our eyes locked, and we both burst out in laughter. "Tell me about baseball."

"You really want to talk about that?" I asked with a snicker.

"I know nothing about what you do. I don't follow sports. But you're a shortstop, right? I think I remember that from high school."

"Yeah. I play for the Coyotes. I just signed another five-year contract."

"Word about that got around town. A lot of people are proud of you."

"What about you?"

"What *about* me?" she asked as we took the ninety-degree blind turn in the road that I always hated. "I told you everything about me. I'm a farm girl, remember?"

"You never wanted to do anything else?"

"I didn't really have a choice, Owen. Some of us aren't talented enough to do more than what we're handed."

Turning in my seat, I leaned toward the center console. In the confined space, her clean scent filled my lungs. "If you could do anything, money was no object, what would you do?"

"Why do you want to know?" she asked incredulously.

"Humor me."

She puffed out a breath, before replying, "Travel."

Her answer surprised me, and I made it known in my response.

"I've always wanted to see the world. Not just the tourist sites, I want to explore everything. Owen, I've never been out of this area on my own. It's only ever been family trips or something like that. But, yeah," she said, as if catching herself exposing more than she meant to, as we turned onto a dirt path off the main road. "I'd want to travel."

"You should."

Her shoulders moved upward toward her ears before falling back down.

We didn't speak any more on the ride, but I contemplated the kind of life Aspen lived. She was the quintessential good girl. She didn't go causing trouble, unless it involved terrorizing me in school, but even then, she was never malicious. Aspen seemed to think the farm was her duty, her contribution to the family. I almost felt bad for her situation, but right now, it was going to work in my favor.

She pulled the car around to a few row homes on the Sunny Brook Farms property. I didn't recall them being there from when I'd sneak onto their land, but these were off the beaten path.

"How far away are we from the main house?" I asked as she turned off the car and exited. The darkness of the space was eerie. I hadn't been around this utter and complete blackness in years, and it was jarring as I stepped out of the vehicle. Not a single light was on in the house, but Aspen seemed like she knew exactly where she was headed.

"It's right down the hill. We're a lot closer than you think."

"Where are we exactly?" I asked, suddenly afraid I walked into a horror film and was about to be the victim.

As if sensing my emerging fear, Aspen took a step closer to me and whispered, "Scared?"

"No," I lied as my voice shook.

Then, without a sound, all the lights around the house illuminated, including a few inside. My heart jumped into my throat.

"For fuck's sake." Leaning over, I rested one hand on my pounding heart and another on my knee as Aspen's laughter swirled around me.

"There's a motion sensor on the outside floodlights, and a timer inside for the living room lamps. I'm normally asleep by now."

"And they just happened to go off at the same time?"

"As luck would have it," she said through a giggle as she stepped onto the tiny porch. "Come on, scaredy cat."

My steps were slow as I made my way to the front door, but I hesitated at the threshold. Reality hit that I was stepping into Aspen's space, a place I imagined numerous times as a teen. Most of the boys in school did, even though she was apparently clueless of their admiration. But what I imagined was nothing like what greeted me on the other side.

Shutting the door behind me, I glanced to the right, where there was a small makeshift kitchen with a sink, two lower cabinets, some shelves, and a hotpot. Across from me was a living space that I assumed also served as a bedroom. The entire thing was no larger than some New York City apartments.

But even in the limited space, I could see that Aspen had made it her own. It was light and airy with the longest wall decorated in a dozen or so pictures. The images depicted famous cities, all in black-and-white prints, with the name of the location written in bold lettering below.

Anyone who walked into the space would immediately guess that Aspen was well-traveled. It was such a shame that reality was the opposite.

"Welcome to my humble abode."

I watched as she toed off her boots, then slinked farther into the room, tossing her bag onto the two-person table in the corner.

"I like it," I replied genuinely. For all it lacked in space, I could tell the place was a home. Which was a far cry from the mansion I owned in Los Angeles.

"It's small. And I have to go to the main house for a regular meal. The other row homes have a stove and microwave. I chose this one because…"

She was rambling, and it was adorable. Casually, I walked over and reached out to touch her bare arm. The gasp that left her lips was unexpected but not unwelcome.

"There's… uh… a bedroom in the loft. I don't know why I told you that." She shook her head, the soft curls of her hair stroking the back of my hand. "Can I get you a water, soda, or beer?"

"A beer, if you don't mind."

Aspen's hips swayed as she walked, and unlike most of the women I ran into tonight, her movements were completely natural and unforced. She had a natural sex appeal that was untapped. As she leaned into the small fridge, I found myself staring at her round backside, imagining what it would look like beneath those denim shorts.

I darted my eyes over to the couch as she stood up straight with the beers in hand, to keep from being caught checking out her ass.

"Have a seat. Now, what did you want to talk about?"

The couch dipped as she sat beside me, a little farther than I was used to people wanting to be to me, but I couldn't expect her to treat me like her new best friend overnight. Well, actually, I needed her to do more.

"I was thinking about both of our… predicaments."

One of her naturally arched eyebrows cocked as her lips pursed.

"Look, my ex won't stop calling. Every message is more desperate than the last. Her cheating on me made me realize I never really loved her. I think it was the thought of being married to her is what drove me, and probably her too. But I need her to realize that I'm *not devastated,* nor do I want her back.

"And I also have the issue of women throwing themselves at me now that I'm single."

She grunted, and I thought about how cocky that must have sounded.

"Aspen, you saw how the women were tonight. That was over the course of an hour. I even got propositioned by the flight attendant on the plane home. Don't get me wrong; I'm not mad about it. But I need to focus on baseball while I'm here. Not sidestepping every woman who wants to give me her number."

"Okay, but what does any of this have to do with me, except being witness to the throngs of women vying for your attention?"

Chugging my beer for liquid courage, I smiled as I finished and set the bottle on the coffee table.

"I am so glad you asked. In return for helping me, I will help you get the guy of your dreams. All by agreeing to fake date me. It will keep the girls off my back, hopefully, and I'll teach you how to talk to men and flirt. It's a win-win."

With an unladylike snort, Aspen lifted her beer to her lips and took a healthy gulp. Her eyes were trained on the opposing wall of photographs, and I couldn't get a read on what she was thinking.

Either she was going to laugh in my face, or she was going to laugh in acceptance. Regardless, I was waiting to hear the chime of her melodic giggle.

"What?" she squeaked and then cleared her throat. "What would all of this entail?"

Her question gave me pause, and I leaned forward, rubbing one finger across my bottom lip as I pondered my answer.

"Honestly, I haven't thought it out that far. I would think a couple of dates in town with some posts on social media. Maybe seen around shopping or at the market. That's still a thing, right? The Saturday farmer's market?"

"Yeah," she whispered as she tucked a loose strand of hair behind her ear. "What... um.... I mean, how would you teach me?"

"Well, during these dates, we can use them as classes. I'll teach you how to talk to a guy, what to wear, things like that. At the end, we can stage a breakup, and you can pursue the suit."

"Hm...."

Reaching out, I grabbed her knee farthest from me and used it to twist her body to face mine. I took a moment to appreciate the feel of her soft skin beneath my fingers. "What's the hesitation? We both get something out of it."

"First, I'm trying to figure out if you're really serious about this. Not only am I unsure that anyone in town will buy this charade, but I am a far cry from the women you've dated. Owen, I am the opposite of those supermodels. I'm just... me."

Before I had a chance to argue, Aspen continued. "And secondly, I feel like I'm getting the better side of the deal."

"I promise you, you're not. As long as my ex believes I've moved on, then the entire scheme is working. And leave the convincing everyone part up to me. I'll lay it on as thick as I need to."

"There is one more problem you haven't considered," she said, leaning closer to me with dilated eyes from the dim lamplight.

"Yeah, what's that?" The huskiness of my voice reached my own ears, and it was a sound I was unfamiliar with.

"I don't have the time."

Her gaze penetrated something inside me, and I found myself leaning closer to Aspen until our faces were only a few inches apart.

"Here's the thing about time, cricket. It's always fleeting. And I understand the dedication to your family's farm. I'm just as committed to my team, but *you* are more than the life you've been handed."

"I don't know how to be anything else."

"Then let me teach you. When we make this agreement, you can be whoever you want. And when I go back to training in five months, you can decide which cricket you want to be."

Our talk had taken on a serious note, and I threw out her nickname to get the reaction I was hoping for. Otherwise, I was likely to start our lessons sooner rather than later, because I wanted nothing more than to seal my mouth against hers.

Of course, I'd have to be careful. In the future, she'd be likely to hold a razorblade in her mouth to slice off my tongue.

But thankfully, Aspen leaned away from me with a sneer.

"I really hate when you call me that."

"I know, but I enjoy riling you up, so…."

As she stood from the small love seat, I followed her movements, grabbing her now empty bottle along the way.

"Can I think about it? Maybe give you an answer in the morning?"

"Sure."

I held up the bottles, a silent question for the location of the trash can, and she pointed me toward the cabinet under her sink. Spinning around, I leaned my body against the countertop. The entire thing shifted, and I worried I'd break the Formica.

"I guess I'll be heading out."

Rolling her eyes, Aspen moved toward a small chest and pulled out some blankets and a pillow. "You can stay here. I'll take the couch, and you can have the bed."

"Absolutely not." Eyeing the two-person loveseat, I knew even tiny Aspen was too tall to sleep comfortably on it. We'd both be uncomfortable. "You take the bed. I'll make a pallet on the floor. So long as you don't kill me in my sleep."

I could see she wanted to argue, but she relented and placed the blankets and pillow on the couch. "Okay, though I want it to go on record that I at least attempted to be civil and offered you the bed, whenever your trainer tells you that you've screwed up your back."

Little did she know sleeping on the floor wasn't nearly as bad as sleeping on the wet ground outside your family home in the hopes of avoiding your father. At least here, in her home, I'd be warm.

People tended to think my life was amazing, but they had no idea what I saw behind my eyelids every night when I fell asleep.

Aspen slipped into the small bathroom while I took the stack of blankets and laid them on the rug in the middle of the room. Shoving the coffee table against the wall, I sorted the pallet until I had a makeshift bed set up.

"Here," Aspen said, reappearing with a freshly cleaned face and an oversized shirt covering her body. In her hands, she held a mass of material. "It's a pair of basketball shorts and a T-shirt of Andrew's. You're around the same size."

"Thanks." Reaching behind my neck, I fisted my shirt and tugged it over my head. I was proud of the dips and planes of my defined muscles. The hard work I put in over the years paid off as I watched Aspen's eyes widen in shock. It made it all the more satisfying.

"I'll take these," I said as I grabbed the change of clothes and sauntered past Aspen toward the bathroom. Her mouth hung open as I closed the door behind me.

On the counter, she thoughtfully left a spare toothbrush. I prayed our truce remained intact as I brushed my teeth. I didn't need a reenactment of sixth grade, when she added Methylene Blue to my drink and left me with Smurf-colored teeth for a week.

I quickly changed out of my shorts and replaced them with the loungewear Aspen provided. By the time I made it back out to the small living space, she was nowhere to be found. There was a lamp on the end table, illuminating the room just enough for me to keep from bumping into things in the unfamiliar space.

Situating myself on the pallet, I reached up and switched off the lamp, casting the room in utter darkness except for a dim light coming from the upstairs loft area where Aspen slept.

"Goodnight, Aspen," I called out as I turned onto my side, my eyes adjusting to the darkness and focusing on the pictures across the way.

"Goodnight, Owen," she hollered in return. "Goodnight, Fred."

That gave me pause, and I found myself asking, "Who is Fred?"

"The little mouse that scurries around the house. Don't worry; he's harmless."

Was I scared of a tiny mouse? No. But did the thought of sharing my bed with a rodent keep me up half the night? Absolutely.

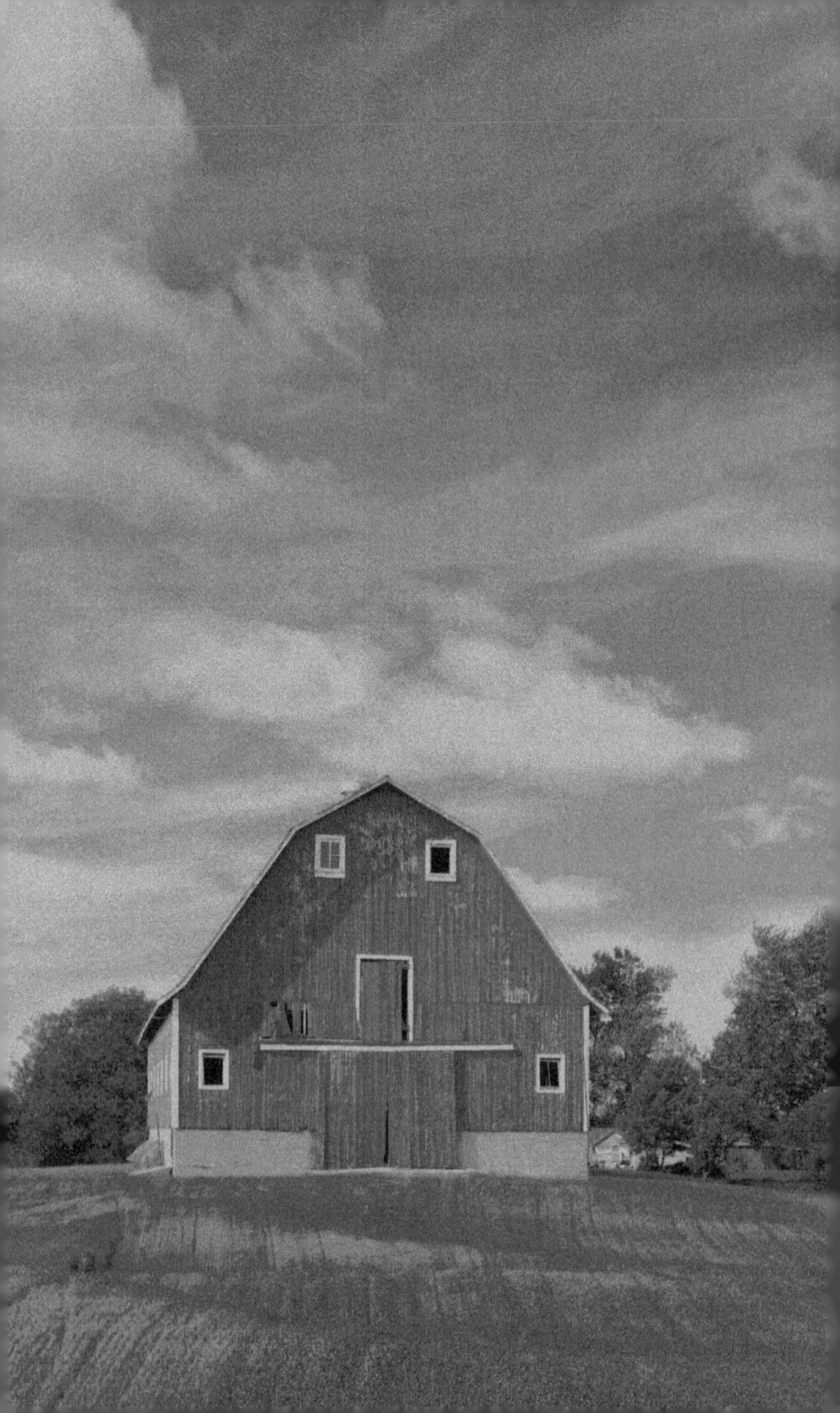

Chapter Seven

Aspen

Sleeping in the same space as Owen proved to be as impossible as I expected. I was a little ashamed of the mouse joke I threw out the night before, but he couldn't expect our truce to cancel out all the pranks. There was no mouse to be found, now that I'd moved into the old property manager's house. It had been vacant for years, ever since my parents built their new farmhouse. There had been a small animal infestation when I first took it over, but after having someone come in and set a few traps, I'd been pest-free for the last two years.

Regardless, I wished I'd set up a camera to witness the look on Owen's face at my end-of-the-night joke.

I was surprised to have slept at all by the time my alarm buzzed. I turned it down as low as possible to keep from waking Owen, though I heard him turning and grunting most of the night. Guilt flooded through me a few times, but he had the luxury of hanging around town today, whereas I had to work. Just like I did every day.

Thankfully, by the time I got dressed and made my way down from the loft, any residual consequences from drinking the two beers last night were long gone. Working and testing the soils with a headache was never a fun task. Especially when it was self-induced.

I tried to move around as quietly as possible, and I'd be sure to let him know later about my courtesy.

After brushing my teeth and grabbing a bottle of water, I crept from the house and made my way toward the main barn. This was where we kept some of the equipment, but my favorite tool, a robot created by my brother-in-law, was stashed in a locked room in the corner.

My dad and the ranch hands loved working with the oversized tractors and combines, but I enjoyed getting my hands dirty with the tools and smaller machines. It was probably why I loved working in my great-great-grandmother's garden the most.

My fascination and care with that particular space had been my downfall. The vested interested made my family assume I'd want to take over Sunny Brook. And while I did love working the fields and managing the little livestock we kept, I preferred tending the garden.

Unlocking the room, I flipped on the fluorescent light and grabbed the oversized remote. It reminded me of one of the RC car remotes my brother had when he was younger. But while it had a nostalgic feel, its large computer screen was a treasure trove of analytic data. Nate had set it up to feed all the information to a computer and backup server kept in my dad's office.

My dad didn't quite understand all the statistics it shot out, but I'd been working on a program to consolidate it all into more manageable information.

"Come on, pretty girl. Let's go take a walk." The agriculture robot resembled one of the robotic vacuums people had in their houses. Only this one was massive in comparison, with little compartments that compared the soil in eight different areas at one time.

When I tapped a button on the remote, the device came to life and began to follow behind me. It used an internal mapping tool to follow along by tracing the path of the remote.

Today, I needed to test some of the soil on Owen's family land. Now that the sale was finalized, I could finally start working on ideas for its use. From memory, I knew Owen's father tried to do various things with the acreage, none of which took. My father believed it was because the land was too far away from the creek that ran through our property, leaving it with more clay than soil. But I believed it was because it was nutrient-deficient. If I was correct, then it was a quick fix to grow whatever we wanted. Clay, though, would limit its use.

On my way out of the barn, I grabbed the keys to one of the UTVs parked just outside the door and lifted the robot inside to save her battery. A few of the ranch hands were milling about, prepping for the harvest. Dad hired a couple of new men who appeared closer to my age, and I wondered what their stories were. What brought them here? Were they stuck in the farming business like I was?

I waved at the crew as I drove past, heading down the dirt path that separated the fields. Sunny Brook Farm was massive, and with the purchase of the

Ramsey property, we were the largest functioning farm in the county and surrounding area.

Thirty minutes passed before I made it to the parcels of land I wanted to test. I came out to the property last week and mapped the fields out into eight large sections, using one of the tractors to cut the paths. Setting up the robot, I let her get to work selecting the eight samples. She'd cover roughly three miles to gather all the data, which left me perched inside the UTV in the peace and quiet for the next hour.

I scrolled aimlessly through social media on my phone. There were old classmates with pictures from recent weddings and baby announcements, while some were jet setting around the world, living their best single life. By the time the robot was finished, I was depressed and hungry.

With no stove or microwave in my house, I usually ventured to the main farmhouse to make a meal like I did when I lived there, but I hadn't been motivated to do so this morning. My aching stomach was payback for that poor decision.

Back at the barn, I parked the UTV in its spot, then I tucked the robot in her closet and plugged the data cable into her remote. This transferred the findings from a server in the barn over to the main computer at the house.

I followed the pebbled path from the barn to the mudroom of the house, noticing my father's boots were still sitting by the door, which meant he was making it a late morning or taking one of the days off my mother had been begging him to over the years. She was the biggest reason he planned on retiring, though his love for the land would never allow it fully. My dad would most likely work until he took his last breath.

The door connecting the mudroom to the main house squeaked as I pressed it open. As I crossed the hallway, I noticed my dad sitting at the kitchen table with a newspaper in hand and a cup of coffee resting on the wooden table. It was a new purchase by my mother to accommodate all the new members at our weekly family dinners every Sunday.

"Hi, Dad," I called out as I slipped into the kitchen.

"Morning, sunshine. Just getting started?"

"Nah. I spent the last hour over on the Ramsey property, testing the soils. I should have some data to look over in a bit."

"That's good. It will give us an idea of what we're working with."

"I'm hoping it's salvageable enough to plant corn for next season. If not, we could look at bringing in some cattle for the area for regenerative seeding."

"You think that's a better idea than using soy or wheat?"

"I do. We could always rent out the space to the Jacksons for their cattle. The expense would be fencing, but the turnaround on the soil is faster."

I could tell my dad was skeptical of my suggestion. We kept a few livestock on our land for the same purpose, but not on the scale we would need for the Ramsey area.

"Well, let me know what the data shows, then we can discuss it further. The leasing of the land will help pay for the fencing. But we'd need to get started soon, and with harvest starting next week, I'm not sure we would have the time."

Nodding, I turned around to head toward the fridge, using the distraction as a way to hide my disappointment. That was one thing about working for your father; he was set in his ways. He had decades of experience, but any time I suggested something that would incur an upfront cost, it was normally turned down.

I already knew that for my suggestion to work, I'd have to scour the financials and see where we could cut costs. Even though we'd charge for leasing the land, we'd need the upfront money to pay for the fence installation. It was something we could do in-house and just pay for the materials, but my dad was right. The harvest was going to take all hands on deck. With Autumn pregnant and Alex up to her neck at work, we were going to lose some of the family for labor.

The fall harvest of the corn we produced was a family tradition at this point. Though most was done by machine, we all helped. There was a factory in Knoxville that collected our supply by the truckload every year for commercial use. We only kept a small supply to distribute to the local grocers.

Just thinking about all the work I had in store in the upcoming months left my mind spinning. Why was I even considering accepting Owen's proposal?

I knew why. I was desperate.

I wanted the relationship my mom had with my dad. My sisters had with their husbands. Someone there to support me, love me, care for me, and who never felt like my life choices were a burden.

"Good morning, darling." Mom's gentle voice wrapped around me like the softest blanket as she stepped into the kitchen. She pressed a kiss to the top of my head as I walked over to the stove with the carton of eggs and a packet of bacon in my hands.

"Good morning, Mom."

"Just getting up?"

I snorted in reply. She already knew I'd probably been up for hours. I couldn't remember the last day I slept in. Christmas?

"Can I make you anything?" I asked.

"No, we're headed over to the bed-and-breakfast. The chef is trying some new recipes, and we get to be the guinea pigs."

"Oh, that sounds nice."

I cracked the first egg into a mixing bowl a little harder than I meant to, and the shell fell into the yolk and membrane. Cleaning it up quickly, I mumbled to myself how it would have been nice to be invited. I suspected the rest of my family would be there except for Rory, who was in Knoxville with her husband.

Thinking of my sister, I pulled my phone from my back pocket and sent her a message asking about any rental properties she knew in the area. Not expecting a reply right away, I was surprised when my phone practically jumped in my hand with her response.

Smiling, I placed the cell back in my pocket and went to work, cracking a few more eggs before whisking them together. In the distance, I could make out the hushed tones of my parents as they discussed an article in the paper.

Footsteps echoed down the hall as the mudroom door hinges squeaked.

"There you are." Owen's deep voice shocked me as I peeled open the packet of bacon with a yank of the plastic, sending it flying in his direction. Thankfully, none of the strips came free from the package as it rested just in front of the toes of his sneakers.

"Oh my God. I am so sorry," I apologized as I stumbled over to him and picked up the packet.

"Didn't mean to surprise you. I couldn't find you this morning, so I figured I'd try here. Though, I did start with the barn." A strangled gasp sounded from the dining table, and Owen twisted his head with his signature cocky smile in place. "Oh. Hi, Mr. and Mrs. Easterly. I didn't see you there. I apologize for not greeting you first." He walked over, hand outstretched, and both of my parents must have been in a deeper level of shock than I was as they returned his greeting. "How are you this morning?"

Behind my scrunched face, I felt disgusted. And as they fed into his suave introduction, I wanted to vomit into the trashcan. Owen always had that effect on people. He could "charm a snake," my mom used to say. Seems that sentiment hadn't changed much at all.

The trio chatted for a short time while I went back to placing the bacon in the frying pan, ignoring the sizzles as they popped on my skin. I was too busy trying to listen to their conversation to care.

From what I could hear, Owen was busy apologizing to my parents for his outburst yesterday at the B&B, even though they weren't there. Smartly, my mother suggested to him that he speak with his mother, who was now one of her close friends. I could tell by the change in his tone that he wasn't quite over her betrayal. His reaction to finding out we now owned the land would probably send him over the edge.

Busy flipping the bacon strips, thinking he was still on the other side of the kitchen, I nearly jumped a foot when I felt Owen's hip nudge mine.

"Oh my gosh!" I cried out as I placed a hand over my racing heart.

"Sorry."

A few deep breaths helped me get my wits about me as I turned to face Owen. "You know, my parents now probably think you stayed the night last night."

He smiled casually as he leaned his body against the counter, crossing his feet in front of him. "I *did* spend the night last night."

A slap sounded as my spatula collided with his arm. "Not like that, you didn't."

He simply shrugged as if he didn't care, rubbing the spot on his forearm where I smacked him. My gaze landed on the numbers and long-stretched line there, where the woman from the night before had drawn on him. His eyes followed mine, then he sighed.

"I tried scrubbing it this morning, but it's permanent ink."

"Sorry." I wasn't, really. "It should wear off in a few days."

"Maybe. Or I'll just grab some nail polish remover from the drugstore. That usually works."

Gesturing with the spatula, I asked, "That happen often?"

"More than you'd think."

Silence grew as he watched me cook the bacon and plate it, then went to make the scrambled eggs in a clean pan.

"I didn't know you could cook," Owen added, sounding more impressed than anything. It was a tone I'd never heard from him before.

"There is a lot of things about me you probably don't know." Quiet for a moment, I pushed around the egg mixture in the hot pan. "I'm assuming you want some breakfast?"

"I wouldn't turn it down."

"Think you can make some toast? The bread is in the bread box over there on the counter." I pointed to the wooden box that had been in my family for generations, then told him where to find the toaster.

He dropped four slices into the appliance and moved back toward me. "You know, I used to cook breakfast for me and my mom growing up."

"Really?" I murmured in surprise.

"Yeah. Sometimes...," he began, then paused, running his hand along the back of his neck. "There were times she didn't come join me, so I'd leave the plate outside her door."

The words he didn't say filled the room with heartbreak. I knew exactly what he was implying, even though he had no idea I knew the extent of what he and his mother endured.

"Owen…." His name was nothing more than a sigh, but its weight felt like an elephant sitting on my chest.

Suddenly, the toaster snapped, and the four slices popped up from their slots.

"Where can I find the plates?"

My mom answered as she entered the kitchen area. "The cabinet to the right of the sink. It's nice to see you two getting along. Your mother and I hoped it would happen one of these days.

"Aspen, we're off to the bed-and-breakfast. We'll be back around lunchtime. Maybe find something to do in town? I don't think Owen's had a chance to see all the new stores and restaurants."

"See you later, Mom. I've got data to run for the Ram—" I stopped suddenly and corrected my words before I let it spill that we bought his family's land. "For the robot."

Thankfully, my mother seemed to pick up on my blunder and played along. "Owen, it was nice to see you. Don't be a stranger. Unless your plans include releasing a bunch of crickets in her backpack again. I still have nightmares about that."

"Sorry, Mrs. Easterly."

"You can call me Marisol. And I'm sure you've grown out of that phase of terrorizing just like Aspen has."

Little did she know, there was a reign of terror we were considering unleashing on the entire town. A friendship between Owen and me.

My dad joined my mother and said goodbye to Owen with a hearty handshake just as I scooped the eggs onto the plates Owen had been setting out on the kitchen island. Grabbing the plate of bacon, I added it to the counter, then followed that with two glasses of water. When I returned, Owen was already seated at the island, buttering his toast.

"Thank you for this."

"You're welcome," I mumbled as I sat down.

As I snatched a piece of bacon, Owen lifted his forkful of eggs to his mouth. We ate quietly, both of us enjoying the meal as if his moans of gratitude with each bite were enough of a conversation. I stared out the window above the kitchen sink, watching the large oak tree sway in the fall breeze.

"What time did you get out there this morning?" he asked as he reached for his glass of water.

"I was up at 4:30 and did a few chores around the farm, then ran some soil samples with our testing robot."

"Wow. Okay, two questions. One, what is a testing robot? Two, why did you willingly wake up at the crack of dawn? It's Sunday."

Heaving a sigh, I described the robot and what data it's capable of collecting, explaining its primary function was for analytics. I was surprised as Owen hung on every word, but then I remembered him excelling in our technology course in high school. Him meeting Nate would probably be a dream come true.

"And I was up early because chores wait for no one. Animals have to be fed. Pens and stalls mucked. The typically day-to-day at the farm."

"Don't you pay people to do that? What exactly do you get? Do you get paid for all this?"

"I get free housing and food, and my parents pay me a small amount."

It was more like an allowance, but I didn't want to call it that. They valued my hard work. I was a big part of the farm's function, and I took over a lot of the menial tasks my dad used to perform.

"Not enough, if you ask me. None of that equates to a healthy lifestyle."

It wasn't worth arguing with Owen, since his comment was the same one that had been running through my head since he laid out his proposition last night.

"So..." Owen prompted, as he helped me carry our empty plates to the sink. "Have you given my proposal any more thought?"

I shrugged as if I hadn't and turned on the faucet to wash the dishes. Owen brought over the two pans without being asked, then gently nudged me aside as he poured soap into the sink and grabbed the sponge.

"You cooked. I'll clean."

I watched as he worked, then I dried the dishes with a towel as he handed them over. We made quick work of it, and soon we were setting the items back where they belonged.

"Owen?"

"Yeah?"

"Yes."

Turning around, he pinned me with his steely gaze and reached out a hand, latching onto my wrist. "Say it again."

"Owen Ramsey, I agree to fake date you to help me get a boyfriend and keep your ex away."

Suddenly, I was tugged forward, and my body collided with his. My free arm wrapped around his waist on instinct.

"You won't regret this, cricket." Then he proceeded to noogie my head like we were in freaking elementary school.

"I already am," I mumbled with a smile on my face as I reached under his shirt and pinch the skin on his side to get him to end his torment.

Then, as we pulled apart, both of us gasping for air, it felt like the world stopped spinning. Because I just agreed to pretend to date Owen Ramsey, bane of my existence—and part of the reason I was still a virgin after all these years.

Chapter Eight

Owen

When I'd woken in the morning to the sound of tractors outside the window, I was shocked to find Aspen already left. I even climbed into the narrow loft to double-check, and lo and behold, she'd already made her way out of the house.

There wasn't much time spent lingering in her sleeping space other than to notice a few travel books on an end table.

Outside, I stood in the morning sun. It was warm, even though there was a crispness in the air giving a hint of the upcoming fall season. I hadn't felt a day like this in years. My time in LA usually revolved around going to the beach and the training facility.

That was something I'd have to sort out soon while I was in Ashfield. Training in the off season was just as important as training during the prime season. My bats were still resting inside the trunk of my rental car, and I felt anxious not having them within reach.

It was the one thing that irritated my ex the most—she claimed I loved my sport more than I loved her.

She may have been right.

I needed to speak with my mom, but as I followed a path over the hill that gave way to the main farm property, I knew that was going to be toward the bottom of my list of things to do. First on my list was to track down Aspen.

The oversized barn filled with equipment was empty, and an employee pointed me toward the path leading to the family farmhouse as where I would find Aspen. The moment I walked through the side door leading to what I determined was a mudroom, I instantly felt like I stepped into a well-loved home. Work boots, sandals, and sneakers were haphazardly strewn across the floor. A few rain jackets hung on pegs above the shoes. Baskets were filled with gloves and hats. The entire room was a mess but in the best way. It reminded me a bit of our locker rooms at the stadium. Though chaotic, everything had a place.

When I stepped into a hall and found my way to the kitchen, it was clear I was an unexpected visitor. But the Easterlys greeted me warmly just after I surprised Aspen, who kindly threw a pack of bacon at me.

That was something I was going to have to remember for later.

She even went so far as making me breakfast, though she'd probably already been at work for a few hours already. I'd never been a morning person, but I couldn't imagine having to do it every day because you'd fallen into a role within your family.

But the biggest surprise of the morning was hearing her agree to my scheme. I was so thrilled I pulled Aspen into my arms and hugged her close, verifying she was onboard for the farce we were about to perform. After a few seconds, she stepped away, and I wanted nothing more than to kiss her plump lips. But I knew she wasn't ready for that.

I had a feeling Aspen was more innocent than she let on.

"So," I began as I took a step back, hesitating as I released the hold on her wrist. "What's in store for today?"

The corner of her lip twisted like an evil queen's, and I worried for a second that she had something nefarious planned. Color me surprised when she said, "I'll be busy running data most of the morning and then checking the books for some way to move around the budget."

"Oh, what for?" I studied finance in college as a way to learn how to manage my money when I went pro.

Aspen licked her lips and glanced out the window for a split second, before replying, "I would like to lease some farmland to some local cattle farmers. I need to see if it's in the budget to add a fence and shelter."

"Well, what if I helped you?"

I stunned her silent, as her eyes widened, staring at me like I'd grown two heads. "You want to help me?"

"Sure. I mean, I'm not a professional, but I'm pretty good with finances. It was my major, after all."

Aspen paused and seemed to weigh her decision, her teeth nipping at her plump bottom lip. "Okay. I suppose you owe me anyway, right?"

"Owe you? Our deal is mutually gratifying."

She giggled, and I was turning into a fool for that sound. "I wasn't talking about that deal, Owen."

"Yeah? Then why do I owe you, cricket?"

She moved around the kitchen and back toward the main hallway, calling over her shoulder, "I found you a place to rent while you're here. Now, let's get started. My dad's office is this way."

Her dad's office was a combination of both organization and chaos. I didn't know how anyone could find anything beneath the stack of papers and books, but Aspen skirted around that space and moved toward a computer in the far corner. It was more modern than the ancient desktop on the oversized wooden desk in the center of the room that looked like it came out in 1994.

She sat in the chair and then swiveled toward me, gesturing for me to grab one of the extra chairs against the wall. It wasn't nice like hers, but it was cushioned enough that I wouldn't lose all sensation in my ass.

"So, my brother Andrew and I have been working to move all the books for the last ten years into a computerized system. It makes it easier for both us and the accountant. It makes sense to Andrew, but to me, it's just a bunch of pie graphs and dollar signs. Finance was not an area I excelled in, and Andrew has been swamped with new contracts for the farm."

As she mentioned her brother, I wondered why he wasn't at the forefront of taking over Sunny Brook. But I didn't think we had moved far enough away from rivals to a friendship to ask those personal questions about her family.

She flipped open a laptop that I hadn't noticed and logged into the device before shifting it over toward me.

"I'm looking for a range of ten to twenty thousand that we could maneuver. The bookkeeping software is on here, as well as the manufacturer and wholesaler catalogs for the items we use on rotation. You're also welcome to search for a better deal anywhere else. If you find them, then that's up to Andrew. I just want to see if we can come up with a proposal, you know?"

"Sure. Sounds easy enough." I watched her boot up another desktop with a thin, sleek monitor. "What will you be doing?"

She went on, talking about the robot she sent out to test some fields this morning and how she wasn't sure of the quality. The details were vague, but it seemed she was hoping to add new crops to the land. "Essentially,

I'm running some data and comparing it to our control field, which produces our healthiest crop of corn."

"That sounds neat, actually. I didn't know things like that existed."

"They didn't until recently. Nate sold the patent to a huge firm with enough investment to keep it affordable to farmers. We're the backbone of the country."

"You're proud of that, aren't you? You like being a part of something that's a legacy in its own right."

"Yeah," she whispered. "I'm surprised you figured that out. It's why I'm afraid to… leave. What happens if I do? The alternative scares me."

"That's something for your family to figure out, Aspen."

The moment the words slipped from my lips, I immediately regretted them and tried to apologize, but no sound came out.

"Let's… um… get to work. Then we can grab your car and check out the rental."

I spent an hour analyzing all the numbers for Sunny Brook Farms. There was a large lump sum withdrawn recently, which gave me pause, but I knew none of that was my business. Clearly, they were in the black and doing well. I did not need to question what they spent their money on.

I glanced over at Aspen a few times, enraptured by the way she pursed her lips and twisted her hair as she compared multiple data points on the screen. It looked like a mashup for line charts, but she seemed to know what she was looking for.

"Any luck?" she asked, spinning around in her chair, catching me red-handed while staring at her profile.

"Yeah. I've typed up a few areas where you could tighten dollars by saving on delivery fees, all by changing the purchase date of some items. It may take a few of weeks, but in the long run, you'd have a couple thousand extra.

"Now, I also researched a few new manufacturers for your ancillary items, and some look like they offer steeper discounts for bulk ordering than the ones you've used in the past."

"Can I see?" Aspen pulled her chair closer to mine and leaned over my arm, getting a better look at the document and the information I pulled.

"It's all there for you to review with your father, but I think with these changes, you could make it work."

She twisted her head to glance over her shoulder, bringing our mouths mere inches apart.

"Thank you," she murmured, her eyes darting down to my lips, then back up again, before she righted herself.

"You're welcome," I squeaked like I was going through puberty. Clearing my throat, I asked, "How was it for you… with the data, I mean?"

"It was… satisfactory. I think what I'm looking for is there."

For a moment, I didn't think she was referring to the data.

A startled gasp sounded from across the room, and both Aspen and I jumped in our chairs. Her sister, Alex, stood at the threshold, looking like she'd seen a ghost.

With her eyes narrowed and pinned on me, she sneered as she asked me, "What are *you* doing here?"

Before I had the chance to answer, Aspen stood from her seat and shut down her computer. "Shut it, Alex. Owen was helping me with something."

"Right. Just like he helped himself to the bottle of ketchup in middle school and convinced everyone you had your period and bled through your clothes?"

Oh shit. I'd forgotten about that stunt in the sixth grade. It had been a prank I saw in a movie at the time and thought it was harmless fun. I was too naïve at that age to know what a period even was.

Aspen got her payback though. During the championship baseball game for the all-star team, she lined the locker-room bench with brown furniture polish, which left me with a huge brown stain on my white baseball pants. Right on my ass. Actually, that was a genius move on her part.

"Alex, we were both eleven years old. Didn't we all do stupid things at that age?"

"Sure, but that was malicious."

I watched as Aspen shrugged and turned her back to her sister.

"You need to leave, Owen Ramsey," Alex protested, and I stood from the office chair and shut down the laptop I'd been using.

"No, he doesn't. He's with me, Alex, and I don't need to ask your permission. You've never given two shits about what happened to me before. I don't understand why you care now. I'm telling you it's water under the bridge, so let it go."

Her sister's cheeks reddened at Aspen's defense.

"Look, I'm just trying to—"

"If I wanted your advice, I'd ask for it. Besides, Owen and I are…" She paused and looked over at me with wide eyes.

"Dating," I interjected.

"Dating?" Alex repeated in shock.

Aspen turned back to face her sister, hip cocked and fist resting on the curve. "Yes, dating. Is it so hard to believe that someone might be interested in me? I realize I'm not as pretty as the rest of you, but still."

"That's not what I meant. I just…. This is a surprise. That's all. He's only been home for two days and was supposed to get married right before."

"And he stayed with me last night."

I could feel the tension growing in the room, and it was not something I wanted to be a part of. Sisterly quarrels weren't necessarily my forte, having been an only child myself.

"I think maybe we need some clarification. Yes, I was supposed to get married. My ex cheating was the best thing that's probably ever happened to me. Aspen and I have kept in touch since she tried to run me off at Frannie's wedding. Animosity turned into friendship. And when I came home yesterday, she was there, and we decided to try something new."

I felt both Alex and Aspen's eyes on me as I wove the lie. In my head, it seemed probable enough, but as the words left my lips, I second-guessed myself.

"Mommy," two young voices called out on repeat, bringing all the attention away from me.

Just as the voices stopped, two little girls popped around the corner and collided with Alex's legs. They looked nothing like Alex, but I'd clearly heard them call her Mommy.

"Aunt Aspen!" they cheered as they darted into the room and ran in our direction.

Alex must have noticed my curiosity, which did not play well into our scheme. After a year, I would've surely heard about two nieces at this point.

I tried thinking back to any and all conversations I'd had with my mother over the years, and I only vaguely recalled Alex eloping last year.

Taking a chance, I looked at the little girls and turned on my charm. "These must be your stepdaughters. Hi, I'm Owen."

They giggled at my outstretched hand, and I crouched down in front of them, bringing me to their eye level.

"I'm Eloise," the one with cute pink glasses said as she gently shook my hand.

Nearly pushing her sister out of the way, the other girl with haphazard braids falling on either side of her head grabbed my hand and shook it with gusto. "And I'm Molly. Our dad said you play baseball. He doesn't like your team, but he likes you."

News of my return had traveled fast, it seemed.

"Well, I'm glad to hear that."

"What are you doing with our Aunt Aspen?"

Aspen gripped my arm and pulled me toward the opening. "We were just leaving, actually. He's going to be staying at Aunt Rory's house for a few months."

"Yay!" the girls cheered as if I was their new best friend.

There was no fighting my smile as I passed Alex, despite her down-turned mouth. It was clear she didn't approve of any sort of relationship between me and Aspen. Which left the two of us faking it as hard as we could to convince everyone.

I stayed silent as we trekked back to Aspen's house, but as we settled into my car—her in the driver seat, since she refused to relinquish my keys she still had—she paused before shifting the gear into drive.

"I'm sorry about that. You did good… covering, I mean. It's an easy-enough lie to remember."

"Your sister was kind of…"

"Mean? Yeah, the two of us have never gotten along. Not since I put pink hair dye in her shampoo when I was five. In my defense, I thought she'd like it. I didn't realize the dye was for marking animals. Her skin was stained for the entire summer."

"So, I'm not the only one you wreaked havoc on?"

"Clearly not. You were just the only one who gave it right back. I still stand by the fact that you initiated our rivalry."

She finally started the car as I laughed while rolling down the window. It was another gorgeous day in Ashfield. I'd forgotten how beautiful it was when the end of summer met early fall.

"In my defense, how else was I going to make sure I won the line-leader spot for a month?"

"So you came up with breaking all the crayons and blaming me?"

"Yep, and it worked, didn't it, cricket?"

"You know, I've always wondered why you gave me that nickname. The pranks involving insects didn't start until later."

"That's my secret. Maybe I'll share it with you one day."

Her lips pursed as she clenched the steering wheel. I knew this was something that had been on her mind for a long time, and I wasn't ready to tell her why I'd fallen upon that name. I didn't think she was ready either.

In town, we picked up her car first, and I was immediately sad she wasn't here, confined with me anymore, instead of in her little tin can on wheels. Not that my rental was anything to write home about, but it was at least built within the last five years. I'd need to look around at buying one while I was here. I could hand it off to my mom in my absence.

Just thinking about my mom forced my mood to take a nosedive. There were more secrets at play than just the house being condemned and her needing a job because she didn't want to use any of the money I sent her over the years. Stubborn woman.

Evidently, that was who I got it from.

I followed Aspen to Rory's house, which was only a short drive from the downtown area and the school. Once we arrived, Aspen explained Rory and her husband—hotel heir, Talon Beckett—had built a new house for themselves on the family property just as Alex had. She'd been thinking of renting out this small craftsman-style home, where she lived before they got married, but hadn't taken the leap yet. I was her first renter.

Surprisingly, Aspen helped me sort through my few pieces of luggage. The house was the perfect size for one person. I was surprised Aspen hadn't tried to snag this place for herself.

Rory had given the space a mid-century modern aesthetic. Aspen pointed out that her sister took the pictures on the wall, which showcased her photography skills.

Talent ran deep in the Easterly family.

Aspen left soon after, but not before I laid some ground rules for our mock relationship. We had to be seen in public twice a week. My goal was for people to post on social media that they'd seen us around town. I wasn't a fan of tabloid photographers, and I knew it wouldn't be long before they caught wind of my location and came to Ashfield, but it was an unfortunate part of getting Vanessa off my back. In the time it took to place my clothes in the dresser, she'd called, then texted fourteen times. Which was fourteen times too many.

Another rule was that Aspen had to do whatever I said when it came to teaching her how to date. I'd never had to work to get a girlfriend or a date, even before landing my multimillion-dollar contract with the

Coyotes. If she was going to learn everything I knew, then she was going to have to follow my lead.

And lastly, we'd stage a breakup where she was the one dumping me. Unlike Aspen, I was leaving once my season started. She'd be stuck with all the rumors in town. For her sake, it was easier to have her end things.

That night, I ordered takeout from the Indian restaurant, but even the spicy flavors and the football game on the TV couldn't pull my attention away from the constant ringing of my phone.

Knowing I was going to regret my decision, I picked up.

"Owen?" she squeaked before I could even say a word.

"Vanessa, stop calling me."

"But… Owen, I—"

Frustrated, I hung up immediately, knowing all I did was add gasoline to the fire. For the life of me, I couldn't figure out why she was so adamant about speaking to me. She made it very clear on our wedding day that the vows we rehearsed meant nothing.

I had never been more thankful that I discovered her deceit before we officially exchanged the declarations.

A bullet dodged.

Now, I just needed to convince her we were over for good.

Chapter Nine

Aspen

My usual Sundays were filled with finding ways to occupy myself around the farm—either checking inventory, cleaning storage areas, or prepping for harvest or soil rotations. But once I helped Owen sort through his things at Rory's house, I'd driven to my favorite overlook and sat on the makeshift bench I put together when I was a teen.

I found this spot during a hike while on a field trip in middle school, and I'd been coming back ever since.

I was pretty certain I wasn't the only one who used the jutted-out rock formation as a resting place, but it was so far off the trail that it was usually empty when I arrived.

The overturned log had weathered from the sun and rain, but it was still sturdy as ever, and as I laid back on the blanket I draped over the surface, I stared up at the cloud formations high in the bright-blue sky. All the while trying to convince myself that my truce with Owen was just that and nothing more.

I knew I was getting the better part of the deal we made. Not that I truly had time for a boyfriend, but I wasn't a one-night stand kind of girl. I wanted to *be* with the person I lost my virginity to. Tryston had been the only person so far who piqued my interest. But the entire process of dating and forming a committed relationship, all for the sake of experiencing sexual intimacy, seemed like a scheme itself.

I could only hope that whatever I formed with Tryston would be long-term, but I knew it was probably unlikely. From the rumor mill, I learned he worked just as much as I did. And while that would be ideal in most situations, I wanted someone who could partner with me on the farm. Or, at a minimum, help with kids if we ever had some. And I had a feeling Tryston would find that emasculating.

Without provocation, my thoughts immediately conjured up a vision of me and Owen with a family. Just from my memory, I recalled how great he was with kids during his summers running baseball camps. I'd seen him on television enough times to know he was amazing with his young fans as well. Owen was definitely going to be one hell of a father one day, even though he'd grown up with a horrific man as his own.

"Stop thinking about him," I murmured as I sat up. My skin was tan from working in the fields all summer, but tinges of pink spread across my legs and arms after being out in the sun today.

Sitting up, I wondered why Owen popped into my mind while I'd been daydreaming about Tryston. I chalked it up to the fact that I'd been with him for the past two days. Thankfully, I wouldn't have to see him again until Tuesday, when he was taking me out on our first date.

I had no idea what that entailed, but he told me to dress "casual but nice." This was his first test; otherwise, he said he'd be taking me shopping for new clothes.

And as nice as that would be, I knew it would be a waste of his money. They'd probably get one use and then sit in the back of my tiny closet.

The alarm on my phone sounded, and I knew it was the preset to remind me of my family's Sunday dinner. I was dreading it, especially after the run-in with Alex earlier today. I'm sure, between her and my parents, the rumor of me and Owen being a thing was spreading like wildfire. Good in theory, bad in reality, because I was not the kind who enjoyed being the center of attention.

Probably because that was never my role in our family. I was in the shadows. The afterthought. The one who picked up pieces when no one was looking.

But Karma must have been on my side after helping Owen, because as I arrived back home for dinner, only a few ranch hands, plus Autumn, Colton, and Beverly, were seated around the table with my parents. Owen's mom was quieter than usual as my mom passed around the pan of stuffed peppers. She was normally the most talkative during meals, but her eyes kept glancing over to the empty chair beside me, then casting downward.

It took me a few minutes to realize my parents and Beverly hoped Owen would be joining us for the meal. An invitation I hadn't considered when I left his place, which was bad if we were supposed to be dating.

I tried to cover up my mistake by explaining that he was busy unpacking and speaking with his coach. Only the smallest of fibs, and thankfully, they seemed to buy it. Everyone but Autumn. I had a sneaking suspicion that Alex already spilled the beans to our eldest sister. Neither of them was a fan of Owen's. It actually surprised me that my parents liked him so much. They always had. Growing up, they used to explain his picking on me was a way for him to tell me he liked me. I never understood that logic.

Dad and Colton were on dish duty, and I spent the evening moving around some cattle in preparation for the harvest. We didn't raise them for milk or beef but for sustainability of the farmland. After a fall harvest of the corn, the cows were experts at clean-up duty, grazing on the leftover corn kernels and plants. It not only helped the soil but the cows as well.

As I drove the fence, keeping the cows away from the creek that ran along the back and west side of the property, I noticed a break in the wire. Aesthetically, we ran a wood fence along the parameter of the fields and property, but we kept a wire fence a few feet inside that line. It was double protection for the animals—keeping them in and predators out.

I usually took care of fixes like this in the daylight. The setting sun made it difficult to see clearly to tie the barbed wire, but it had to be done.

There was a small spool of wire in the back of the UTV, and I ran it from one post to the other, making sure it was taut. This was a smooth cord, and I'd have to clip off and tie portions to create barbs.

Carrie, the cow who loved to test my patience the most, moved toward the newly attached wire, lifted her back leg, and kicked. That asshole repeated the movement three more times—with what I'd swear was a smug grin—until the twist finally popped free.

"Dammit, Carrie! Do you want foxes or coyotes coming after you? Can you please not be a jerk today?"

The cow walked off, head held high in the air, and that's when I saw the fencing was about to split open. And that's also when I did the stupidest thing ever. I'd left my gloves in the truck, but that was an afterthought as lunged forward, and I grab the released barbed wire, rolling around my arm and wrist to force the fencing back together. By the time I was done and my adrenaline waned, I finally felt what I'd done to myself.

Along my arm, a deep cut was sliced into my skin. I was going to need to bandage it up as soon as possible. The blood dripped down my hand as I carried the wires to the back of the vehicle, and though I never had issues with blood before, I started feeling woozy.

"Shit," I mumbled as my vision blurred while I tossed the bundle into the open bed of the UTV. "Freaking Carrie." The cow meandered close by again, her white head a contrast to her brown body. It was the only way I could pick her out from the blackness closing in. It was as if the cow got some sick enjoyment out of seeing me lose it.

I stumbled over to the passenger side, where we stored a first aid kit under the seat. I rooted in the box for some of the large bandages but came up empty. What we had in stock was something that could cover nothing more than a splinter.

Thinking quickly, I wrapped my arm in gauze, ignoring how the blood immediately seeped through the white cloth. I continued wrapping until the spool ran empty, then used the medical tape to secure the top and bottom.

I bent forward and lifted my arm in the air, doing my best to decrease the blood flow to the area and restore it to my head. Closing my eyes, I tried to take my mind off the throbbing sensation.

I could hear the mooing in the background as if Carrie now felt some sort of regret for her actions, but then again, she was more likely mooing in victory. She hated whenever we moved them over to a new field, and she was the ringleader for the six of them. Whenever they were moved, the herd acted out for about two weeks before settling again. All of them, except Carrie. She had it out for me all the time, even though I was the one who fed her most days.

Opening my eyes, I sighed as my vision returned. Leaving my left arm in the air, I scooted over to the driver seat. I held onto the top of the vehicle, as I started the ignition. Knowing I'd have to patch the broken wire in the morning, I prayed nothing would breach the barrier during the night, or that Carrie would break more wires loose. It was too late in the evening to send any of the ranch hands out there. The sun had been setting when I first arrived; now, twilight gave way to a navy abyss.

The dirt path led me toward the main barn, but I turned off just before I reached the wooden structure, heading to my house instead.

I didn't think twice about my outside lights being on, my mind solely focused on my arm and getting it cleaned up as soon as possible. Fear of a tetanus shot pumped adrenaline into my blood as I scooted out of the UTV and rushed toward my door.

Most days, it was unlocked, since we knew who was coming and going on the property. What surprised me was finding Owen sitting on my couch, reading one of my travel books.

I stood just inside the house with my arm lifted high in the air when our gazes collided. His smile fell from his face as he took me in. I could imagine how pale my skin had turned, and by the way he frowned, I was certain I didn't look as alive as I had earlier today.

"Aspen? What happened?" he asked, rushing over to me, his hands cupping my cheeks in a way I'd have to think over later. It was almost caring. "Who did this to you?" He was staring at my arm still hovering above my head as if a tether in the sky was holding it up.

"No one," I whispered. "Just a demonic cow and some barbed wire."

"Fuck, should we go to the hospital? Is it bad?"

"I'm… I'm not sure, but I need to get it clean. Shit, I'm getting woozy again."

My body started swaying, and I closed my eyes, only to feel myself lifted in the air. I could tell by the smell of the sunscreen I applied every morning that he carried me into the tight bathroom. There was barely enough room for one person, let alone two.

My bottom hit the toilet seat cover, and Owen lowered my arm to rest along the edge of the vanity. I leaned my head back against the wall, hearing the cabinets under the sink slam closed, and then a gentle hand ran through my hair.

"Stay with me, okay? Where's your first aid kit?"

"In the upper cabinet, next to the sink."

"Okay. I'm going to help get you cleaned up, and we'll see if we need to go to the ER."

I winced at that thought. The closest ER was an hour away. That was the downfall of owning a rural farm. Accidents happened, and unless it was during business hours, there usually wasn't anyone close by to treat farmers.

He pulled his hand away, and I pouted, missing his touch.

"All right, pretty girl, let's see what a mess this demonic cow caused, shall we?"

As he began tugging at the medical tape, I explained how the cow hated me, and his chuckle was like a numbing salve. I focused on it instead of the throbbing in my arm.

With the tape free, he held my arm up to unravel the gauze. I cracked open my eyes and immediately closed them when I noticed red painting across all the white material like I was the freaking Queen of Hearts from *Alice in Wonderland.*

"Damn, cricket," he mumbled, and I felt his fingers trace around the skin. It heated under his touch, and luckily not from infection, but from my reaction to him. "This is pretty deep. I think we need to go to the ER."

"Too far away," I whispered. "I'll be fine. Just put a couple of bandages on it."

"It's going to leave a nasty scar if I do that. Is there a farm medic I can call?"

There was, but he was out of town, expecting a grandchild at any moment.

"Not really."

"What does that even mean, cricket? Look, I'm going to call your dad."

"No!" I jolted and immediately regretted it. If my dad thought I couldn't handle the farm, he'd take on my hours, which would defeat the purpose of his retirement. And Mom would throw a fit. "Please don't. Just… wrap it up, and I'll grab some liquid stitches at the pharmacy tomorrow."

"Pretty sure it will be too late by then."

Silence grew around us. The only sounds were my deep panting to keep from passing out and Owen's steady breaths.

I heard shuffling, then I felt his hand caress the side of my head. For someone who used to torment me, he sure was attentive.

"Sit tight, cricket. Don't do anything stupid."

"I make no promises." I smiled and opened my glassy eyes to watch him smile in return.

I tried my best to stay awake by listening to Owen's soft murmurs in the other room. I wasn't sure who he was speaking with, but he wasn't gone long.

"All right. First, we're going to work on stopping the bleeding, which seems to have slowed a lot. Then I'll start cleaning it, okay?"

"Yeah," I replied, licking my lips nervously. "I'm usually not so bad with blood. Guess it's different when it's my own."

Chuckling, he confessed he was the same way. "You were smart to keep it above your heart. I think we'll get this stopped quickly. I'm going to wrap it up again and apply some pressure. Do you want something to hold on to while I do that?"

"Your balls," I joked through gritted teeth as he wrapped clean gauze around my arm.

I felt every tug and pinch as he tightened it around the wound, doing his best to stop the bleeding.

"I'm such a wimp," I whimpered.

"You're perfect, cricket. Now, tell me something about you no one knows."

"We already did this. I told you I wanted to travel."

"No. Something personal. Something that no one would ever guess about you."

I opened my eyes again to find Owen's gaze pinned on my face. His eyes were filled with concern and care… and something else I couldn't quite pinpoint.

There weren't many secrets I kept close to my chest. If anything, Jenna knew every deep and sordid detail of my mind. She knew I was only a virgin because the one guy I dated in my early twenties turned out to be a douchebag with another girlfriend on the side. Even though I was conservative in my thoughts that I wanted to wait until marriage. But my outlook was thinning on that aspect. I would probably remain a virgin forever.

That was a secret I could tell Owen, but I hesitated. Instead, I spilled something that only my mom knew.

"You were the reason I went to our senior prom."

Owen's grip loosened, only slightly, but enough for me to feel the blood rush back to my arm. He quickly adjusted his hold and regained the tension.

"But I—"

"You didn't go, even though I heard Tessa waited for you before she came alone. She started the rumor that you showed up at her house drunk."

"Yeah, I remember hearing about that from my coach. I wasn't. I mean...."

"I know. It didn't sound like something you'd do."

Owen glanced down, focusing on my arm while I focused on him. His hair had lightened a bit since he was in high school. I attributed it to the California sun and all his time spent in it. There were blond streaks mixed in with the dark-brown. For a moment, I wondered if he had it done professionally.

"You really went to prom because of me?"

"I mean... I didn't have a date or anything. I wore my sister Autumn's pink slip dress. But I thought.... I don't know. I just wanted to see you in a tux, to be honest." I followed the confession with a giggle and felt relieved when Owen smiled along. It was his eyes that told me it was only for my benefit though.

Just when I thought he would say more, there was a knock on my door. Owen stood up immediately with a look of relief.

"I'll be right back."

There were two voices mixed with his, and just as I mustered the energy to look over at my door, I found three sets of eyes staring at me.

"Oh dear," Beverly said as she moved into the room. There was a young man with her, who I recognized from the doctor's office in town.

Owen moved into the space, his body seeming to fill every crevice once he stepped inside. I felt his leg press against my body as I continued sitting on top of the toilet seat. Embarrassment overwhelmed me, and I ducked my head.

"What happened?" Beverly's gentle fingers pried the layers of gauze from around the wound, hissing when she saw the slice through my skin.

"Long story short, the demonic cow and the barbed wire won this round. I'll have my vengeance… eventually."

She nodded, then gesture for her sidekick to hand her a small bag. "I'm going to clean the wound and surrounding skin with some saline and antibacterial ointment before I stitch you up."

Out of instinct, I jerked my arm back.

"Careful, dear girl. I was a nurse in my past life. Kevin was able to get these supplies over to help. Thank goodness Owen called me."

She pulled out a squirt bottle and cleansed my arm before wiping something on my skin. When she pulled out a syringe, I nearly passed out, but Owen crouched next to me and grabbed my free hand. I turned my face toward him, distracted. I never even felt the pinch.

"That was to numb you. Now, I'll stitch you up. I've had a lot of practice doing this," she said solemnly, and I wondered how often she had to stitch up her own wounds... or her son's.

"Thank you," I whispered to Owen, whose eyes were still filled with worry. His hand shook in mine. I wondered if he was reliving moments of his childhood by watching my arm getting stitched up.

"You doing okay?" Beverly asked. "I've only got a few sutures left."

"Yeah, I'm fine," I squeaked, feeling the tug on my skin. It wasn't painful, but the sensation wasn't completely absent.

Owen pressed his head against mine and whispered, "You're doing great."

My body heated at the compliment, and I felt my cheeks burn.

"All done. I brought some fresh bandages. Take some pain meds and get some rest. Okay?"

"Yes, ma'am."

"When was your last tetanus shot? You may need to get one tomorrow."

"I had a booster last year."

"Oh, good. You should be covered then. Let's not wrestle with barbed wire anymore, shall we?"

Chuckling, I leaned my upper body against Owen's hip, my energy already drained.

"Get some sleep," she said, and then I was abruptly lifted in the air and deposited on my couch. "Thank you for calling me, Owen," I heard her tell her son.

"Well, I figured if anyone could stitch her up, it would be you."

Even I felt the subtle dig, but Beverly replied gracefully, which surprised me. "Years of practice." She leaned over me. "Make sure to get extra rest and be careful with that arm over the next few days. It will be sore."

"Okay." My response was garbled.

I felt the couch shift, then heard Owen's deep voice off in the distance. He was likely saying goodbye to his mother. Opening my eyes, I examined the dressing on my wound, wondering how I could have done something so stupid. I'd been rewiring the fences since I learned to use the metal cutting sheers when I was ten. It was a stupid mistake I made, and now I was injured because of it.

Owen closed my front door and then sat beside me. The couch cushion dipped dramatically under his weight.

"Thank you, Owen."

I leaned toward him, resting my head on his shoulder.

"You're welcome, cricket. I was worried you'd go nuts once you realized I called my mom."

"You did the right thing. I'm sure she appreciated it too."

"Probably."

We stared at the black screen of the television. The only sound in the living room came from the large clock on my wall that ticked quietly with each passing second.

"You know, you never told me why you were at my house in the first place." I stifled a yawn, using the back of my good hand to cover my mouth.

"You're exhausted. How about I help you get to bed, and we can talk about it tomorrow?"

Yawning again, I agreed.

He argued to carry me up the loft stairs, but I protested enough he let me go on my own. By the time I reached the landing, I was woozy again and even more tired than before. It took me twice as long to remove my clothes, since I had a numb hand and arm.

Owen called up to me twice to make sure I was okay.

"Yeah," I mumbled as I finally released my bra and slid it down my arms. My sleepshirt rested around my neck as I tried to maneuver my arms through the holes. The first went through fine, but I struggled to get my injured arm through the opening. It took an extra minute, but thankfully I tugged the shirt down enough to cover my panties just as Owen climbed the stairs.

"Good. You're dressed. Now, get into bed." He brushed past me and tugged down the covers for me to slide in.

Once I was settled, he moved around the bed and sat down. I couldn't see what he was doing, but then I heard two thumps. Shoes.

Then… he stretched his large body across the other side of my bed, on top of the covers.

"What are you doing?"

"Keeping an eye on you."

"Owen, that's ridiculous."

"Sorry, Mom's orders. Now get some sleep. If you need some pain meds during the night, wake me up. I'll get them for you."

There was no point in arguing. Owen was just as stubborn as I was. Instead, I turned over and faced him, my injured arm draped over my body. Gently, he slid a small, decorative pillow under my arm to help it stay elevated, then turned to face me.

Any other night, I would have protested his staying over, or at least take the opportunity to stare at his handsome face. But as soon as my body relaxed in the bed, I was lost in slumber.

Chapter Ten

Owen

The sound of large machines outside the small house woke me from one of the best nights of sleep I'd had in a long time. Even better than some of the five-star hotels I stayed at with Vanessa.

Staring up at Aspen's ceiling, I wondered how many missed calls or messages I'd find on my phone this morning. I purposely left it charging in the kitchen area.

Turning over, I saw Aspen was still asleep in the same position as the night before. Her eyes were pinched shut as if she was in pain, and knowing the stubborn woman, she was hurting but refused to ask me for anymore help.

It was a humbling experience to have her require my assistance last night. Just imagining what would have happened if I hadn't been there was all I needed to finally call my mother.

That in itself was humbling enough for me. But just as I knew she would, my mother came at my first request for help. I remembered her having to stitch my wounds a few times growing up, when my dad got reckless with a pocketknife. Shaking my head, I ridded my thoughts of my mom having to stitch herself up when my father would go after her.

Stretching, I climbed out of Aspen's bed, doing everything I could to keep from waking her up. As I slipped on my shoes, I watched her eyelids tighten even more and her lips flatten into a line.

Out of instinct, I shuffled over to her side of the bed and gently ran my hand across her hair. Her body immediately relaxed beneath my touch.

She really was beautiful, especially when she wasn't out to get me. Though, those were some of my favorite memories. Her comment the night before about prom was something I was going to keep locked away for good measure. It was the most honest conversation

I'd ever had with Aspen, and I knew she told me that in confidence. I wasn't even sure if she would remember it when she woke.

Downstairs, I cleaned up the mess left in the bathroom from the night before, then left the house. The large farmhouse was my destination. I hadn't been lying when I told her I cooked breakfast for me and my mom growing up.

Settling for something sweet, I went about gathering the loaf of bread, making a note to myself to restock it for Mrs. Easterly today. Then I gathered some eggs, milk, vanilla extract, and cinnamon.

It took me a couple of minutes to find everything I needed around the kitchen, but before long, I was making enough French toast to feed an army.

As I plated the first batch, I was surprised there didn't seem to be anyone home in the house. With all the banging around I was doing, I would have woken everyone up. I glanced at the clock on the microwave and saw it was 9:30 a.m. Not too early in the morning, but definitely late for Aspen.

Just as I plated the last couple of batches and found the syrup, the sound of the front door slamming forced me to look down the long hallway leading to the front of the house. Mrs. Easterly and her three other daughters stared back at me in surprise.

I felt like I'd been caught stealing.

"I'll... uh... replace the loaf of bread."

Marisol smiled gently, then walked down the hall toward me, her daughters trailing behind her.

"You made French toast?" she asked.

"Yes, ma'am. I was going to take it over to Aspen's." Now, looking over the multiple platters of food, it was far too much for two people. I might have gotten carried away.

"She's still asleep?" Autumn asked as she not-so-sneakily snatched a slice of the French toast. One of her hands rubbed her expanded belly as she moaned with each bite. "This is delicious, by the way."

"Thanks."

Marisol drew my attention once more. "Is she sick? Aspen has never slept in."

"Yeah." Unsure how much to disclose, I hesitated. "She got a small injury last night while out in the fields, repairing a fence."

"What?" Marisol's face turned an ashen hue just as Nash walked into the room through the back door.

"Aspen got hurt last night," Marisol told him, not looking at her husband, who was loading up a plate with the French toast, but at me. "Is she okay? What happened?"

All eyes of the Easterly family were on me. All except Nash's. For some reason, I had a feeling he already knew what was going on. Nothing took place on this farm without him knowing. My mother and the medical assistant driving through the main gates would have been on his radar.

Thankfully, I was saved by the pixie in question as she walked casually into the room. "I'm fine, Mom. Just a nasty scrape that needed stitches." She showed her wrapped arm and went into a *Cliff's Notes* explanation of what happened. I watched Nash out the corner of my eye. He nodded slightly as he smothered his breakfast in a month's worth of syrup.

Turning to her father, she told him she'd fix the fence this morning after moving Carrie the cow to a different field.

"That dang cow has had it out for you since she came to this farm," Marisol inserted as she started filling her own plate with the toast. Her other daughters did the same. "Should we look at rehoming her, Nash?"

"Mom, she's fine. I just need to make sure she's not in a field where I'm working. It's not her fault. She thinks I'm encroaching on her territory."

I could tell there was more Marisol wanted to say. Even I had a few thoughts, but I kept my mouth shut. This was family business, and I was just a fly on the wall.

Aspen filled a plate, and then I finally grabbed some breakfast for myself. Before I knew it, all the toast was gone, and Nash was cleaning dishes.

Marisol and Aspen's sisters had been out at the hair salon that morning, and I noticed how Aspen deflated at the knowledge. Even though I liked her long waves, I knew she felt passed over next to her sisters.

In my quest to take her from the house, I thanked the family for allowing me to use their kitchen and then ushered Aspen away. I was pretty sure I even saw Alex crack a knowing grin in my direction.

I was still in my clothes from the night before, but I didn't mind, as Aspen and I loaded into the UTV parked at her house. We stopped by the main barn to restock the wire, and then we were off to repair the fence she'd been working on.

This time, she used a pre-barbed wire, so all we had to do was wrap it around the posts and pull it taut.

As we were finishing up, a large brown cow with a white head meandered over to the UTV, her eyes trained on Aspen.

"That's Carrie," she said as she tossed the spool back into the UTV.

"Well, aren't you a pretty girl?" I said to the cow, pulling her attention away from Aspen. It was as if the animal had just then noticed my presence. She cocked her head to the side, then strutted closer.

"Don't let her nibble on you. She's been known to bite."

Nodding, I let the cow get within a foot before I stood straighter. Carrie was large, but I was taller. I could see how she wouldn't be intimidated by Aspen, but she seemed curious around me.

Reaching out, I stroked the top of her head, and I swear I heard her purr.

"God, you even put Carrie under your spell. How is that possible?"

"It's a talent. What about you? Do I have *you* under my spell?"

Giggling, she smacked my stomach gently with her good hand. "You wish, Casanova."

Carrie turned her head toward Aspen, and I wasn't sure what the cow was thinking, but her eyes followed every move she made.

"Hey, girl, you have to be nice to my friend. She's here to take care of you and keep you safe, okay?"

The cow looked at me and stared for a minute before her head dropped once, then she wandered away.

It was fucking weird, but maybe I made things easier for Aspen. Or worse. There could be a jealous cow on the loose at Sunny Brook Farms now.

Back at the barn, we dropped off the UTV and walked back to Aspen's house, where I gathered up my few things and stored them in my car. We stood on her small porch like nervous teens finishing up their first date. I'd never been anxious around Aspen until now.

"About last night," I started. "I don't know why I came over initially. I just…. I don't know. I wanted to see you. You're the only one who will treat me like a normal person. And our truce has been a nice change of pace."

"I get it. The last couple of days have been… nice. Weird, but nice."

"Maybe we can hold up the truce whenever I come back to visit?"

She laughed and made no promises.

"You remember I'm picking you up at 6:00 p.m. on Tuesday, right?" I asked.

"Yep. Still not going to tell me what we're doing?"

"Not a chance. See you then, cricket."

"Bye, Owen. Thank you… again."

I left her house filled with emotions I couldn't place. Maybe this was what a blossoming friendship felt like. I wasn't sure.

***

After two days without seeing Aspen, I actually missed her. I wasn't sure what the fuck that was about. I'd missed no one in my life—except my mom, when I went to summer camp as a young boy.

As promised, I showed up at Aspen's house at 6:00 p.m. I knocked on her door, and she called out for me to come inside. The living area was barren, but I saw a light coming out from beneath the closed bathroom door.

I had ideas for tonight, and I planned on testing Aspen's limits a bit. I needed to know what I was working with.

With my back turned, I heard her call out my name. Spinning around, I nearly lost my balance as she appeared in a short denim skirt and a flowy shirt covered in flowers. It was the perfect mix of casual and feminine, and a complete one-eighty from the outfits she normally wore.

"Will this work for tonight?" she asked, her fingers nervously skimming along the hem of her skirt.

"Yeah," I croaked, then repeated the word more clearly. "You look great." Her makeup was done. Her mascaraed eyelashes fluttered, and I saw her lids were a shimmering gold color. Aspen's hair fell in soft waves down her back, and I was stunned by her appearance.

It made me wonder how she looked at prom, all done up.

"Will you tell me now where we're going?"

"Not yet."

"Well, what shoes should I wear? Sandals, sneakers, or my boots?"

"Whatever you're most comfortable in."

"Boots it is," she said as she quickly ran up her stairs. I averted my gaze, not wanting to focus on her backside right in my line of sight. She dashed back down, carrying a pair of socks.

After slipping everything onto her feet, we were out the door.

"New car?" she asked as she ran a finger over the hood of the McLaren. I'd found the car for sale in Nashville and used the last two days to seal the deal. I contacted my old friend in town, Chris, and he and I went to pick it up this morning. Chris worked at the police department in town and had the next couple of days off, so I promised we'd spend some time catching up.

I realized since I'd been home for four days, I'd made a lot of promises I wasn't sure I could keep. My coach had scheduled a video call for next week, and there was a chance he was going to want me back in L.A. sooner rather than later. There were a few charity games and press events he wanted me to attend. At least, that was the gist I received from his assistant.

As I watched Aspen lower into the bucket seat, her skirt exposing more leg than any man could resist eyeing, I realized I wasn't quite ready to get back to reality.

We didn't drive long, just enough to bring us toward downtown, and I stopped at the bar where Aspen and I started our deal.

"What are we doing here?" she asked as I parked the car out front.

"This isn't our final destination. But it's our first lesson. I want you to go inside and sit at the bar. Your goal is for someone to pay for your drink."

"What? How do I do that? Owen, you know I'm not good at this. I've never even asked to borrow a pen from someone, let alone to buy me a drink."

"You can do it. I'll come in just a minute behind you. You won't be alone. Okay?"

"What if no one buys my drink?"

"Then I'll do it." I shrugged. "You'll get a free drink either way."

The leather squeaked as she sunk against the seat, her eyes closed. My gaze traced the gentle slope of her nose and the long line of her neck before trailing down her shoulder. Her wound was covered in a few large bandages that matched the color of her skin.

Sitting upright, she unlatched the seatbelt and reached for the door handle. "All right. Wish me luck."

"You can do it, cricket."

"Gah, I hate that name," she mumbled as she opened the door and stepped out of the car.

"I know."

She leaned down and shook her head when she found me grinning like a loon. I had faith that Aspen could work her natural charm and get someone to buy her a drink. I just needed her to have faith in herself. Her lack of confidence astonished me.

Scrolling through my phone, I gave her three minutes before I left my car and slunk inside the bar. The light was dimmer than I remembered, but it was easy enough to spot Aspen. She was perched on a stool at one corner of the bar. She might not have noticed, but every male's eyes in the place was locked on her. She was like the first flower in bloom after the winter cold. With her blonde hair and innocence, she stood out, whether she wanted to or not.

I scanned the place as I took a seat at a high-top right near the entrance. This left her in my direct line of sight.

"Can I get you a drink, sir?"

"I'll take a water," I said to the female server. Just as she started to walk away, I added, "You see that girl sitting at the bar in the white flower shirt?"

"Yes, of course."

"In five minutes, if she doesn't have a drink, will you please get her whatever girly drink is popular right now and put it on my tab? But don't tell her it's from me."

"Of course. Sister?" the woman asked with hope.

I shut her down real fast when I replied, "Girlfriend."

She walked away, glancing over her shoulder at me in confusion… twice… before pushing through the doors to the kitchen. She returned quickly with my water, and I sat at my table in the dim light, tracing the woodgrain lines of the tabletop. Looking down at my outstretched arm, I focused on the mountain landscape that wrapped around my forearm. A world-renowned tattoo artist etched the intricate details into my skin. She added everything in the design that I requested, even some hidden features that only I knew existed.

When my phone showed that five minutes passed, I glanced up to the bar to find a bored Aspen swirling a straw around in her soda glass. The server I'd spoken to earlier slipped behind the counter and prepared a drink, then handed it over to her with a smile. Aspen looked up to ask her who sent the beverage, but the server only shrugged.

Looking to her left and right, Aspen caught the eye of a table of young guys, and she smiled sweetly at them.

I knew then that I could never tell her I was the one who sent the drink.

After twenty minutes passed and Aspen finished her drink, I asked for the check from the waitress, who informed me there was no bill for the water. When I asked her about the drink, she confessed another patron ordered the one she served to my girlfriend.

Instead of feeling pride for her accomplishing her first task, I felt… jealousy. Didn't they know she was here with me?

My chair scraped loudly as I stood from the table, grabbing Aspen's attention, then she slid off her stool, wearing the brightest smile I'd ever seen.

Fuck, I couldn't even be mad, because I'd do anything to make her smile like that again.

She waved at the group of guys as she made her way toward me, but her eyes never left mine, and when she reached out her hand to me, I took it without a second thought.

"I did it, Owen! At first, I thought you may have sent the drink to boost my courage, but then I realized you would have ordered me a beer."

She was right. I remembered that was what she was drinking last weekend. But that would've only happened if I ordered the drink on my behalf. A cocktail could've been from anyone else.

"I'm really proud of you, cricket," I said as I held the car door open for her, just as the suits from Saturday exited a brick building down the block.

They stole her attention immediately, and she stiffened next to me. The men were chatting, but the short one quickly noticed the car and then me. My fan gestured to his friends, and all their eyes turned toward us.

"I'm going to kiss you, Aspen."

"What?" she whispered.

"Just play along, okay?"

"Okay."

I cupped her face and twisted it toward mine, and I brushed my lips against hers. She opened up hesitantly, and my tongue dipped inside, tasting the sweetness from her drink.

The kiss didn't linger, and I pulled back with a grin. Her smile matched mine, and I ran my thumb along her bottom lip.

"That okay?"

"Mmhmm," she replied, as if in a daze.

A car horn sounded from down the road, bringing Aspen and me back into the moment. She immediately sank down into the car, then I shut the door and moved around to the driver side.

I was thankful for the interruption, because I could have stood there kissing her sweet lips for hours if she would've let me.

Soon, we were driving down the alleyway toward a warehouse-looking building in town. I looked up the old place and saw a young couple bought it and were working to fix it up. They already restored the old signs and woodwork.

I'd never tell Aspen, but I was a little excited to check it out. When I lived here, the place was too derelict to ever visit and was never open. Though I did recall one hell of a party taking place in the building, before it was broken up by the cops.

"We're going bowling?" Aspen asked as I pulled into the lot. It looked completely different from what I remembered. Fresh paint. A new retro sign. Neon lights. The couple who bought it dropped some serious cash.

"We are. And you can play one-handed. Have you been here since it reopened three years ago?"

Her energy never wavered as she told me that I already knew the answer. It was clear she wasn't exaggerating when she said she didn't get out much.

The timing was perfect, because as my phone switched to 7:00 p.m., Jenna's car pulled in beside mine with her date, Derek, in the passenger seat.

"You invited Jenna?" Aspen asked, leaning across the center console, gripping my forearm with her injured arm's hand, and waving to her friend with the other.

"I did. I thought a double date would be a good way to get the relationship rumor mill going. If we can convince Jenna, then we can convince everyone else."

"Good idea," she said, smiling up at me before sitting back in her seat.

Exiting the car, I walked around to the other side and helped her out of her seat. The two women hugged, and then we walked inside.

I didn't spend a lot of time lingering on the looks of the place as I paid for a lane and the rental shoes. Bowling wasn't a sport I excelled at, but I had fun either way. And that was the point of our date tonight.

Derek and I chatted as we ordered some food for our lane, along with a pitcher of beer. I wouldn't drink more than one or two glasses, since I was driving and under advisement from my coach to keep up my training regimen.

The girls giggled as they tied their clownish-looking shoes, but I had to admit these weren't as hideous as some of the ones I'd seen on television or in the movies.

We played a few practice rounds, Aspen nearly releasing her ball behind her twice. And that was with her good arm—the right one, and she was righthanded. She confessed to never having bowled before, and it showed, but as we all teased her, she laughed, knowing it was all in good fun. I wanted her to see that a date could be something amusing and spontaneous. Even if it was something new, she didn't have to be so apprehensive. Not all dates had to be formal and serious.

It was also nice to see her let loose. Jenna leaned toward me once the food arrived and told me this was the happiest she'd seen Aspen in years.

When I ran into Jenna at the grocery store yesterday, I broached the topic of a double date. She was skeptical of me going out with Aspen after all the torment we caused each other growing up. But when she agreed, I made sure that Betsy, the town gossip, overheard us. I was sure the news would spread like wildfire by the end of the week.

Which was most likely the reason no one was on the lanes closest to ours. Everyone requested lanes on the complete other side, knowing the chaos that surrounded us whenever we were in the same room together back in the day. I was thankful the owners hadn't grown up in Ashfield with us. They probably wouldn't have let us into their establishment together at all.

Two rounds, a large pizza, and two pitchers of beer later, we were laughing so much we didn't notice the group of college-aged kids who took up the lanes close by. There were no colleges in Ashfield, but there was a small private university in the next town over, which catered to kids who were born with a silver spoon in their mouths.

I worried they'd recognize me when a few of the guys started eyeing our lane, so I turned my back to them, unsure if I should suggest ending the game. We were having a great night, and I didn't want my fame to ruin that. I was used to being noticed, but I knew from my time with Vanessa that not everyone could handle it.

"Everything all right?" Aspen asked as she took the seat beside me, leaning her head on my shoulder.

"Yeah, I just think those frat guys might've recognized me. I… uh… just wanted to have some fun, you know?"

Reaching down, she used her right hand to squeeze mine before standing and walking away. I didn't dare turn around to watch, but I was certain the group was watching her every move. Across the way, Jenna's attention was on Aspen, which gave me peace of mind.

Suddenly, the entire room was bathed in blackness, before purple-tinted lights clicked on.

Uncontrollable laughter bubbled to the surface, and I bent over to catch my breath. I knew this had to be Aspen's doing, since I'd seen on a sign that Cosmic Bowling wasn't until tomorrow evening.

What better way to keep people from recognizing you than to make it dark enough no one could see you?

The only thing that stood out was my white Henley shirt and the laces of my clown shoes.

Soon, Aspen was back, and I immediately reached out and pulled her close.

"You're the fucking best. Thank you," I told her before I pressed my mouth against hers in a chaste kiss.

She looked a bit surprised when I pulled away, before she mumbled, "You're welcome. Now… I challenge you to the next round."

"You're on."

An hour later, we left the bowling alley, Derek and I both driving since we limited our beer consumption to two glasses each. I had originally planned on only drinking one, but we stayed until midnight when the bowling alley closed, which was a long-enough time for two beverages.

Jenna gushed about Aspen's and my new relationship the entire way to the car, and as I settled my date in her seat, her best friend exclaimed she wanted to be the maid-of-honor at our wedding. She was getting a little ahead of herself, but the thought of marrying Aspen didn't scare me the way it did when it came to Vanessa.

During the drive home, I thought back to my ex and our engagement. I had never actually asked her to marry me. Instead, she wanted to live with me in my house and said we could only move forward like that by getting married.

The next day, she had a ring on her finger that she purchased with my credit card and gushed to everyone that I proposed to her over dinner the night before. I went with it, because I was happy with Vanessa, but looking back, I realized I was merely complacent.

Looking across the car, I caught Aspen's tipsy smile and returned it. "Have fun?"

"It was the freaking best. How's your shoulder? I saw you wincing toward the end."

Damn her for being so observant.

"It's okay. I probably need to ice it later."

We exited the car together, something that bothered me more than it should have. I wanted to be the one to open her door for her. When we reached her porch, I hoped she would ask me inside, but I also didn't want to overstep. Everything we were doing was fake, and even though I spent the night with her… twice, it was because of unforeseen circumstances.

Bugs danced around the porch light next to the door, buzzing whenever they got too close to the heat.

I pulled Aspen into the shadows. "I had fun tonight."

Smiling up at me, she replied, "Me too, even if it *was* all for show."

"Yeah," I agreed in jest. None of it felt like a show, and it was only the first date. "Maybe on the next one, we'll go to a cricket farm or something."

She reminded me of a tarsier, with her eyes widening and pupils shrinking to the size of a pinpoint.

"You do not joke about that."

Chuckling, my body shook, jostling my sore shoulder. One stupid tweak while I was showing off at the bowling alley, and now I was worried about my throwing arm. It had been worth it though.

"Sorry. I couldn't resist."

"Well, goodnight, Owen."

"Goodnight, Aspen."

I followed after she stepped over to the door, walked inside, and closed it behind her. I stood at the threshold, contemplating my next move.

The light on the porch clicked off either due to the timer or Aspen flipping a switch, and I took that as my cue to leave.

Only… I didn't want to go back to my rental. Not yet, at least. I reached for the knob and twisted. The door was still unlocked. "Fuck it."

Once I opened the door, there she was… waiting.

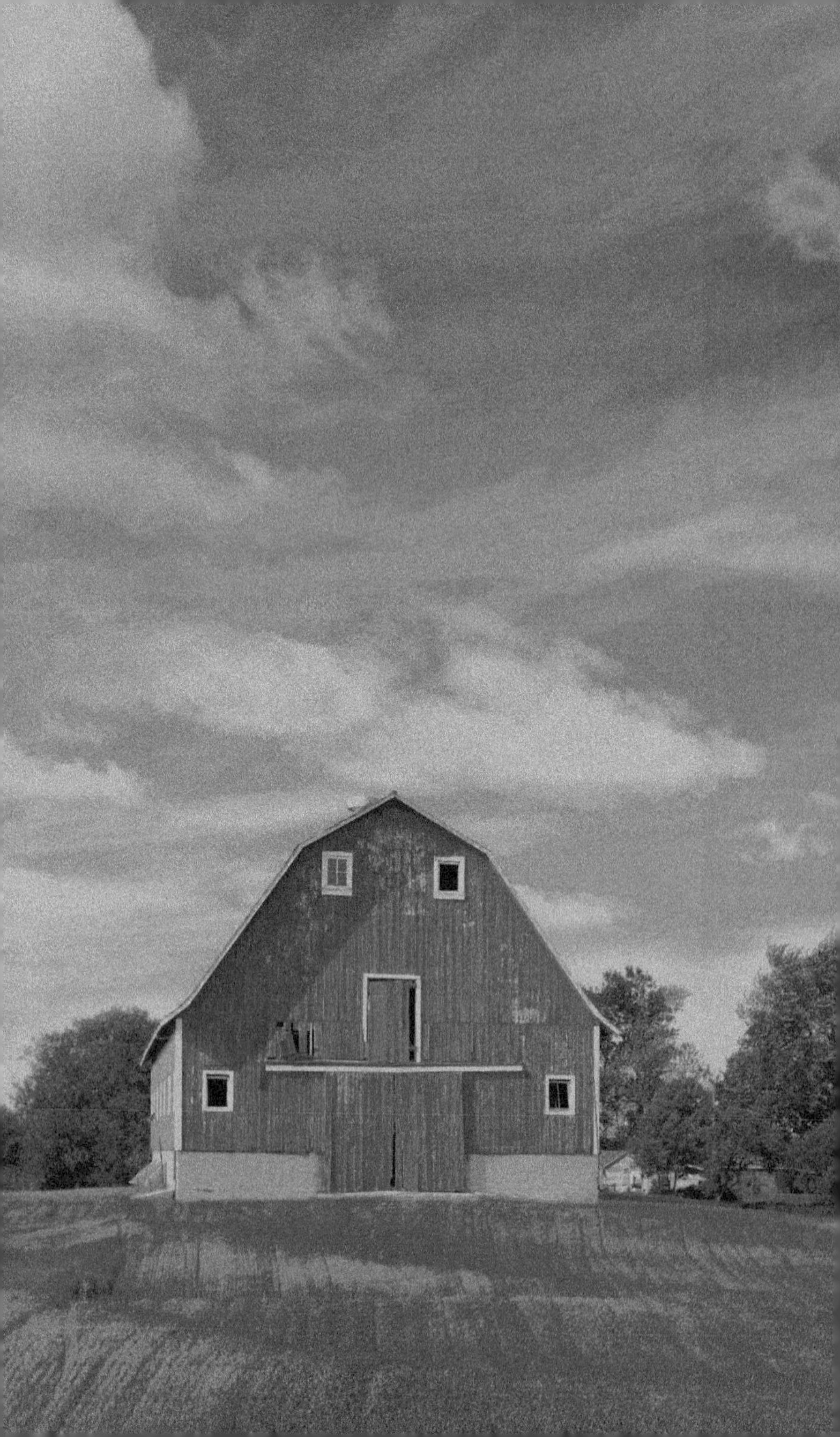

Chapter Eleven

Aspen

My entire body shook as I contemplated rushing back out to flag Owen down. I was so new to dating that I didn't know the etiquette for first dates and the bases, but I knew I wanted more from him. The kisses we shared earlier were just a taste of our chemistry, and I needed another. I was hungry for it.

I should've probably worried he'd pull some stupid prank with garlic or fish breath, but even then, his kiss would've been better than any of the ones I had before.

I'd just turned around at the entrance after depositing my bag on the small console table, when Owen stepped inside. He mumbled a few unintelligible words, and then his body was pressed against mine.

My arms instinctively wrapped around his neck as his hands came up to cup my face. His thumbs pressed against my jawline, tilting my head in whichever direction he craved.

I rocked against him as his tongue swirled with mine, feeling the bulge in his pants against my stomach.

"Owen," I whimpered, needing more of… something. Needing to be closer to him.

His lips left my mouth but trailed down toward my jaw and then neck as his hands skimmed over my body, landing on my backside. He squeezed the globes, and before I knew it, he hoisted me into the air. My back landed against the wall as I wrapped my legs around his waist.

I groaned as my center rubbed the zipper of his pants.

"Ah, fuck, cricket," he moaned as he pinned my body against the wall with his hips. One of his hands reached under my skirt and cupped my thin-cotton-clad ass, while the other slipped under my shirt and palmed my breast covered in a soft but plain bra. Even with our clothing still on, I could feel the heat from his skin penetrating the material. "Damn, you feel good."

His lips were back on mine, exactly where I needed him, as he trailed a finger just inside the elastic of my panties. He skimmed just close enough to tease my center, never giving me what I desired.

My fingers clawed at his hair, seeking a way to pull him closer. His body still felt too far away, though a piece of paper wouldn't fit between us.

"I need more, Owen. Please," I begged.

I could feel myself growing wetter with each passing second. I'd never wanted more than a kiss or some light petting with a man before. Not until now. Not until Owen.

His hips rocked into me once more before he pulled back and settled me on my feet.

"Aspen," he hissed as he reached down and adjusted the bulge in his pants. It had to be uncomfortable confined behind the zipper and waistband. "I… need to go."

"Are you sure?" I whispered, unwilling to believe there was a man alive who was willing to stop when a woman's body begged for so much more.

"Yeah. I don't think me staying here tonight is the best idea."

He was right. I knew he was, but my ego took a hit, regardless.

"Okay."

He paused at the doorway, then left without a backward glance. I didn't even care enough to turn the outside lights back on—I'd go without the motion sensor for one night. It would leave me and my scorned self hidden in the shadows, where I felt at home.

I tried not to shed a tear as I got ready for bed. They didn't need to be wasted on Owen and my inability to experience anything further than kissing tonight.

Owen was sweet and attentive the entire evening, but just like every other relationship I'd been in, we never made it farther than second base. There was one singular time I gave Tony DiComaro a blowjob the summer after high school graduation, but for me personally, I'd never felt anything past second base. Which was hilarious in my mind, since Owen played shortstop for the Coyotes. It was like he had been subliminally blocking me since childhood.

If this had been a lifelong prank, Owen definitely had the one-up. Now, I just had to figure out how to pay him back.

***

I made it five days before I saw Owen again. I tried to stay on the farm, and when I had to venture out, I did my best to steer clear of everyone.

My mom had already harassed me about the rumors involving me and Owen. Someone embellished the dating rumor so much that the town of Ashfield thought we were engaged to be married. Thankfully, that gossip hadn't made its way to the magazines… yet.

I didn't pride myself on the fact that the last time I was at Chuck's Grocery, I grabbed the few tabloids that had a grainy picture of Owen and me alongside a picture of his distraught ex-fiancée. She was playing the role of an innocent victim.

I wondered if Owen had seen the articles yet, but I didn't want to reach out to him. I couldn't. Everything that happened Tuesday night left me embarrassed. I wasn't even sure I could follow through with our charade any longer. I could hide at my farm, but Owen had to go back to that life. And if Vanessa was going to play the casualty of their botched wedding, then it was only going to get worse for him.

The magazines sat in a stack on my coffee table, staring at me every time I walked into my living room. Vanessa's watery eyes focused on me everywhere I went. It was like living in my own haunted house.

A knock sounded on the door just as I stepped out of the shower. I spent the weekend mucking the cattle stalls, and surprisingly, Carrie gave me no issues. It was the first time in history.

Wrapped in a towel, I went to answer the door, surprised to find Andrew on the other side of it. A part of me wished it was Owen, but seeing my half-brother was a much-happier shock.

"Andrew! What are you doing here?" I exclaimed as I hugged him with one arm and held my towel together with the other.

"Just returned from California and Florida. Man, I'm beat," he said as he crashed onto my couch. "Maybe I'll stay here tonight. Traveling is exhausting."

Chuckling, I added, "Especially at your age." Andrew had just turned forty-two. Not old by any sense of the word, but he'd been single as far back as I could remember.

"You're hilarious. I'm thinking of cutting back. Talking to Dad about hiring someone to handle contracts. It's just… a lot."

Sighing in desolation, I shifted my towel tighter. "Yeah, I could see that." I mentally added one more thing to my massively overfilled plate.

"You want a drink while I get dressed? I have a beer or two, I think."

"Sure, that sounds good."

Andrew called me snowflake since I was born as platinum-blonde "towhead" in the middle of a snowstorm. He was eighteen years older than me, but he was the sibling I was closest to. And probably the only one who understood the pressure of taking over the farm.

As I dashed up to the loft to change, I shouted down to him, "I wanted to talk to you about the farm, actually."

Struggling to pull my jeans up my slick legs, I hobbled around, knocking into my dresser a few times as I explained my thoughts on hiring more staff and freeing up my time. The night out with Owen and Jenna transformed something inside me. It was like I saw a movie playing in fast-forward, and it was my entire life… spent on the farm. I wanted more than that.

I wanted what everyone else in my family had. Everyone else but Andrew. I hadn't quite figured out what kept him single. He was a good-looking guy, objectively speaking.

"We can talk it over with Dad. I heard you had a proposal for the Ramsey land as well."

"Yeah, the stats came back super clean. I think just rotating the plants like we do now would be enough to keep it enriched. One season of cattle grazing, one season of soybeans, then we can plant the corn."

"And how does Owen feel about this?" he asked, as I made my way down the steps to the main floor.

"What do you mean?"

My stomach clenched at the thought of tearing up his family's land, but it needed to be done. The soil was rich with nutrients, his father must've just mishandled everything he planted. But it wasn't my job to tell him his mother sold it to us. Not that she'd had much choice. Thank goodness my father swept in when he did, because Jim Ramsey had been close to making the entire property a nightmare for Beverly and Owen, from the grave.

"I heard you two were seeing each other."

"We're... dating, if that's what you're inquiring about."

"And does he know we own his family's land, even after he's been sending money to his mother for the last four years, ever since he went pro?"

"No. I just…. I think he needs to talk to his mom first. There's *a lot* he doesn't know," I said, twisting my fingers together in front of my clenching stomach.

"I agree, but don't let it get back to him that you knew all along and said nothing. He'll blame you, regardless of if you were the instigator."

Andrew was right. Biting my lip, I snatched his beer from my coffee table and took a hearty sip.

"I should tell him."

"No, you should explain to Beverly that you need *her* to tell him."

Nodding, I gulped down another mouthful before setting it back on the table.

"I like him for you, you know."

"Really? I thought you hate all guys we date."

"As a generality, yes, but Owen's a good kid. I can't tell you how many nights I stayed at the ballpark watching him from the bench with Coach Rudicell long after the practice ended, and then he'd practice with a few younger kids who showed interest."

In my head, I wondered if it was because he hadn't wanted to go home.

"Yeah, he loves baseball."

"Anything he sees worth in, he loves. Sad to hear about his wedding though, but in the end, everything works out, it seems."

"You're being awfully calm, knowing I have a boyfriend."

He shrugged and chugged the rest of the beer. "Mom's making chicken pot pie, and I don't want to be late. You ready?"

"Yeah."

When we arrived at the house, there was a slew of extra place settings, plus an extra table extended off our normal dining table. This wasn't completely abnormal. We always fed the workers and their families during the harvest. And as the groups started to arrive, the space in the open-concept dining and living rooms dwindled into practically nothing.

The workers gathered in clusters. My siblings, their husbands, and the kids collected near the large fireplace, and my parents stood together in the kitchen, watching everyone mingle.

Andrew and I stood off to the side like the outcasts we were. Even though we were together, it felt... lonely.

Mom called out to everyone that dinner was ready. The groups started gathering around the tables. Once we were all settled, I noticed two extra seats, one of them being next to me. Andrew and I locked eyes across the way. I wasn't sure who else we were expecting to dine with the family that evening.

"Sorry we're late," a gentle voice called out as she entered the dining area, Beverly's eyes twinkling with happiness.

Quickly, I spun around in my chair to look at the main hallway. Owen walked in behind his mom, chin tucked toward his chest, avoiding eye contact with everyone in the room.

"It's nice to see you again, Owen," my mom said as she gestured to the open seat next to me. "You can take the seat next to Aspen. Beverly, you can join me over here."

Owen lifted his head, and our gazes locked as he walked toward the open chair and sat down. He greeted everyone in our area nicely, then leaned to whisper in my ear, "You've been ignoring me this week."

I had been. Ever since our make-out session on Tuesday night, I made myself scarce. I avoided his calls, cringing whenever his name popped up on the screen. He even tried to track me down on the farm on Friday, but thankfully, I'd been away, negotiating the delivery and pickup schedule for the start of harvest this week.

"I have," I whispered back, as Mom set out the rolls. Andrew snatched the basket off the table the second she stepped away and grabbed two handfuls of the homemade goodness.

"Why?"

Exasperated, I turn to face him, the tips of our noses nearly brushing against each other. "Because I was embarrassed, okay?"

"Nothing to be embarrassed about, cricket."

Across the way, Andrew snickered. "Trouble in paradise?"

"Nah, all is good," Owen replied before I could start verbally attacking my brother. He stretched his arm along the back of my chair, running his fingers along the exposed skin of my upper arm. My body immediately erupted in shivers.

"How's your arm, dear?" Beverly asked from her spot six chairs down and on the other side. Her skin was no longer the ghostish pallor it had been a year ago when she began working for us. Her sunken features had plumped, and she looked the healthiest I'd ever seen her.

"It's healing well. Thank you."

"My pleasure. I'm glad Owen thought to call me."

The table erupted in chatter about Beverly's prior nursing experience, and Dad even asked if she'd want to come assist as a medic on the farm. Owen's mom lit up at the recognition.

Mom and Alex served the individual dishes of chicken pot pie. It was one of my favorite comfort foods. Alex had been toying with my mother's recipe. Though I knew my sister's tasted just as good, something about it wasn't the same, and I couldn't quite put my finger on it.

"This looks great, Mrs. Easterly. Thanks again for having me," Owen said as my mother set his pie dish on his large plate.

"Thank you, dear, but this one was all Alexandra's. I simply watched over."

"Oh. Well, compliments, Alex."

I could tell he was being sincere, but Alex narrowed her eyes quickly before thanking him.

Just as the dinner was served and a family prayer said, the door to the mudroom opened. From my seat, only my dad and I could see the person walking down the hall. Andrew's back was to the new arrival, but I watched, fascinated, as he tensed before a single word was spoken.

"I hope there's room for one more!"

Colton bounded from his seat and wrapped his half-sister in his arms. He'd been in foster care most of his life, never knowing he had a sister. Until she found him five years ago.

"There is always room for you, Sadie. Let me grab another chair." Mom dashed out of the room and returned holding a wooden chair from the formal dining room. "Where's Jacob?"

Andrew's fork clattered on his plate at the mention of Sadie's boyfriend. The two had met on a humanitarian project in South America last year and had been together ever since. She was there studying soils and teaching the civilians to make better use of their land to grow their crops. Jacob had been there providing dentistry services. Surprisingly, he recently moved to Nashville, and the two had been renting an apartment in the bustling city.

"He has poker night with his dad and brothers tonight. So I thought I'd make the trip. Is that okay?"

"Of course, it is. We're always happy to have you."

Mom placed the chair at the other end, next to her brother. Colton looked as happy as he had the day Autumn told us of her pregnancy.

When Sadie reached across the table, I noticed a very large, sparkling diamond on her left ring finger. Just as I was about to ask, Rory beat me to it.

"Oh my gosh, are you engaged?"

The striking brunette nodded and held her hand out for all my family to "ooo" and "ahh" over, but Andrew was quiet. I knew he had a special relationship with Sadie. Though many people thought it was romantic, I knew it was nothing more than him seeing her as another sister to worry over.

Andrew always considered himself like a second father to us all. He'd had years to learn and perfect how to treat me and my three biological sisters, but when Sadie came along, she threw his world into a tizzy.

And though there may have been a crush on her end at some point, I knew Andrew would never act on it. He barely got over the age difference between my sisters and their significant others. He and Sadie had a sixteen-year age gap.

Nudging Andrew's foot under the table, I whispered, "Everything all right?"

"Of course." He smiled, but it was forced. Something was going on with my brother, and I was determined to get to the bottom of it.

During the meal, I tried to add to the conversation flowing around the table but was always ignored or spoken over. Something I was all too familiar with. Even Sadie and Owen were able to get a word in edgewise.

As I was pushing the peas, my least favorite vegetable, around my plate, Owen seemed to pick up on my dejection.

He reached under the table for my hand, intertwined our fingers, and rested them gently on his thigh. I looked up at him, but his face never steered away from the conversation he was having with my brother-in-law Talon.

I'd never had my hand held like that. Not even the date who took me to the movies for a matinee showing.

It felt foreign, strange, but I never wanted him to let me go. I squeezed his hand softly, letting him know I appreciated his attention, and he broke his discussion to face me and smile.

For the rest of the meal, Owen held my hand the entire time. I wasn't sure if it was for his comfort or mine, but it was nice to have someone seemingly on my side. A few times, I caught Beverly's eye, and I silently begged that she explain everything to her son. I wasn't sure what his reaction would be, but I knew he'd approach me about it, regardless.

"Dad, have you given anymore thought to the data I gave you?"

Andrew caught the tail end of my question and gave me a look. Pure panic and fear bubbled in my stomach, hoping he wouldn't bring up what I told him earlier. Of course, it was my fault for saying anything in the first place, and now I couldn't back out.

I wasn't overly religious, but a guardian angel must have been on my side during the exchange of looks, because suddenly Owen's phone rang, and he left the room to answer, explaining it was his trainer.

With whatever spare minutes I was granted, I gave Dad the lowdown about how Owen was in the dark about all of it.

"You need to tell him," Andrew reiterated from our first conversation about the subject.

"I will if I have to, but *again*, I don't think it's my responsibility."

"Do you want me to talk to Beverly?" Dad asked, but I could tell he was wary about it.

I couldn't understand why she held back. Were there deeper secrets that forced her to withhold the information? Either way, Owen was going to find out soon, and I felt like I was going to take the brunt of the blame.

"No, I'll talk to her and give her a deadline. But if I end up having to break the news, then it might help to have you there."

"Okay, I can do that for you. And I think your data, along with the budget proposals, are solid. I'll have Andrew look them over, and we'll work up some of the contracting changes."

"The goal is to get the fencing in before the first snowfall, then, in the spring, lease the land."

Minutes passed, and Owen was still missing, but my dad and Andrew began collecting plates while I waited to pull Beverly aside. It would be difficult to broach the topic with her, but I was tired of being in the middle. And with the harvest starting up, my focus needed to remain on that. The next month was going to be chaotic.

I wasn't even sure how I'd have the spare time to keep up the charade with Owen.

When she ended her conversation with Autumn, I asked her if we could speak privately for a moment. Thankfully, no one paid us any mind as I pulled her toward the back hallway.

"Beverly, I really need you to speak to Owen about the land purchase."

"I know. Owen may hate his father, but… it's the only thing the two of them did together. You know that's the only time Jim showed pride—whenever Owen would win a county fair competition and beat out everyone else. Those were things he grew up doing with his dad. I know Jim wasn't perfect, but there are still good memories there."

I snorted. "Nothing Jim Ramsey did was on the up-and-up. You and I both know that. Remember those years something mysteriously went wrong with our small garden?"

"I'm not saying Jim was an angel. He was the devil in human form. But I…." She looked down at her twisting fingers, then back up at me. I'd never noticed the two of us were almost the same height, and it made me remember how small and frail she had been when we saw her right after Jim died. He'd put her through hell 'til the very end. "I'm making excuses. You're right. I need to tell him, especially with you two together. He's going to be upset that you didn't say anything."

"Probably, but I can handle him. I have been since we were six."

She smiled genuinely. "I like you two together. Whenever you two were competing at the fairs or just making each other miserable in school, your mother and I always talked about how cute you two would be as a couple."

My heart twisted. None of it was real, even if my stomach clenched whenever I watched Owen walk into a room. I blamed my social anxiety for the feeling. It had nothing to do with an attraction toward the man. At least not a mutual one. Because what in the world would *the* Owen Ramsey see in me?

Chapter Twelve

Owen

The Sunday dinner with Aspen's family had been a tradition as long as I could remember. It was something I'd been envious of as a young boy. When I was in elementary school, I used to pretend I was invited to the soiree. Sometimes, I'd sneak over to their house and watch from a hiding spot behind their back deck. Other times, I would set up the table at my house for the three of us like they did theirs. We didn't have the fancy plates or utensils like the Easterlys did, but I still tried to wrap the plastic forks in paper towels like we were at a restaurant. Mom would join me sometimes, but mostly it was just me and whatever meal I could come up with.

It was different being on the inside and took all my willpower to not feel any resentment toward the large family. None of my family issues were their fault.

Leaning against their porch railing, I looked out over the expanse of their farm. Unlike the one I grew up on, the Easterlys didn't utilize all their land. A lot of it was sectioned off for other purposes. The main front fields were covered in wheat that swayed in the breeze with each gust. It was picturesque.

"Here you are."

My mind immediately calmed when Aspen stepped up beside me. I'd noticed over and over she had that effect on me. Knowing she had been avoiding me the last few days bothered me more than I told her.

"Everything okay?"

I had to think for a moment and remember I ducked out of dinner to answer a call from my trainer. He was sending someone local to help me work out my shoulder and verify I didn't have a rotator cuff injury. The therapy would be good during my downtime. They also sent me a list of exercises to focus on.

"Yeah. Everything is good."

I winced as I shrugged my shoulder in a circle, and Aspen's large brown eyes narrowed.

"I promise," I added. "My trainer is sending someone out next week to help me exercise it."

"You have a call with your coach next week too, right?"

"Sure do. He'll probably call me back soon. My agent said there are some new sponsorships on the table."

"That's good news," she chirped without a hint of malice. It was strange to hear someone's wholehearted excitement for something related to my job without a single question related to pay or social media following.

"It is. I can't play the game forever, so it will be nice to add extra funds to the bank."

Aspen's sisters and the ranch hands began trickling out the front door toward their vehicles. I knew a few of the Sunny Brook Farms employees lived on site during this time of year with the harvest happening. Their families went on their own way while the workers strode toward their bunk houses.

My mom wasn't far behind. I picked her up from the bed-and-breakfast and intended on taking her home.

As I said goodbye to the Easterlys and thanked them for dinner, I pressed my lips to Aspen's cheek on the way out, telling her I'd message her later and making her promise she'd reply.

The ride back to the B&B where my mom lived—something I still hadn't come to terms with—was awkward. I didn't know what to say, and Mom seemed just as conflicted. She practically jumped from my car when I pulled up to the front of the historic farmhouse.

I contemplated driving back to Sunny Brook Farms and spending the night with Aspen but opted to head to my rental.

Instead of going inside, I ventured to the fenced-in backyard and grabbed my bats from the small deck. I pulled a weight from my bag and slid it into position. Over and over again, I practiced my swing, grimacing with each pull of my shoulder.

I looked over toward the neighbor's house when one particular swing left me seeing spots and met the eyes of a little boy who couldn't have been more than ten years old. He had stars in his eyes as they shimmered brightly in the dimming daylight.

"Wow. I want to be a ballplayer like you when I grow up," he said, awe filling every word.

"Yeah? Do you play?"

"Yep! I'm a shortstop, just like you. Well, when my coach lets me. He always wants me in the outfield, because I'm the only one who can throw far. But that's okay. Mom said he has to let everyone play all the spots."

"I remember playing like that. It helps you appreciate the role everyone plays in the game."

"My mom said something like that too."

The little boy looked eager as he leaned over the fence. I wondered if he stood on a chair or ladder to get a better view. I hoped it wasn't something dangerous.

Off in the distance, a stern voice hollered, "Roman Elias Spiegel, you better get your feet back on the ground!"

"Oops," the boy chuckled without moving an inch from his perch.

Walking toward the fence, I rested my arms on the top, my bat dangling from one hand.

"Ma'am!" I called out and waited until a frazzled woman with two babies in her arms came out to their porch. "Sorry to bother you. Do you think Roman could practice some swings with me? I can come over there."

"Are you sure, Mr. Ramsey?" she asked as one of the babies tugged at her brown hair. "I don't want him to be an imposition."

"It's no problem. I need to practice, and I heard he has quite the throwing arm."

The woman sighed with a growing smile as she glanced at her son. "That would be great. Thank you. His dad should be home soon. He got called out to an emergency."

"Cop?"

"Firefighter."

"That's some hard work."

She nodded, then looked to her son. "All right, Roman. Please listen to Mr. Ramsey and be on your best behavior."

The young boy dashed over to his mom, wrapping himself around her legs. She looked down at him with so much love I felt like *I* was imposing on the moment.

"All right, kid. Go grab your bat and a ball."

***

I gave Aspen a pass on dating lessons the next day, since I knew her family was launching the harvest of the corn. The large trucks for transport had been seen all over town. I still didn't know how they maneuvered the vehicles around the ninety-degree turn that gave most people difficulty in normal cars. But the drivers were skilled—that I knew for sure.

I messaged her that night, just to check in, though I wanted nothing more than to see her face. She had quickly become someone I looked forward to seeing.

> How did things go today?

Cricket
> Good. Tiring. I'm ready for a bath.

> Can I come wash your back?

> <deadpan emoji>

> I met with Coach Rudicell at the high school today. The kids seemed excited.

> I bet they were. They look up to you.

There was a long pause in the texts where bubbles would pop up and then disappear. After ten minutes, I finally caved and sent one first.

> Can I see you tomorrow?

It's my turn to pick up sandwiches for lunch. You can take me, if you want.

> Sounds like a plan. Pick you up at 11?

Sure. I'm heading to bed. Exhausted.

> Night, cricket.

Are you ever going to tell me why you gave me that ridiculous nickname?

> Maybe one day, but that day isn't today.

G'night, Owen.

Now here I was the next morning as I laid in bed, scrolling through our messages one more time, the sun casting the entire bedroom in a yellowish hue. I'd always enjoyed talking with Aspen, even when it was something cruel she was spewing at me. It was the only time I ever saw her with a backbone.

Dinner Sunday night was eye-opening. Though she continued to chime in on conversations, Aspen was usually ignored. I was sure they weren't doing it on purpose, but by the end of dinner, Aspen's face was one of dejection. It wasn't until she asked her father something directly that anyone paid her any mind.

I'd never experienced living in the shadows of anyone. Not only because I was an only child, but I'd always been a leader. My personality surpassed others'. I wasn't being egotistical; it's just how things were.

It also helped me understand why Aspen was so willing to take the role her family assigned her. She was paid so little attention that if things failed, there was a chance they'd barely notice until it was catastrophic.

Tossing my phone aside, I made my way toward the bathroom for a shower. Just as I stepped out of the warm spray, a knock sounded on the front door. Quickly, I wrapped a towel around my waist and went to answer. My mom stood on the other side with a cardboard box in her hands.

"Hey, Mom," I said as she stood across from me, looking as if she'd seen a ghost.

"Hi. Can I come in?"

"Sure." I ushered her inside and gestured for her to take a seat while I changed into some clothes. I hoped she didn't plan on staying long. I wanted to get as much time with Aspen as I could. I also had a stop to make on the way to Sunny Brook Farms.

In the five minutes it took me to change, Mom hadn't moved an inch on the sofa. Her eyes were trained on the images hanging on the opposite wall. Seeing her with her shoulders hunched, I realized how small and frail she truly was. Nothing like the mother I remembered when I was little. Even though she'd been going through her own hell, she still did her best to fight my father off whenever he focused his anger on me.

"Would you like a drink? Water?"

"No, I'm fine. Thank you though."

I grabbed myself a glass, because I was purposely prolonging whatever brought my mom here. I surmised it was related to the ongoing drama with the house and my father.

"What's in the box?" I asked as I took the empty seat next to her. My large frame sank into the cushion, nearly causing Mom to slide into me.

"Just a few things from the old house I thought you might want. Trophies, certificates, pictures."

"Cool. Thanks." I grabbed the box and flipped one pane open to explore inside. The first item I grabbed was my trophy from winning the National Championship when I was a senior in high school.

"I've been working with the kid next door, Roman. He's pretty good."

Mom nodded and gnawed on her bottom lip, but she didn't reply.

"I know this isn't the only reason you came by."

"You're right. You've always been very perceptive."

"Well, might as well rip off the Band-Aid and get it over with. That's what you used to tell me."

Mom pushed up from the couch and stood, then walked toward the sliding glass doors leading to the back deck and yard. Her back was to me as she said, "You know, you were born at twenty-eight weeks. The tiniest little thing. I was so worried about you, thinking I'd done something wrong. Every day was a challenge.

Every day, I was worried when I visited you that they'd have something heartbreaking to tell me.

"But now, here you are. No one would ever know how much you struggled that first year of life."

I listened intently, even though her story was one I'd heard numerous times. Usually, it accompanied a milestone event, like graduating to the next grade in school.

"That was when everything changed with your father."

My ears perked up. That was not her typical statement made after the flashback. Normally, it was the level of pride she felt for me that followed it.

Mom had my complete attention.

"He wasn't a bad man before. Never raised a hand. Now, I don't want you to believe *you* were the cause of his anger. It was *never* you. He was angry at me, because he thought I couldn't give him a healthy son."

Her sniffles echoed around the room.

"I let it go on for so long. Too long. The day he left was the happiest in my life… until I learned how devilish he truly was.

"Your father had a whole other family on the side. A wife, stepchildren, two dogs. The sad part was she knew about us the entire time. She relished the weeks he didn't return to her."

"He... he hit her too? And the kids?"

"She and I never went into the details, but I assume so."

"Do I have siblings?" I choked out the words.

"No. They were hers from a previous relationship."

"Wow," I whispered, leaning my elbows on my knees as I ran my hands through my hair. Talk about an overload of information.

"I'm sorry, sweetheart. That's not even the worst of it."

"What?"

How was the man causing all this devastation from the grave? Did he make a deal with the devil?

Unable to process what she told me so far, I stood, chugged my glass of water, and walked back to the kitchen. I needed something stronger. Grabbing a beer from the fridge, I cracked it open and gulped it down, then followed it with another. I didn't care it was early in the morning.

"Owen?" Mom questioned as she stood in the opening between the living area and the kitchen. I rested back against the closed fridge, craving the distance.

"Just... get it out, Mom."

"When your father died, I thought it was the best thing that could have ever happened. By the time you left for college, he was never around, so I lived in peace for those few years. Then the first letters and calls started up right before you were drafted by the Coyotes."

The letter and calls she told me about when I first got to Ashfield, the conversation that sent me storming off to the bar that night. Collections, banks, pretty much anyone my father owed money to. All those years he tried to do something with the farm, he'd taken out loans in my mother's name.

She continued, "Now, Jim never gave me access to any of the bank statements. Anytime I asked or questioned where the money was coming and going, he would blow up. It was easier to stay quiet.

"I told you he had two mortgages against the house and some personal loans. But what I didn't get the chance to tell you, because your reaction to only those was bad enough, was he also had two more on the land alone, and he put the farm as collateral on a business loan."

The bottle of beer nearly slipped from my fingers as I stared at my mother in shock.

"He…? That bastard! How much money? Why didn't you use the money I sent you? How much do I need, in order to get us out of this hole?"

"None." My mother smiled sweetly, as if she were in on some secret. Then my entire world exploded as it all hit me like an asteroid.

"It was the Easterlys. They bailed us out, didn't they? I should have fucking known."

"They did, and it was the nicest thing anyone has ever done for me, Owen. They paid far more than that land was worth, and the house isn't even inhabitable."

Pushing past my mother, I brushed her shoulder harder than I intended in my anger, but she stood there stoically, like the rock she was. The sliding glass door banged against its frame as I made my way outside.

I didn't care that the worn wood of the deck might leave splinters in my bare feet or that the morning sun was blazing down on me. I'd sat through worse.

Lifting the bottle to my lips, I stewed over the knowledge that Aspen knew about my family farm all along and said nothing. She'd had so much time to tell me. I'd been home for less than two weeks, but we'd spent a lot of that time together.

Less than two weeks, and *everything* had changed.

A friend would have told me. A true friend wouldn't have kept the secret this long.

"I told Aspen not to tell you. She'd been begging me since the sale went through to say something," my mom said, as if reading my thoughts as she sat beside me with her own beer in hand. Neither of us seemed to care that it was barely nine in the morning. "That's on me, not her. I also can't say I expected y'all to form a friendship, much less so quickly after your return. So don't hold it against her or the Easterlys. This was a decision *I* made when your father died."

I wondered what would've happened if my father hadn't died. Would my mother have continued working odd jobs to try to pay back all the loans? My father put them all in her name. Did he do this to his other family too? I was riddled with questions that would never be answered. The bastard died and took it all to hell with him.

I'd bring him back to life one more time just to send him to the grave myself.

"I hate him." My words faltered, and a took a breath, looking up to the sky through a glassy view. "I hate him so much."

"I do too. The only good thing that man did in my life was give me you."

Finishing my beer, I spun the bottle back and forth between my palms, watching as my forearm flexed with each turn. The veins made the mountains and trees of my tattoo look like they were moving.

"Why didn't you use any of the money I sent you every month?"

Instead of answering, she repeated what she told me the day I got home. "I put it in a trust in your name at the bank. You're the only one who can access it."

Nodding, I wished she kept the money for herself. My mother had been through too much to be living in a bed-and-breakfast where she worked. A job she didn't even need to have.

"You should renew your nursing license. Maybe you can take over this rental when I leave."

"I'm happy, Owen. I enjoy working at the B&B. And I'm the only one living there full-time. It's like living in my dream home. Entertaining the guests is one of my favorite things. I always wanted to host Tupperware parties like those moms on television. When we moved out here, I thought that would've been be my chance. Never occurred to me we moved here because your father was out-schemed and needed to hide.

"Anyway… I'm perfectly happy with how my life is right now."

Turning my head to stare at my mother, I could see she was telling the truth. Even after everything she told me, this was the happiest I'd ever seen her. The healthiest too. I was no longer afraid I'd find her ankles covered in rope burns or a boot mark along her stomach. Her brown hair was soft and shiny, not the dull, lifeless strands I remembered growing up.

"I... I don't know what to do with all this information," I confessed. "I don't know how to process it all."

"I understand," Beverly replied. "I need to run a few errands, but if it's all right with you, maybe you could join me for lunch tomorrow."

"Sure. That sounds nice."

"I love you, sweet boy," she said as she stood up, and then she made her way back through the house.

I sat there for a moment longer, and then something inside me snapped.

I darted around the outside of the home, flung open the fence gate, and made my way toward her car. I met her there just as she stepped off the front porch, her face one of surprise. And then my arms wrapped around her tightly, her breath leaving her body in a whoosh.

"I love you too, Mom."

Chapter Thirteen

Aspen

Sitting high in one of the combines, I watched Owen's car fly through the driveway to the main house. The McLaren kicked up a ton of dirt that would leave the maroon paint filthy, but I knew he would have it spotless by the next day.

Glancing down at my watch, I noticed he was nearly an hour early. Using a walkie-talkie, I radioed my dad and Andrew to let them know I was taking a break and to send someone out to finish this portion of the field. Soon, one of the veteran workers came out, delight filling his eyes when I handed over the keys.

The UTV made quick work of moving me across the fields and over to the house, where I found Owen and my mom sitting out on the front porch in rocking chairs, drinking lemonade.

They looked adorable.

"Oh, Aspen. Good, you're here. Let me run inside and get you the list of sandwiches to grab from Ernie's."

Mom scurried out of her chair so fast it continued to rock while she made her way inside. I was too busy looking at her retreating back to notice Owen stood up until I turned and found him only a foot away.

"Hey," I said, just before his hands came up to clasp my face, and he pressed our lips together.

The kiss caught me off guard, and when my lips parted in surprise, Owen's tongue veered inside. My arms hung loosely at my sides, but as the kiss grew more zealous, I reached for his waist, leaning my body against his.

"Oh!"

Owen and I jumped apart at my mom's sudden return. While I kept my gaze trained on the wooden planks of the porch, he snickered.

"Sorry. I didn't mean to interrupt. Here is the list," she said, holding it out for me to take. My eyes looked everywhere but at my mother's as I reached for the piece of paper.

"Anything else you need, Mrs. Easterly?"

"Oh, maybe a half-dozen pies from the store? Everyone is working so hard. I'm working on the stew for dinner, so that will be a great dessert."

"Sure. Can I grab a couple of bottles of wine for you as well?"

"Oh, that would be wonderful, Owen. You're such a kind man. Don't you think so, Aspen?"

I looked at my mom in shock and then over at Owen, wondering if she witnessed him mauling my mouth. Though, I didn't regret it for one second.

"Yeah, he's a gem."

"Okay. Now you two be on your way. Lunch is in two hours. I gave Ernie a heads-up, so he knows you're coming."

Before Mom could say anything more, I gripped Owen's hand and dragged him down the stairs toward his car. I would have offered to drive, but I knew he'd protest.

During the drive, we talked about the harvest and his neighbor. Owen was hoping to get some practice in using the high-school batting cages while he was here.

He was just waiting for the go-ahead from his temporary trainer.

We walked hand in hand inside Chuck's while we looked for pies. The fact that holding his hand felt so right was an observation I was trying my best to ignore.

What was impossible to overlook was that everyone around sprinted in the other direction whenever they spotted us. Not in a silly way, but because people were completely terrified.

"You know, you'd think by now that everyone would've forgiven our chaotic behavior from when we were kids."

Owen laughed as he stacked the six pies against his chest with a single arm, never dropping my hand. "It seems our reputation precedes us."

"It seems."

Leaning down, his lips brushed against my ear. "We should give them something to talk about."

"Are you talking about…," I started as Owen pulled away and stepped around one of the displays. I peered at him in confusion, then suddenly felt something soft and squishy press against my cheek.

Peeling away from me with laughter, the pies in one hand and a squished cupcake in the other, he ran toward the registers. Grabbing a cupcake of my own, I gave chase. Two families moved out of the way as I bolted after him. I cornered him in the checkout line as Mrs. Henson stood at the register, writing out a check for her groceries.

"Owen Ramsey, you're going to pay."

He ducked and veered at my attempts, but I used the conveyor belt as leverage and hoisted myself high enough to smash the chocolatey goodness into the side of his face and hair.

"Oh dear!" Mrs. Hensen exclaimed, and I realized I smashed the cake so hard that bits and pieces flew into the air behind Owen, some landing on Mrs. Henson and the teen working the register.

"I'm so sorry," I apologized between fits of giggles.

Owen stepped forward, and for a moment I wondered what other tricks he had up his sleeve. He surprised me as his fingers forcefully slid into my hair and yanked my face toward his, crushing his mouth to mine.

"Oh dear," Mrs. Hensen repeated, but this time her voice was breathy.

I pulled back from Owen and went in search of paper towels to clean ourselves up while he paid for the pies and two cupcakes.

By the time we got back to his car, we looked as good as new, minus the brown streak along Owen's shoulder from the chocolate. He didn't seem to care and shrugged when I brought it up.

At Ernie's, a newer sandwich shop in town, Owen and I were on our best behaviors. While we waited for the staff to finish making the thirty sandwiches Mom called in, we strolled up and down the block. Most of the people we passed waved and smiled. Only a few pulled out their phones to snap a picture. Most just wanted to leave us alone.

As we walked back to the shop, a group of women stood just outside the doors, blocking the entrance. I knew immediately they were hoping for a chance to get to Owen.

His hold on my hand tightened, and I knew he must have noticed them too.

"Owen!"

"Owen Ramsey!"

The group shouted his name over and over as they waved to get his attention.

I tried to slip my hand free, to give him a chance to greet his fans, even the female ones, but he squeezed my fingers, dragging me along with him.

"Good afternoon, ladies."

Within a second of his greeting, they began asking for pictures and autographs. One even pulled her shirt down to reveal her lacy bra and round breasts.

"Sorry, ladies. I'm at lunch with my girlfriend right now. If you're looking for an autograph, I'm helping the high school run a conditioning camp over the weekend. I'll hang around for an hour or so to sign things for the kids."

Without listening to a single word they spoke, he brushed past them with me in tow and slid us into the sandwich shop. I was thankful the women didn't follow us inside.

"I didn't know you were doing a camp this weekend. That sounds fun."

"Coach Rudicell asked. I remember learning a lot at those camps. You should come. Be my own personal cheerleader."

Barking out a laugh, I replied, "You and I both know that I was never a cheerleader, nor do I have the hand-eye coordination for baseball. But I am sure you'll have a great time."

"I'll get a bat in your hands one day."

"Only if I get to chase you with it," I said and smiled while pursing my lips. Something about Owen brought out a saucier side of me I never knew existed.

"We're going to the movies tonight, by the way. The theater is showing one of my favorite movies as a kid."

"Yeah? And what's that?"

Smiling down at me as the shop worker handed over five bags filled with sandwiches, he replied, "*Angels in the Outfield.*"

"Of course they are. You're like a hero to the people of Ashfield. I am 100-percent certain they chose that movie with you in mind."

"Don't care. We're going to see it." Leaning down as we exited through the back door to avoid the crowd out front, Owen added, "And maybe if you're a good girl, we can make out in the back row."

***

I was lying to myself by saying my cheeks were red from the sunburn I received from working on the farm, but I knew it was from listening to Owen's promises running through my head over and over.

Even as I tried on my third outfit of the night, I couldn't shake the natural blush that flushed even brighter when I thought about sitting in the movie theater with Owen.

With a glance at the clock on my nightstand, I knew he would arrive at any moment. Sighing a heavy, desperate breath, I yanked a black spaghetti strap dress from my closet and tugged it over my strapless bra and lace panties. They didn't match, but none of my undergarments were a set, so I was working with what I had. I only owned anything lace because Jenna insisted I buy them the last time she and I went to the big city.

Staring at my reflection in the mirror hanging from my closet door, I pulled at the hem of the dress. I didn't remember it being that short. So much of my legs was exposed. My normal attire of cut-off denim and tank tops beckoned me from the dresser drawers, while my cowboy boots taunted me from their spot by my front door. The semi-dressy sandals I owned were waiting to be slipped on, just as my doorbell rang.

Rushing down the steps, I nearly slid on the rug covering my hardwood floors. Thankfully, I caught the corner of the wall with my hand and propelled myself forward.

My hair laid like a curtain over my face, and I was busy brushing it away as Owen opened the door and stepped inside.

"Everything okay? I thought I heard some slamming."

"Yeah, sorry. Slipped on the rug." I pushed my hair back one final time and glanced up at Owen, but my eyes only made it to his hand holding a bag from one of the boutiques in town. "What's that?"

"Something I picked up for you this morning."

"Before lunch?" I asked, almost scared something was going to pop out of the bag.

"Yep." Owen smirked in the way that could either be described as sexy or mischievous. Neither appealed to me at the moment. "Do you want to see what it is?"

"No. Not really."

He laughed, one of those deep belly laughs you felt down to your soul. I couldn't help but join in.

"Come on. Don't you trust me?"

"That's a loaded question, Owen."

"Fine. I'll take it back."

Reaching out, I snatched the white bag out of his grip. "Never." When I felt inside, I held my breath, secretly praying my hand would not come in contact with a bug or something else equally as gross. Instead, I was surprised to feel the softest of materials.

Lifting the fabric in one hand and dropping the bag to the floor with my other, I was stunned to find a lovely silk dress. The color was the most beautiful shade of purple, between eggplant and maroon. I couldn't decide, as the light from the setting sun hit it in different areas.

"Owen, this is gorgeous. Thank you."

"You're welcome."

"Did you pick this out yourself?" I asked, inspecting the dress closer. The sleeves would hang off my shoulders, and the hem would hit just above my knees.

"I did."

The tag hung loosely around the underside of the sleeve, and I tried my best to ignore it, but the triple zeroes immediately caught my eye. The silk was the nicest I'd ever felt, but I wasn't sure I would be willing to pay a couple thousand dollars for it. I'd stepped into Nicole's Boutique in town, and she sold all sorts of items. Some bargain and some high-end. She catered to everyone. It was why her store was a success. But I'd never looked at the racks with the designer labels. Not because I didn't have the money for them, but because working on the farm didn't necessitate that sort of clothing.

"I want to argue about you spending this much money on me, but I'm not going to," I explained as I hugged the dress against my body.

"Really? I expected a full-blown shitstorm to be honest."

"I can give you one, if you'd like, but I'd rather just thank you again. I've never had something this nice before." Stepping toward him, I stood on my toes, my lips barely reaching his jawline, and I left a lingering kiss. "I'm going to wear this tonight. I'll be right back."

I hurried up the stairs, whipped my black dress off my body, and replaced it with the purple garment. Standing in front of the mirror, I twisted back and forth, admiring the way it set on my body. The silk dress looked like it had been made for me.

I considered pulling my hair up into a twist but instead left my hair in long, loose waves. Trudging through my closet, I reached for a pair of black-and-tan espadrilles that were a gift from Jenna I'd never worn. Slipping them on my feet, I walked back and forth in the wedges to make sure I would not topple over, then made my way back down the stairs.

I felt like Lainey Boggs from *She's All That* walking down the steps, and Owen was my own Freddie Prinze Jr. In my head, "Kiss Me" was playing on repeat.

"Wow," Owen breathed. "You look beautiful."

"Thanks." Just then, my stomach chose that moment to chime into the conversation. "Sorry. I haven't eaten yet."

"That's okay. I thought we could stop by Angelo's then hit the 9:00 p.m. movie."

Internally, I counted the hours of sleep I'd get if I got home by midnight. Wake-up was usually at four or five. Normal Aspen would have complained. Normal Aspen would have asked to skip dinner and head to the movie early. Non-social Aspen would have suggested skipping it all together.

But the new Aspen who was trying to live her life smiled at her fake date and grabbed his outstretched hand as he guided her from her house. New Aspen ordered a glass of wine with her baked ziti. And the new Aspen chose a seat in the back row of the movie theater, where she and her fake boyfriend could make out through the entire movie.

At one point, we even knocked the tub of popcorn to the floor.

The old Aspen really liked this new Aspen, regardless of the fact that things would likely go back to the way they were when Owen left.

But this Aspen was going to live for the moment, no matter how few hours of sleep I was going to get.

And when Owen asked if I wanted to go back to his place for a bit after the movie, I immediately accepted.

Chapter Fourteen

Aspen

Rory's house was dark when we arrived. I followed Owen up the front porch and over the threshold, where he switched on a lamp that rested on a small console table by the door. I was already familiar with the layout of the house and set my purse on the table, then walked over to the living room.

"Can I get you a drink or anything?"

"Um… whatever you're having is fine," I replied. I was more nervous now than when he picked me up. There was something different about being in his place. Here, we weren't faking it for anyone. There were no cameras or gossipers. No girls eagerly waiting for him to sign their breasts. It was just us, and I didn't know where in the sand to find the drawn line.

"Here. It's a vodka soda."

"Thanks."

My hand shook as I took the glass from him. He had to have noticed, as the ice clinked in the glass, but he didn't say a word. Tentatively, I took a sip of the drink, surprised when I found it cool and refreshing.

"So..."

"So...," I repeated.

"Do you want to watch a movie or something?"

"Um... no... not really." Setting my glass on the end table, the clunk reverberated in the room. "Sorry. I'm nervous."

"Why? We're just hanging out."

"That's what makes me nervous. I've never just... hung out with a guy."

Owen hummed, rubbing one of his thick fingers against his bottom lip. "How about we work on another lesson?"

"What was the first lesson?" I asked, trying to remember if we actually made a list.

"Teaching you to be more confident. Men are attracted to confidence. That's why I sent you to the bar alone."

"Oh."

"The second was going to teach you to be accepting of gifts and compliments, but you didn't have any trouble there. So, I think we can move on to lesson three."

"Yeah, and what's that?"

"Knowing what you want and being vocal about it."

My palms immediately went clammy at the thought of telling anyone my desires.

Licking my lips, my voice croaked as I tried to speak up. "Are you talking about not allowing a date to order dinner for me or something like that?"

Owen took a step closer, setting his drink on the end table next to mine as he leaned over me. His lips brushed against the soft bare skin of my neck. My body quaked at the gentle touch.

"You know what I'm talking about."

"I… I'm confused. Is… isn't this all supposed to be fake?" My eyes closed as I tilted my head toward the ceiling. The feel of his lips burned along my skin in the best possible way. Unexpectedly, his hands reached for my hips, gripping the silky material in his fists as he drew me up against him. The outline of his cock behind his pants pressed against my stomach, and I immediately clenched my legs together.

"It's as fake as you want it to be. I can stop, and we can keep this professional, or we can explore this. Tell me what you want, cricket. Tell me if you want me to stop."

Hesitantly, I touched his shirt-covered chest. Our kissing at the theater and the few stolen kisses before that… they'd all been fake, right? It was all pretend. But now, with his mouth tracing paths along my neck, collarbone, and shoulder, it sure didn't feel like a game.

"I… I don't want you to stop. Teach me, Owen."

"That's my good girl," he said as he pulled back and released my dress from his fists. He covered my cheeks with his hands as his mouth met mine. Caution was thrown to the wind as our tongues swirled, my arms wrapping around his waist, and I held on for dear life.

Without breaking our kiss, Owen released my face and lifted me into his arms, mine circling his neck as he carried me to the bedroom.

Reluctantly, I released my hold once he pulled back and settled me on my feet.

"All right," he whispered, pushing my hair back from my face and shoulders. "Tell me what you want."

My nerves popped and pinged at the thought of describing the things I wanted Owen to do to me, with me. There were things I'd only heard about in books and movies.

"W-What do you mean?" I asked as he took a step back and rested against the dresser, crossing his arms against his chest and his feet at the ankles.

"Tell me what you want to happen tonight. I can keep kissing you, finger-fuck you, eat your pussy, fuck you until you can't remember your name…."

My entire body heated at his words, though Owen didn't even bat an eye as he spoke. My body squirmed beneath his gaze. I couldn't comprehend how or why this gorgeous man wanted to do something so intimate with me.

"Is there something in it for you?" I murmured. That was one of my biggest fears, being used for a game of some sort. But Owen and I were already playing a game to fool everyone else. I worried about fooling myself in the meantime. I knew from town gossip and tabloids that Owen wasn't a playboy. Not by the common definition. Before they broke up, he planned to settle down with and marry a woman I couldn't compete against, so I had no idea what he wanted with me.

"Just the pleasure of making you come."

I gasped. No man had ever spoken so bluntly to me. Of course, I'd never given them the chance to. Immediately, I felt my core tighten and my stomach clench at the thought of Owen touching me, tasting me.

"Tell me what you want, sweet girl."

Closing my eyes, I thought about my end goal. How I wanted to be intimate with someone and how I didn't want it to be awkward. With Tryston, I'd have to get to know him first, but with Owen, I'd known him most of my life. It was both awkward and exhilarating.

"Take off my dress," I mumbled, my sweaty palms fisted.

Owen reached out and pulled my body against his. I didn't hear or feel the zipper make its way down my back. All I felt and heard were his gentle fingertips sliding down my bare skin and the soft sound of each of his breaths.

The material pooled at my feet, and Owen took a step back, admiring me as I stood before him in my strapless bra, lace panties, and wedges. It took every ounce of self-control to keep from covering myself with my hands and arms. Though still not completely naked,

I'd never felt so exposed as I did at that moment. Owen's eyes traced over every inch of my body as if he was saving it to his memory.

"Take off your clothes," I requested, my voice trembling as I tapped out a rhythm with my fingertips on my thighs. I had no idea what the song was, but it kept me from completely abandoning ship, grabbing my dress, and running for the bathroom.

The smirk I'd started to grow fond of appeared on Owen's lips just as he reached behind his head, gathered the material of his shirt, and pulled it off effortlessly. If I tried the same thing, I would have ended up in a tangled mess.

"Damn, you're hot," I said, not realizing I uttered the words aloud until I heard Owen's chuckle as he toed off his shoes and socks. He made quick work of his pants, and they landed in a heap atop his ankles.

I counted an eight-pack. Eight mounds on his lower abdomen and a freaking line darting down from each hip. He had the body men desired and women dreamed about.

"You know, I used to think they worked magic with some sort of editing software on the images they put of you in magazines, but no. Of *course* you actually look like a freaking Greek statue."

Owen looked down, his brow furrowed like he was seeing himself for the first time. Following his movement, I did the same. I was toned from years out on the ranch, but Owen's body was on a whole other level.

His boxer briefs rested low on his hips, and the cotton did nothing to hide his large cock pressing against its confines. Most women probably would've quivered with anticipation if the chance of having Owen's dick was on the night's dessert menu. Unlike them, my throat dried up, and my core clenched in fear.

Thank goodness I was saving myself for Tryston, or whatever steady boyfriend came along after Owen's and my fake relationship ended. This man would've been too much for me.

"Cricket. Eyes up here," he said, pulling my thoughts back to him instead of his almost-naked form.

"Sorry," I mumbled, my eyes focusing on his chiseled face.

"What do you want next?"

My teeth chattered, and I clenched my shaking hands, as I whispered, "Touch me."

Owen took a step closer, his bare feet almost making contact with the tips of my espadrilles. "Where?"

Our breaths mingled, and my skin grew warm all over as he lifted his hand toward my neck. Even though his fingers didn't touch my skin, they left a heated path along each centimeter they moved across. The electricity jumped off my skin in waves, leaving prickles in their wake.

"Everywhere," I moaned in anticipation.

He finally made contact, his fingers drawing around my clavicle, then a line down the middle of my chest between my breasts and to my navel, where he swirled around the soft skin. The sensation nearly made my knees buckle.

"You're going to have to be more specific."

My impatience was growing as his fingers glided along my hips, slipping just inside the waistband of my panties. "Take it off, please. The bra and panties."

"My pleasure," he responded with a cunning smile.

"I think it's the other way around," I said, my voice hitching when he unhooked my strapless bra. It toppled down my body, exposing my breasts I now fought not to hide.

"Fuck. Stop distracting me," he groaned with a lusty gaze focused on my chest. My nipples pebbled under his stare.

"I'm not doing anything," I replied with a chortle.

"You certainly are. How am I supposed to focus on the task you've given me, when you have these perfect breasts to distract me with?"

I never thought my breasts were anything to write home about. They were always on the smaller side, and most of the time, I felt self-conscious when I wore a tight shirt. But with the way Owen was staring at them, I wondered if I'd been wrong all these years.

"Sorry." My apology for distracting him was just for show, because I *liked* the way he looked and appreciated my body. It left me wanting more.

With a powerful breath in through his nose and out through his mouth, as if to calm himself, Owen slipped both his index fingers into the waist of my panties and tugged them down my hips until they fell at my feet on their own.

His body descended, his hands softly sliding down my sides until they cupped my ankles. My breath was coming in heavy pants by the time he gazed up at me. Lifting one of my espadrille-clad feet, he slipped it out of the panties and then repeated the action with the other, tossing the lace and my bra over toward the dresser.

I was stark naked in front of the most gorgeous man in baseball—and definitely in Ashfield—and he was licking his lips like he'd just been invited to an all-you-can-eat buffet.

"Shoes," I mumbled. It was unintelligible to my own ears, but Owen seemed to understand, as he unbuckled each strap and slipped the shoes free.

I dropped almost three inches in front of Owen, where he kneeled on one knee before me after setting my shoes aside. His eyes were patient, but his body was wound tight. His jaw ticked, and I felt my core grow wetter.

"Owen," I pleaded, wanting him to do anything he pleased with me. I was at his disposal. A willing student ready to be taught.

"Yes, cricket?"

"Touch me."

"What do you want?" he asked again, leaning back only slightly and clasping his hands together. His erection tented his boxer briefs. "Where? How? Tell me what you need, sweet girl."

"I need it all, Owen," I whimpered. "I'm begging you to put your mouth on me."

"God… damn," he growled.

I thought he'd go straight for my breasts, which had garnered so much of his attention the peaks were straining for his touch. But Owen glided his hands up along the back of my legs until he reached my thighs. Then, in a flash, he lifted one over his shoulder.

Before I could take my next breath, he settled back onto his ankles and ran his nose along my wet, hot slit.

"Oh my gosh," I cried out, nearly falling backward the moment his tongue ran across my center, but he immediately reached up and gripped my ass in one hand to steady me. He used the other to slide a finger back and forth over my clit.

Moaning out his name, I reached up and cupped my breasts with my hands, rolling my nipples between my fingers before I even realized what I was doing.

"Mmm. You taste so good. Like spun sugar." He pulled back slightly, his finger still swiping along my folds.

"What does that mean?"

Suddenly, I was lifted into the air and tossed onto the bed. As I bounced, Owen crouched between my legs, bending them at the knees as he spread me wide.

"That I have a sweet tooth, and I plan to spend a lot of time devouring your pussy."

I didn't know it was possible to grow wetter than I already was, but I was mistaken as my inner walls compressed, and I released more.

"Show me how you get off, baby. I need to see it." He sounded like a crazed junkie waiting for his next hit. I'd never been big on masturbation, only doing so when my body was too tight to ignore and I had no choice but to give myself a release.

"I thought I was in charge," I joked.

"Oh, you definitely are. You drive me wild, cricket. I want to make this good for you. Show me how."

Slowly, I slid one hand down my stomach, running my middle finger in circles around my sensitive clit, while my other hand caressed one of my breasts, tugging and pinching the sensitive peak.

My hips started grinding against my hand to increase the friction. I crept a finger inside my channel, coating it in my slickness, then drew it back over my clit, repeating the process until my knees shook.

"Yeah, baby. Make yourself come. You're fucking beautiful." I was surprised to find he wasn't looking at my hand between my legs, nor the hand on my breast. Instead, his eyes were trained on my face, darkening with each heavy, quick breath I took as I reached the edge.

"Owen?"

"Yeah?"

"Kiss me."

He crawled up the bed and laid beside me. Forcefully, his mouth descended on mine. There was no sweet or gentle pecking, only the hungriness of longing and desire.

The hand on my breast reached for Owen's head, and I held him steady against me as our tongues dueled.

Without warning, my body exploded, and I pulled my lips away to gasp for air.

"That's it. Ride it out," he commanded as I gyrated my apex against my hand.

Just as quickly as it rose, my orgasm came down, and I was left feeling unfulfilled. Usually, I was good for weeks before I needed another release.

But this time, I wanted… more.

"That was," I mumbled, unable to tell Owen what I needed, because I wasn't sure what to ask for.

"Hot as fuck," he supplied for me as he rolled his body over mine. His very large, very hard cock settled between my legs, and without a second thought, I rocked myself against him.

"Oh, hell," he said, clenching his eyes shut. "Steady, baby."

"I need more, Owen."

His lips brushed against mine in the sweetest way, like the caress of a flower petal.

"I know you do. I won't fuck you tonight, cricket, but I'll make you come as many times as you need. My hand, my tongue, my leg. You can ride every part of me but my cock."

"Geez. I don't know what to say to that."

"Say, 'Yes, Owen, I want you to make me see stars.'"

"Yes, Owen, make me see stars."

"Your wish is my command," he replied as he dove between my legs again and showed me exactly how magical he could be.

His mouth did things I never imagined, and it felt like heaven. I couldn't get enough of it. My hips rocked and swirled against his face as he fucked me with his tongue and fingers. By the time he added a second digit to my tight sheath and sucked on my clit, my second orgasm made itself known.

I cried out Owen's name and arched my back, reaching down to grip his hair with one hand while the other fisted the bed covers.

"Oh my gosh, I feel like a limp noodle," I told him after he went to the bathroom to clean his face, which glistened with my wetness, and to retrieve a warm washcloth to clean between my legs. Owen was surprisingly tender in his care. "I'm not sure how I'll get dressed," I cried as I tried to lift my body off the bed and failed.

Owen fell upon the bed with a flourish and tugged me against his semi-naked body. His erection was still hard and thick inside his boxer briefs, and it throbbed against my hip.

"Stay," he told me against my hair as he draped one strong arm across me.

"Owen," I scolded. "You know I need to—"

He quickly hushed me by pressing his lips against mine. His kisses purged my mind of every thought, question, and scenario until it became a blank canvas.

"Please," he whispered as his mouth brushed back and forth.

I should've been leaving to get a good night's sleep. Work started bright and early on the farm, and I was already cutting it close. But as I gazed at Owen's shimmering gray eyes, I couldn't say no. Instead, I asked him to grab my phone for me and turn off the lights.

By the time he returned with my phone and blanketed the room in darkness aside from the moonlight coming from the window, I was tucked under the covers with a corner pulled back for him to slide into bed.

In the subtle blue glow, Owen tugged down his last remaining stitch of clothing and slipped in beside me. He trailed his fingers up my exposed arm until they reached my shoulder, then neck, the face. They combed through my hair as he leaned forward and pressed his mouth against my lips again.

I moaned in contentment until he pulled back and tucked me against him.

"This changes things," he murmured.

And though I felt the same, I kept reminding myself this thing with Owen was temporary. He was leaving, probably sooner rather than later if his coach got his way.

And every once in a while, the nasty reminder that he was about to walk down the aisle just a few short weeks ago to marry another woman would make itself known. It was clear to me, and most people who knew him, that he hadn't loved his ex-fiancée, but he had planned to make the commitment regardless of how he felt.

And that made it impossible for me to believe he was ready for something more than a quick fling. Even though my heart strangely decided she wanted a piece of Owen.

Chapter Fifteen

Owen

My days felt lighter since the night Aspen stayed over at my place. I'd woken at four in the morning, only a couple hours after we'd fallen asleep, with her delectable mouth on my cock.

It was the fucking best blowjob I'd ever had. And not because Aspen was skilled, but simply because it had been from her. I knew she was as innocent as they came. The moment I pushed a finger inside her slick pussy and found it tight beyond measure, all signs pointed to a virgin.

She'd hinted at it enough in the time we spent together, but it was different when I could feel it. I'd had many women claim to be virgins, or claimed I was their first time after the fact, but none were as believable as my cricket.

It still made me chuckle whenever her face hardened each time I said her nickname. But in the bedroom, she nearly purred. Which left me thinking she secretly liked it.

We hadn't spent as much time together since that night. I knew she was busy with the farm, and I tried to give her the space she needed. Not because I wanted to, but because she was purposely ignoring me… again. I was growing addicted to her. Her taste, her smell, the way she made me laugh even when she wasn't trying. It made me realize I'd been pretending with Vanessa. I guessed I wanted it to be real, but I never felt an iota for Vanessa what I did for Aspen.

Which caused a whole other problem.

Vanessa reached out to my lawyers. She wanted to fight me for the house and the ring. Which was ridiculous, because the house was in my name, and I had it prior to our engagement. The ring had been a hefty purchase that she selected, but there was no way a judge would rule in her favor. Especially since video of her indiscretions before the wedding started making their rounds. Mostly from guests, but a few of the hotel staff members posted their own takes, catching the couple in multiple areas of the resort.

I was certain her modeling agency and their lawyers were trying to get the videos taken down as fast as they could, but replicas continued to pop up with a flourish.

I no longer cared. My lawyers were certain it was going nowhere, though they suggested giving her money to keep her quiet. I wasn't about to play that game with Vanessa. She graced enough covers and walked numerous catwalks for high-end designers. She didn't need my money.

Or at least that's what I'd been told by her and her "best friend." I never expected something was going on between the two of them, but maybe I'd been blinded by my career. Baseball took over most of my life. If I wasn't out on the field, I was training. There was very little personal time. Though, in hindsight, a lot of my teammates had families and looked forward to each day off they had. Many traveled with us when they could.

I'd never thought about having a family in the stands. Vanessa was only interested when the Coyotes were in the Championships and the game was on national television. Otherwise, she told me numerous times that baseball was boring and that there was no point in her sitting in the family section.

My coach tried to convince me to get my mom to come out, but I'd been hesitant and declined.

With our rocky relationship, I knew she would mess with my game. I'd find myself taken back to a time I'd rather not remember. To this day, I would never know how I held myself together all those years I played while living under my father's thumb.

I was driving my sports car the back way to the bed-and-breakfast, where I was meeting my mother for lunch. Though most roads in Ashfield took a good while to travel, this route took me around one mountain that created a boundary around our town.

Our?

It had been years since I considered Ashfield my home. It was nothing more than a place I once lived. Whenever a fan or reporter asked where I was from, I always said California. But something recently changed how I felt about the picturesque town.

It was… different. Or more specifically, *I* was different while I was here. I'd made friends with owners in the shops. Chuck at the grocery store chatted with me about his grandchildren and their love of science. Garret, owner of the hardware store, emailed me a bunch of links about how to fix things around a home, since I kept coming in and asking questions when I decided I want to replace the back deck for Rory. The owners of the coffee shop knew my order the moment I walked inside their building. And Ronald McEntire now had a signed picture hung of me and him in his restaurant. With a standing reservation.

My teammates were still amazed at that feat.

Ashfield was different. So was I. And I knew exactly why the change happened.

The road swerved and wound around the mountainous landscape, bringing me to the backside of my family's property—or what used to be our property. It belonged to the Easterlys, who now owned a massive expanse of land in Ashfield. As I passed the overgrown grass and the lake that looked like it had seen better days, I tried not to feel a sense of bitterness. I knew selling the land was the best thing my mom could have done. Not only to rid herself of the debts my father left, but to rid herself of my father all together.

God, I hated that man.

I'd slowed down as I crested a hill and stared over at the house that looked worse than when I'd seen it a few weeks ago. I'd done everything in my power to keep from coming back to the property.

What caught my eye was the slew of large equipment parked beside the house. A bright green dumpster stood out against the red brick and changing leaves of the trees.

Anger at what my father had done bubbled up to the surface.

"Fuck you, old man. I hope you're rotting in hell right now."

Off in the distance, a bird called out, and I took it as confirmation that he was decaying away somewhere. Mom and I didn't have a funeral for him. We didn't even claim his body. Once the police identified him in the cheap motel room, surrounded by booze, that was all the validation we needed. It wasn't until we had to collect his things that I even paid much attention to the fact that he died.

My tires squealed as my foot punched the accelerator, propelling the car forward. Traveling faster than necessary, I nearly spun out around a tight turn that led me toward the Easterly event venue.

The renovated barn stood majestically at the top of a hill, with a gorgeous view of the mountain range just beyond. I knew from pictures in Rory's house that the venue was home to some of the best sunset views around.

A few minutes down the road, Sunny Brook Farms came into view, and my heartbeat sped up. With the windows down, the sound of combines and tractors could be heard over the purr of my engine. I wondered if Aspen was out there wearing those denim cutoffs I loved so much.

A car was traveling down the driveway and pulled out behind me as I passed. Behind the wheel of the sleek vehicle that could rival my own, there looked to be a large man. I kept glancing behind me as I followed the road toward the B&B and was surprised when the car pulled off when I did.

Curiosity got the best of me as I peered out my window when the car parked beside me in front of the double-porched farmhouse. I was surprised when I realized Andrew was the driver of the car. I'd only ever seen him driving a beat-up pickup truck.

"Hey, man," I called out in greeting as I stepped free from my car. "Surprised to see you here."

"Hey. Yeah, I needed to speak with Aspen, and Mom said she was here."

"Oh. I didn't know she was going to be here." That was news to me. She mentioned this morning that she was working on the farm all day.

"Something about lunch. I figured you knew, since she's your girlfriend and all." Andrew seemed to still hold some skepticism, as did Alex, while Aspen's other two sisters had come around. Our parents were over the moon with our relationship. If they ever found out it was fake, it would crush them.

None of it felt fake anymore though. At least not to me. Aspen still hinted at future dates she'd go on when I left, asking me for advice, but I shut her down and distracted her.

"I only knew she was working hard at the farm today," I said sardonically. "Why aren't you there working with everyone else? To be honest, why aren't you the one learning the ropes so your dad can retire? Seems strange it's all being left to your little sister."

Andrew may have been older, but as I crossed my arms against my chest and stood to my full height, I had about two inches on him.

"I have my reasons. And besides, this is what Aspen's always wanted."

I huffed out a sarcastic laugh, then said, "Are you sure about that? Have any of you actually *asked* her what she wants?"

"Of course we have," he replied, but his tone made him seem less convinced than before.

"Owen, you're here. Oh, hi, Andrew," my mom called out, breaking the tension between me and Aspen's big brother. I didn't really care what he thought of me and my relationship with his sister. What bothered me was that the Easterlys did not know what Aspen wanted to do with her life.

I knew she wanted to see the world and write books and blogs about traveling on a budget. She'd shown me the few things she's written when she was in Nashville and Knoxville. The towns were close to her, but she wrote in a way that made it seem as if she was seeing them for the first time.

"Are you staying for lunch as well?" Mom asked Andrew. He shook his head as he told her he wasn't, but greeted her warmly with a hug before heading inside.

My mom turned toward me and smiled, but I could see there was still a wariness there. The creases around her eyes didn't divot the same way they did the first day I was home. That was before she threw me for a whirl I wasn't quite ready for.

"I've made some brisket sandwiches with au jus for lunch."

Leaning down, I kissed my mother's cheek and thanked her. I knew she'd chosen my favorite meal as a peace offering. We'd been to a few more Sunday dinners at Sunny Brook Farms, but most of my time was spent with Aspen. Usually, I'd pick Mom up, we'd eat, and then we would leave, before I'd drive right back and stay with Aspen.

Though I liked Aspen's house, it was a little cramped for the both of us. Since the night she spent with me, I'd been asking her if she wanted to stay there while I was still in Ashfield, but she hadn't been throwing off the signals that she was interested in that step yet. I was hoping to convince her soon.

Mom and I strolled inside the house together. A few guests were lingering in the large living space with a local tour guide Autumn commissioned. From what I'd been told, they offered winery and brewery tours, as well as historic outings and hikes.

Farther back in the house, I followed my mom toward the kitchen area. The house boasted a regular-sized kitchen as well as a butler's pantry, which was essentially a second kitchen where staff could eat. That's where we found Andrew and Aspen. My girl looked antsy as she listened to her brother, and I wanted nothing more than to step in, but I knew it wasn't my place. Instead, I followed Mom toward the side deck, where she'd set up the bistro table with our lunches.

I handed her the bag with the potato salad she requested from the store, and she scooped it onto our plates with a spoon she had ready at the table.

"This looks great, Mom. Thanks again."

"You're welcome. I feel like I see you here and there, but we don't get a chance to chat."

She was right, and the words stung. I just didn't know what to talk about with her. The hands of my father bruised and battered our entire relationship. Somehow, our conversations always came back to that time in our lives.

"Well, I've been speaking with Coach Rudicell about holding a few camps. I'm not sure how long I'll be here. Maybe until Thanksgiving. The weather should be nice until then."

"That will be nice. The Easterlys are almost done collecting their corn, so you should have some time to spend with Aspen."

That was news to me. I assumed it would take much longer to harvest, but I'd done some reading about combines and the attachments that pulled the corn kernels and removed the silks and stalks.

"That will be nice," I repeated her words awkwardly. "Of course, I'm sure she'll be busy with something else. If I remember, the farm is always going."

"That's true. I haven't paid too close attention over the years."

Silence filled the air as we ate. This time, it wasn't awkward like it had been in the past. Instead, I listened to the birds chirping and wondered if I could fit in a hike before the leaves changed completely.

"So, have you and Aspen talked about what you'll do when you go back to California? Are you going to try the long-distance thing?"

It's the same question I'd been asking myself but kept having to remember we were only temporary. Apparently, we were just really good at fooling everyone.

"I'm not sure. We're just having fun right now."

"Ah, I see," my mom said as she reached for her glass of water and sipped it with a saucy smile. I knew what she was most likely thinking, and Aspen and I had the furthest thing from that kind of relationship. Hell, I was just happy to be in the same room as the pixie.

"Whatever you're thinking, it's the opposite."

"Sure," she giggled just as Aspen walked onto the deck.

"I just wanted to pop over and say hello before I head back," she said with an infectious smile, her sparkling eyes trained on me. I wasn't sure if men got butterflies in their stomachs, but I had a ferocious nest of hornets buzzing in my abdomen when she grinned in my direction. She wore nothing fancier than a buttoned shirt tied at her waist and a pair of denim cutoffs. And with her trusty cowboy boots and signature hat, Aspen looked like the sexiest cowgirl I knew.

"Hey," I said, reaching out, grabbing her wrist, and tugging her toward me. Aspen fell onto my lap with a grunt. "Have you eaten yet?"

"I was going to eat when I got back to the ranch," she tried to explain as she wiggled on my lap. I tightened my hold around her waist and held her firmly against me.

"No, you're going to eat now."

"Owen," she argued, but I held up my sandwich a couple of inches from her mouth, refusing to move until she took a bite. Her answering moan told me how hungry she was.

With a mouthful of food, Aspen lifted a hand and covered her mouth as she spoke. "I didn't intend to spoil y'all's lunch together."

"Oh, no worry, my dear. I'm happy to have you join us. In fact, I'll go grab another plate and sandwich."

"There's more?" I asked with delight. I really did love this sandwich. Mom chuckled as she stepped back into the house, and Aspen turned her upper body to face me.

"I've missed you," I told her as I set the sandwich back on the plate, swept her hat off her head, and placed it on my own. It was way too small, but I'd do it a hundred times to make Aspen giggle the way she was.

"You know what they say about wearing a cowboy's hat," she implied, and I leaned forward, brushing my nose against hers.

"It's the number one rule, and I always follow the rules. You can expect a good ride later."

Her cheeks reddened like the leaves on the oak tree that currently offered its shade over the deck. "I'm looking forward to it."

I removed the hat and placed it in an open space on the table, then wrapped my other arm around her waist. My thumb brushed against the bare skin of her lower back.

"I told you I missed you," I reminded her, and she moved her arms around my neck.

"You saw me earlier this week."

I shrugged, because I didn't care if I saw her every day. I'd still miss her.

"I miss you too," she confessed.

"Come over tonight."

"Owen, I don't know if…." She closed her eyes, ending her sentence midway. All signs pointed to her turning me down again. Either it wasn't a good idea, or she was busy, or the farm needed her. She was stretched thin, and I was doing a poor job of trying to show her she couldn't be everything to everyone and still maintain a relationship. Something had to be cut, and I prayed Aspen knew love or a relationship shouldn't be that item.

"Owen! There's someone here for you," Andrew called out almost angrily, surprising both me and Aspen. I hadn't been expecting anyone, and my first thought was that Vanessa had shown up unannounced.

"Shit," I mumbled as I gently lifted Aspen off my lap. She weighed no more than a rag doll, but her body was stiff from the sudden news.

"You don't think it's your ex, do you?" Aspen asked, as she followed me into the house.

"I sure as fuck hope not."

Thankfully, when I turned the corner, the woman in question who was chatting with my mother happened to be a solid foot shorter than my ex.

"Hello, I'm Owen." I walked toward the newcomer, not missing Andrew's scrunched face of as he leaned against the hallway wall, hidden in the shadows.

"Hi!" she greeted me enthusiastically as she stepped around my mom. "It's so nice to meet you. Well, again, that is."

"I'm sorry. We've met before?" I asked impatiently and with a harsher tone than I meant, but I felt like I was missing a very important detail in this woman's arrival. How had we met? Was this a crazed fan?

"This is our new guest," Beverly piped in. "She's a physical therapist for the Nashville Bears."

"Oh!" I chimed in. "You're the one my coach was sending."

"Yeah. I apologize. It took a couple of days longer to get here than I planned."

"That's okay." My mom moved toward the check-in area, in full manager mode. Andrew stomped off in the other direction, and Aspen and I both flinched when the mud room door slammed. I imagined the screen door bouncing a time or two.

"I am. I just need to get my stuff, then maybe we can get together to come up with a training plan. I'm Kelsey, by the way. Kelsey Davis. I met you at spring training two years ago. Your athletic director mentioned it's your shoulder you're worried about?"

I nodded and explained I also needed a solid training regimen while I was here. Kelsey agreed, and we planned to meet once she was settled in.

Guess I was spending the day at the B&B after all.

As Mom went to help Kelsey with her bags, I looked at Aspen and shrugged.

"I feel like we're missing something," she mumbled as we made our way back to the porch. Along the way, I grabbed the sandwich Mom was making before Kelsey arrived.

"About what?" I asked her as I sat in my previously vacated seat, then tugged her back down on my lap.

"Andrew's reaction. He was so angry when he found out a woman was here and then stormed off without even meeting her."

I had my suspicions, but I planned on keeping those to myself. Andrew could think what he wanted about me. Even in a fake relationship, I would never cheat on his sister. I wasn't the scumbag he wanted me to be. Although I wished he trusted his sister more. She'd never tolerate a man who gave off the slightest inkling he was cheating. Aspen may have been a wallflower, but that made her observant.

"Yeah. Maybe he just forgot to rotate that stick in his ass or something," I said in jest, and Aspen nearly choked on her bite of food as she laughed.

"He really is so straightlaced sometimes. I bet he thought she was here for you for some... *nefarious* reason."

Leave it to Aspen to come to the same conclusion as me.

"Probably."

We finished our lunch, and eventually my mom came back to check in with us, apologizing a thousand times for Kelsey's interruption.

Aspen and I helped clean up, since my girl claimed she really needed to head back to work. But I hadn't spent nearly enough time with her.

As we finished wiping down the clean dishes, Aspen reached for my wrist and tugged me toward the opposite side of the house. There was a hidden narrow stairwell that my shoulders barely fit through as we climbed.

"This was part of the original design of the house. During the renovation, most everything was knocked down, but Autumn wanted to recreate as many original features as she could. This is my favorite one of them."

I followed along, reaching up to grip her hips a few times, which brought her ass to my chest.

The staircase twisted twice, and by the time we reached the top, I realized we were on the third floor. It was a small room, no bigger than a nursery or an office. The only light came from a dormer window overlooking the backyard. Aspen quickly informed me that when Autumn and Colton lived here full time, they used this as the office. She gestured toward the hidden door that led to the living area my mother now resided in. There were two chairs and a coffee table in the space. It looked like a nice private place to get away and relax.

Aspen stepped toward me, and my hands settled on her denim-clad hips.

"Why'd you bring me here, cricket?"

"Because I won't see you for a while, and I want to make sure you'll be thinking about me when you meet with Kelsey later."

"Jealous?" I asked, smiling as she placed her hands on my chest and slowly trailed them downward.

"A little. She's quite beautiful."

Leaving her hips, I rested my hands on both sides of her face, drawing her attention to me. I waited for her eyes to meet mine. "You're the only one I see, Aspen. I told you the other night that this thing between us didn't feel fake anymore. I meant every word. This is as real as it gets for me. Understand?"

"Yeah," she whispered. "It feels real for me too, and that... scares me."

"Why?"

"Because then it makes everything I'm feeling real. It makes the hurt real."

"I won't hurt you, cricket. Not intentionally. I can promise you that."

It was clear she didn't quite believe me, and not because she'd been hurt before, but because she didn't trust the idea of relying on someone else.

Her hands lingered around the waistband of my jeans, and when a single finger dipped just inside the elastic of my boxer briefs, my cock jumped in anticipation.

"You know what I find interesting?" she prompted, nuzzling her nose against my jaw. I'd never felt so weak in the knees as I did when she sensually ran any part of her body against mine.

"What's that?" My breath caught when her teeth nipped at my stubble-covered chin as her fingertip ran across the head of my cock.

"Even with the girls flocking around you when you're in town, and the social media posts that have shown our pictures—"

I interrupted her immediately. "Grainy pictures in which no one could tell who you and I were."

"Regardless, the articles say I'm just a fling and a way to get back at Vanessa. But you know what?"

Her sultry voice wafted over me in waves of lust, and I was drunk on her words.

"What?" I growled.

Her mouth moved over to the other side of my face, nipping the skin. "I wasn't jealous of any of that. Not a single woman or picture made me jealous… until today."

"Kelsey?"

"Yes. Kelsey. I'd never felt that before."

"Yeah? And what does that mean?" I could barely hold my eyes open as she lightly stroked the mushroom head of my cock.

"I don't know. Maybe I need to mark you somehow."

The thought of Aspen branding me as hers turned me inside out. I was itching to feel her on me and me *in* her.

"Mark me, cricket, and I'll put it on my skin permanently."

"Hmm…"

My brain had entered a lustful haze at this point, but I was doing what I could to pay attention to Aspen as she stroked my cock inside my pants.

"So, if I… let's say, left a bite mark on your cock, you'd get it tattooed on your skin?"

"Um… probably not, but if you bit anywhere else… 100 percent. I'd add it to the others that mean so much to me."

Aspen grew quiet but never stopped her explorations of my dick. After an hour—I swear that's what it felt like—Aspen unbuttoned my pants and pulled down the zipper before tugging my cock free from the confines of my boxer briefs.

"I've been thinking about having your cock in my mouth all day," she mumbled as she stroked my rock-hard dick.

My brain shouted hundreds of questions and ran multiple scenarios as she stroked me, but the moment her delectable mouth opened and slurped me like a melting popsicle on a hot day, I was a goner. All thoughts and left my mind.

"Fuck," I groaned as I watched my erection slide effortlessly into Aspen's mouth to the back of her throat, then back out. She repeated the motion until I was forced to close my eyes and roll my head back.

As one of her hands cupped my heavy, sensitive balls, I felt the tingling at the base of my spine.

Immediately, I dove my hand into her hair, tossing it to one side so I could see her face when I opened my eyes. "I'm going to come, baby."

I thought she'd retreat, but as she continued on, her hand at the root of my cock started increasing its pressure and strokes.

"Yes," I groaned as I pumped into her mouth, and within seconds, streams of my cum shot down her throat, and Aspen swallowed it up with a smile in her eyes.

When she pulled back, my cock popping free from her mouth, she wiped at her lips and a smudge of my cum from her chin with the back of her hand.

"That was...," I started, but I couldn't find the words to explain what her form of branding meant to me. I'd never be able to be with another woman without thinking of Aspen ever again. Not that I could before. I'd always had her with me in some form since I met her.

"Good?" she added as she moved up from her knees to stand in front of me.

"Amazing," I told her. There was no hesitation on my part to kiss her, and it lingered as we stood in the third-floor room. The sun was bright and shining through the window, and I felt like I was on cloud nine.

Slowly, Aspen pulled back, a blissful smile on her lips as she glanced up at me. "Now, I *really* need to head back to the farm. We're just about done, and then we start cleanup. Carrie is most excited."

Her mention of the cow got a chuckle out of me. I hadn't been back to see the heifer, but Aspen told me she'd been on her best behavior recently. The stitches on Aspen's arm dissolved, and now there was a faint line in its place that would eventually fade. I hated that the cow caused her harm, but the injury brought us closer than we would have been otherwise.

"I'm sure the therapist will want me to test my shoulder tomorrow, but can I see you Saturday?"

"I thought you have the camp. Remember, all those fans are coming to get your autograph and number?" She giggled wickedly.

My body shivered at the thought of all those girls showing up.

"Yes, I remember. Can you come in the afternoon, and we can do something after?" I pleaded with puppy-dog eyes that my mom used to say would get me anything I wanted. It may have only worked as a kid, but I was willing to try now too. I could sense Aspen was slowly coming around. I threw out a persuasive "pleeease," then smiled triumphantly when she agreed.

I followed her down the narrow steps that returned us to the main floor and then out the back of the house, where her UTV waited. With a chaste kiss, she was on her way, her hair flapping in the breeze. Her faithful hat was still on the back deck table where we left it. Now I had an excuse to drop it by her house tonight. Just thinking about the taste of her pussy had me adjusting my bulge as I made my way back inside.

Tonight could not come soon enough.

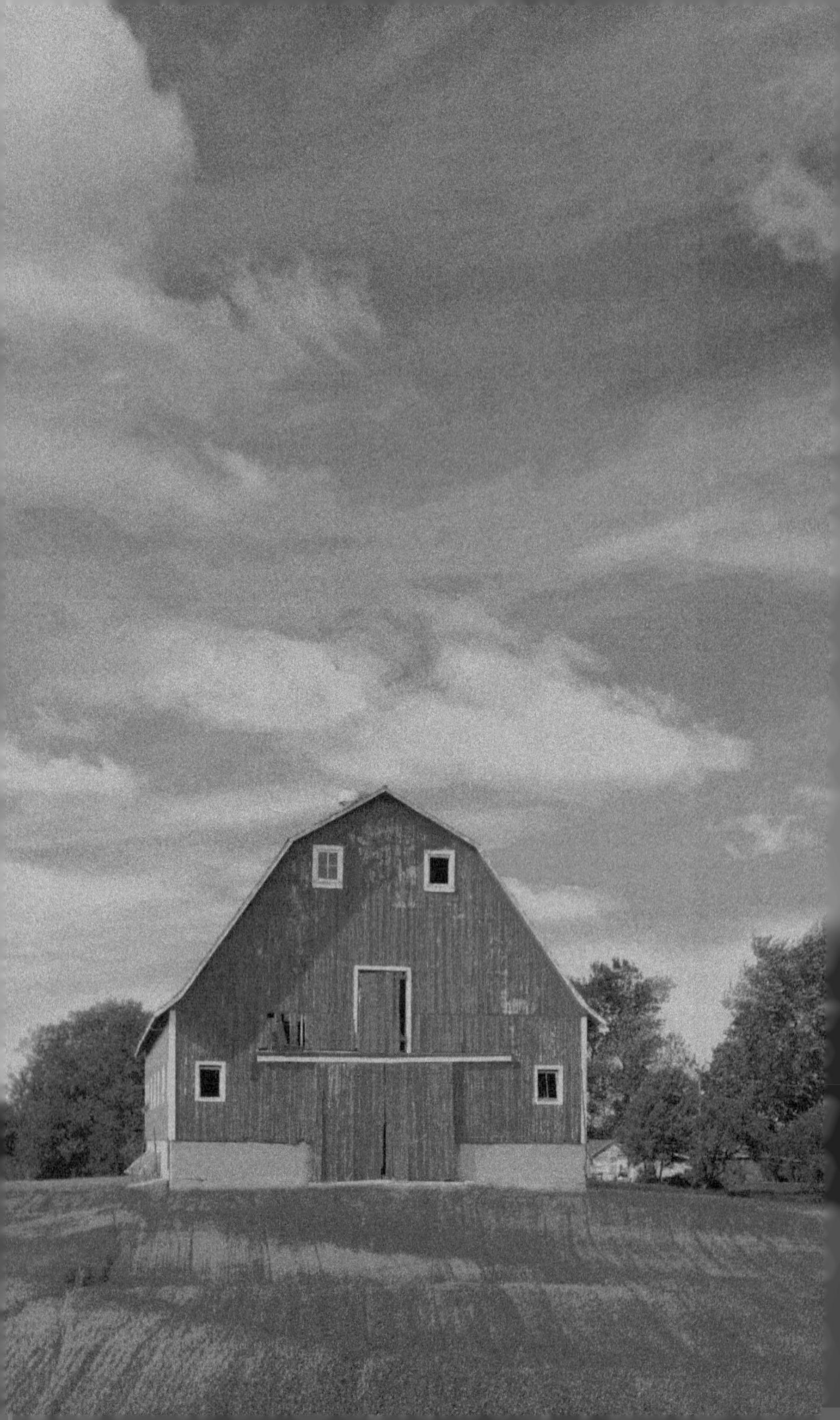

Chapter Sixteen

Aspen

For the first Friday night in years, I was going to spend the entire evening with Jenna. She demanded some girl time and wouldn't take no for an answer. I desperately needed some advice, so I wasn't overly upset to spend my free night away from my own couch.

On my way to pick up snacks for our girls' night, I ran into Tryston. He was busy comparing two different ice-cream brands and just happened to be standing right in front of the black cherry that was my favorite.

I waited patiently for a minute, but then the basket on my arm filled with cookies, candies, and wine started to grow heavy. Switching the shopping basket to my other hand, I took a step closer to Tryston.

"Excuse me," I said nervously, hoping he couldn't hear the tremor in my voice.

"Oh, sorry," he apologized and took a step back.

Quickly, I grabbed the carton of creamy goodness I needed and closed the freezer door.

"Thanks." Taking a deep breath, I thought back to the lessons I'd had with Owen and garnered a bit of the confidence he'd been trying to teach me. We might've decided what we had between us was real, but that didn't mean I couldn't use the new skills just to be friendly.

"Do you need any help?" I asked Tryston, who was still analyzing the nutritional information on the cartons.

He chuckled and admitted that he did. "I'm just trying to see if either of these contain Red Dye 40. I'm allergic." He held out both containers, and I noticed they were plain vanilla. Which was a little boring, though no less delicious.

Leaning forward, I glanced over the ingredients, not finding the offensive additive. While subtly leaning closer, I tried to hide the fact that I was sniffing him, just because I'd always wondered what he smelled like. His cologne was light, almost like the ocean. Nothing nearly as intoxicating as what Owen wore. I wanted to bathe in that scent.

"I think you're safe with either. Though, I particularly like the one made with vanilla bean."

Tryston met my smile and moved toward the freezer. It was when he turned back around that I saw he placed my recommendation back. He didn't seem to notice my disappointment.

"Alice, right?"

"Actually, it's Aspen. I get that a lot though," I lied as I continued to try to hold a conversation with someone I hadn't known my whole life. My frustration was growing by the second at Tryston's disinterest in anything I said.

This was why I kept to myself. Small talk was hard.

"Fun things planned tonight?" he asked, gesturing toward my basket.

"Yeah. Girls' night with my friend, Jenna."

"Well, have fun," he said as he smiled and strolled away toward the registers, leaving me standing in the freezer section with mixed feelings.

Back in my car, still confused over the interaction with the guy I had crushed on for a year, I tilted my head back against the headrest. I always imagined my first real interaction with Tryston would leave me breathless, flustered. I'd been building it up like a mountain of attraction that ended up being more like an ant hill. While collecting my thoughts, I received a text from Owen asking if I wanted some company that night. He'd been at the high school gym all day, working with Kelsey. I was sure he was sore and exhausted, but I found myself tempted to cancel with Jenna.

But I needed her opinion.

Declining his invitation, I thought back to Owen's arrival in Ashfield. He'd been here for almost a month now, and I felt like I'd been exposed to all new sides of him. A caring side. A dominant side. An affectionate side. He may have had them all when he grew up here, but I'd never witnessed them. I needed to talk all this through with my best friend, since he and I were truly giving this a go instead of it being all pretend.

Starting up my car, she shuddered a couple of times before the ignition caught, and I headed toward Jenna's.

My friend didn't live far from Rory's house, where Owen was staying. By the time I arrived, I had another message from him saying he was going to hang with his high-school friend, Chris.

Chris Mathewson was the only one of his friends who had always been nice to me, never once joining in on the teasing or antics that Owen's clique partook in. His wife had been the leader of our debate team, and the two of them now had the most adorable little girl. I was glad Owen was taking some time to see his friend. As far as I knew, if he wasn't with me, Owen had mostly kept to himself since being home, besides hanging with his old coach and the neighbor's kid, Roman.

I let myself into Jenna's, carrying my bags over and setting them on her kitchen counter. We were going to order pizza from Angelo's for dinner, but that didn't stop me from pulling out a large spoon from a drawer and helping myself to a dollop of ice cream before I set the carton in the freezer.

"I saw that," Jenna claimed as she stepped from the hall with a mask of pink goop covering her face.

"Just my appetizer," I explained as the doorbell rang. Jenna yipped as she darted back down the hall, leaving me to answer her door.

Thankfully, she already paid for the pizza, and I carried it into her living room, placing it on the coffee table. By the time she joined me with a freshly cleansed face, I poured us each a glass of wine and had our favorite reality show paused on the television.

I rarely had time to watch shows, but she got me hooked on the series now on its tenth season. The show *Hidden in Plain Sight* followed an A or B-List celebrity as they worked like us common people undercover. Most of the time, the normal people on the show had no idea until the end, but every once in a while, someone would catch on.

This season had been my favorite so far. The celebrity was Chase Duran, one of the most famous action stars in the world and the lead of my favorite movie franchise. He was falling hard for his younger female associate at the library where they worked. She seemed to be clueless. And I was waiting for the episode where he confessed his feelings.

"Oh good, you have the show ready. It's been killing me not to watch the last episode," Jenna told me as she settled on the couch with a slice of pizza.

"I seriously hope he confesses this week. I'm dying to know if she likes him too."

"She has to. What's not to like?"

"True, but I have a feeling Zoey isn't going to care for being lied to, or that he's a celebrity. I mean,

Chase has one of the most recognizable faces in the world."

"You're right. Speaking of dating a celebrity. How are things with you and Owen?"

"Good," I replied hesitantly. I'd been trying to come up with a way to ask Jenna for advice about Owen and my non-conversation with Tryston without giving away the fact that Owen and I weren't actually together—except *now* we were. But we still hadn't talked about what would happen when he left, so maybe we were only together for right now.

Whatever we were confused the hell out of me.

"I like you two together. And so does a lot of the U.S. population," she added as she turned toward her end table. Swiftly, she opened a drawer and pulled out a stack of magazines. As I plucked off the first one, I found my face staring back at me. Grabbing the rest from Jenna, I saw pictures of me ran across *all* the covers. All with Owen, all with me, but some with Vanessa included as well. It was… a lot.

"What's going on? I mean, I knew we'd probably be pictured in a magazine or two, but I didn't expect them to pit me against Vanessa. She's his ex. It's not like we dated him at the same time."

"Of course they did. Plus, she's pretty famous on her own. But from a poll I took on CelebrityBuzz.com, you are winning."

"Winning what?" I asked as I tried to calm my breathing. It was all too much, too overwhelming. I wasn't anyone important, just someone helping a friend keep his ex off his back, but now it seemed the entire world—not just Vanessa—knew we were together.

"The survey of who is best for Owen. Vanessa's affair has been all over the news, so I'm not surprised. Plus, the tale of you being from his childhood hometown makes your love sort of like a fairy tale."

"Love?"

"Oh yeah. You're totally in love with him. Anytime you speak about him, your eyes light up. And, honestly, this past month is the happiest I've ever seen you."

Am I in love with him?

I couldn't go a minute in my day without thinking about him. And even when I tried to ignore him because I was feeling too much, he was still on my mind. Every time he walked into the room or grazed a finger over my skin, the butterflies in my stomach fluttered like they were caught in a strong breeze.

"Shit," I mumbled as the realization washed over me. I couldn't be in love with him. What would happen when he left?

"What's the matter? I thought this was a good thing."

"He's leaving, Jenna. He has no intention of staying."

"So what? You can break up amicably or try long distance. People do it all the time."

She was right. They did, but I wasn't sure I was built that way. There was a bit of a fairy-tale-loving romantic behind the workhorse image I portrayed.

"Oh!" Jenna perked up and grabbed her glass of wine as she focused her attention back on the screen. "Look, he's in the confessional and is asking the producers to remove the disguise."

The part of the show I'd been waiting for was right in front of me, but my mind was still stuck on the fact that I was in love with Owen Ramsey. The kid who made my school years a nightmare and was determined to beat me at every contest we ever entered together. All those county and science fair ribbons that should have been mine, stolen, all because he knew how to sweet-talk the judges.

"Jenna," I mumbled as I prepared for my own confession.

"Mmhm?" she droned with her interest glued to the TV.

"You know how I thought I wanted Tryston to take my virginity, because he is sort of the perfect guy? He has the stable job, and he's attractive…"

"And you've had a crush on him since he moved to town. Well, when Owen leaves, you can shoot your shot with Tryston. He'd be a great rebound, actually." She rattled on about the perks of using Tryston to get over Owen. Jenna swore rebounds could become a long-lasting relationship.

"Jenna," I tried to interrupt her, and when she continued, I repeated myself until she looked my way.

"I think I want to have sex with Owen."

She stared at me, her eyes wide like a doe's, waiting for me to elaborate. When I remained silent, she asked, "You *think*?"

Taking a deep breath, I felt my lungs fill while my heart pumped wildly. It was like a drum being banged behind my breastbone. "I know," I decided. "I want to have sex with Owen. I want him to be my first."

With a punch-drunk smile, Jenna toppled onto me in an embrace, miraculously holding her wineglass in the air without spilling a drop as we fell back on the couch together. "Yes! I'm so happy for you!"

Trying to pry myself free from her grasp, I finally slipped out from under her body and fell onto the floor with a thud. "Jenna."

"What? Why don't you look excited? You've finally found someone to give your flower."

"Oh my gosh, could you not be so corny right now?"

She shrugged as she sat up and explained that she couldn't help it. "Anyway, why the upside-down smile?"

"What if… what if I ask him, and he turns me down?"

"Oh girl, you're crazy. Derek and I could feel the chemistry between you two when we went on that double date. He definitely wants to put his bat in your cage."

"That's a terrible image."

"It's all I could come up with."

"So, what do I do if he says no? I'll be so embarrassed, Jenna. I'd never be able to show my face around town again."

"That man is not going to turn you down. But, if you want to guarantee that he pokes you with his

Johnson, show up at his place naked. He won't be able to control himself."

I sneered at the thought. Though Owen had seen me naked before, being completely clothes-free while asking him to have sex with me was a whole other ball game. I'd feel way too vulnerable… and humiliated if he said no.

"God, I'm nuts. He's not going to want to have sex with me, Jenna. Have you seen the women he's slept with before? Even when he was just in college and not famous yet, I'm sure he snagged the most beautiful girls. I'm just a way for him to pass the time right now."

All my insecurities rose to the surface, and there was nothing I could do to tamp them back down.

"Don't you dare talk yourself out of it. I believe in you. And for someone in love, you're not speaking too highly of Owen. Do you actually think he'd care one iota about your inexperience or what your body looks like?"

She was right. Owen wouldn't care at all. I wasn't giving him the credit he deserved.

I mumbled to myself that I wished I believed in myself as I got up and refilled my wineglass. Jenna was already focused on the show when I sat back down, and we finished the episode, both of us crying when Zoey turned Chase down because she felt like she'd been set up and duped. Jenna was livid at the woman, but I felt for her. I would've felt the same way.

Luckily, there was one more episode remaining, and I had a feeling the couple would work things out.

Jenna and I got into her king-size bed as she went on about her budding relationship with Derek. She was already head-over-heels in love with him, and I was afraid she'd get hurt, because Jenna always thought she was in love within a few days of a new relationship. But in the end, we fell asleep without me raining on her parade.

The next morning, I slipped out just after 5:00 a.m., because my internal alarm clock refused to let me sleep in most days. Jenna knew I'd be gone by the time she woke up, but like the best friend I was, I made sure to set her coffee pot timer and have a cup brewing for her in a couple of hours.

After cleaning up the bit of mess we left in her living room, I made my way back to the farm. Most people might assume our small town would be dead at the early hour, but it was lively with farmers starting their day. Tractors drove down the roads to get to other sections of their land. Pick-ups carried ranch hands to the market to get supplies. I passed more people at 5:00

a.m. than I would've at 5:00 p.m. as I made my way back to Sunny Brook Farms.

When I arrived at the ranch, I quickly made my way toward my house to change and get to work. Now that the harvest was mostly complete, I was due to ride along the fences surrounding the fields where the crops had been removed. These were where we'd allow Carrie and her herd mates to roam for the next month to clean up before seeding.

Next month, I'd start testing the soil for acidity and pH levels to determine if I needed to swap in some soy to give the soil rest. The farm was in a constant state of rotations to keep the soil and land healthy.

I also needed to check the Ramsey property. The demolition crew informed us that the roof had completely caved in, so no one was allowed inside the building any longer. I'd broken the news to Beverly yesterday, and though I could tell it left her bereft, she said there was nothing on the property she needed.

I wasn't sure how I was going to broach the topic with Owen. I had a feeling he was still reeling a bit about everything he learned regarding the land and its sale. He told me he was thankful we were able to help my mother but that he wished she reached out to him instead. I understood his point. He wanted to help. Beverly had been ashamed though. All she ever wanted was for Owen to live his best life and forget how he'd grown up.

As he and I grew closer, I hoped one day he'd open up and disclose all he'd gone through as a child. I thought it might be a way for us to grow closer. But I wouldn't be hurt if he didn't share. That was a part of his life I was never privy to, and if reliving it hurt him, I wanted no part of it.

Thinking about Owen, I stripped out of my loungewear and quickly replaced it with a pair of overalls, a tank top, and a flannel shirt. With fall making her presence known, the mornings were often chillier than I liked. I was definitely not looking forward to the upcoming winter. My name did not reflect my feelings toward that particular season.

Outside, I headed toward the main barn to get a set of UTV keys. We had a few horses in the stables, but I knew the ranch hands preferred to ride, though I took the opportunity when I had the chance. As I grabbed the keys I needed from their hook, I was surprised to find Andrew working in the small office of the barn. I peeked my head inside and greeted him.

"Good morning."

"Morning," he replied, his voice heavy with sleep. Either he got here earlier than I did, or he'd been here all night.

"Surprised to see you here this early. You've been hanging around a lot more. I'm sure Mom is thrilled."

Andrew was born from my mother's first marriage. His dad died as a decorated soldier overseas, and Mom married my dad when they met by happenstance a couple of years later. My dad loved Andrew as if was his own blood, but sometimes I could see how Andrew held himself back, as if he didn't belong with the rest of us.

"It's nothing. Just getting bored in Knoxville. I've been considering moving back home."

"Oh." That was news. Andrew was known to speak about needing his space and wanting to make his own way. Small-town living wasn't for him. While he worked for the farm, sorting and finalizing contracts, he worked with other companies doing the same. I was secretly envious of his ability to have his hands in so many things and still make time to relax and date. Not that he dated anyone seriously, but he always had a date or a woman he was seeing.

"Any particular reason?" I prodded as I leaned my hip against the old, worn desk that once belonged to our grandfather.

"Well, with you taking over, I figure we need to hire a few other people to manage the books and operations. Inventory. Data. Things like that," he said as he typed away on a laptop and shuffled a few papers spread out on the desk.

"So, what would be my role then?" I asked, crossing my arms tersely against my chest. My words were biting. "Seems to me you'd hire people to do the things *Dad* does. Don't you trust me enough to do the job I've been given?"

"Aspen," Andrew said through a sigh. "That's not what I meant. The new hires would be to help you so you could focus on the overall picture. That's all."

My eyes narrowed into slits, and Andrew had the decency to look as if he'd been scolded.

"Look, it's been a record-high profit year for us, but also record-high expenses with the purchase of the Ramsey farm. You did a good job finding wiggle room in the budget and inventory to pay for the fences to mark out that property. And Dad mentioned your idea to lease the land to the local cattle farmers. It's a great plan. I just want this job to be as stress-free for you as possible."

There was something he wasn't telling me, but my anger from feeling like no one thought I could do the job made me fist the keys in my hands. The metal would leave indentations in the callused skin once I unclenched.

But he was right that I didn't want all the stresses my dad handled. Now that I had a taste of freedom, I wanted it in spades, but this job just didn't allow for that.

"I wish you talked with me about it, Andrew. I feel you're going behind my back."

My brother didn't apologize. Instead, he went back to work, ignoring me.

"For what it's worth, which isn't much, *I* think you *should* move back here," I said as I moved toward the exit. "We all miss you." The door hinges squeaked as I shut the door.

With Andrew's news heavy on my mind, I made my way around the property. Thankfully, Carrie hadn't destroyed any more fence lines. She and Owen must have formed some silent truce during their moment together.

The morning sky quickly turned to afternoon, and the sun warmed up the brisk day. I returned the UTV to the barn and followed the pebbled path back to my house. I took a quick shower and changed into a pair of maroon athletic pants and a matching sports bra and crop top. I knew Owen had a thing for my boots, but I laced up a pair of sneakers. If I was going to visit him during the pop-up camp he put together with his old coach, then I wanted to at least look the part.

After I pulled my hair up into a ponytail at the top of my head, I unlocked my phone and was surprised to find a few messages from Jenna and two from numbers I didn't have saved.

Jenna
> Hey, thanks for the coffee.

> What time did you leave?

> Don't go on the internet.

> Aspen, are you okay?

> Answer me.

> OMG you're freaking out, aren't you? It's not true. You know it isn't.

> **I just realized you're probably working. Call me!!!!**

I was concerned after the multiple exclamation points. Jenna was a little over the top when she messaged but was usually reserved with her punctuations.

Skimming through her messages again, I immediately assumed there was something on the internet pinning me against Vanessa. I remembered the gossip sites doing the same to Colton and Autumn, with whatever women he'd been seen with in the past. The longer I thought about it, the more I realized all my sisters had gone through the same situation. All three married high-profile men with exes they left scorned. It was easy news to pin the new flame against the old one.

I texted Jenna back.

> **No worries. I'll check it out, but I remember the game these people play. And you're welcome for the coffee.**

I hesitated before reading the messages I received from numbers I didn't recognize. Like a kid on the first day at a new school, my nerves were getting the best of me. With shaking hands, I pulled up the first message.

> **826-555-4324**
>
> **Hey, it's Tryston. I got your number from the neighborhood chat. Anyway, I was wondering if you'd want to go out sometime.**

The old me would have squealed like a schoolgirl if he sent that message a month or two ago. But now? Now, I was… disappointed? He asked for a date in a text. Why couldn't he call me? And to make matters worse, I didn't think I even wanted a date. Not yet, at least. And for sure not until Owen went back to California.

Plus, I had just come to terms with the fact that I was in love with him, even knowing he was leaving soon. I set myself up for heartbreak.

I left the message as Read but unanswered as I moved to the other unknown number's text.

761-555-8963

<image>

There were no words but a picture of a magazine cover. In big, bold letters read the words **It's back on!** with a formal picture of Owen and Vanessa dressed to the nines. From the background, it looked like they were attending a sports award ceremony.

Wondering if Owen had seen the magazine, I saved it, then forwarded it to his number. I didn't expect him to reply, since he was at the camp, but not a moment later, he replied with a short video of a man rolling on the floor laughing.

Owen

<GIF>

Funniest thing I've seen all week.

You know not to believe that stuff, right?

ALL FOR YOU 309

> Yep. Who did the message come from? 761-555-8963

That's my best friend Marc. I'm pissed someone published this.

> Did you give him my number?

No, but it's not hard to find on the internet, cricket.

> Are you ever going to tell me why you call me that?

Maybe one day. Will I see you soon?

> On my way.

My thumbs hesitated over the letters on my phone. I almost typed out the words "love you" but held back. What would he do if I did? Would he freak out?

Return the sentiment? Run for the hills? The fear of rejection had me sliding my phone into the pocket on the side of my pantleg and grabbing my car keys. Plus, that wasn't really something I should say for the first time over a text. Like Tryston's date proposal, the thought gave me the ick.

The entire time I drove to the baseball fields, I wondered if it was better in the long run to keep my feelings for Owen to myself. Nothing good would come of it. But then I thought about how I'd feel if I were him. He'd been tricked and lied to most of his life. Other than Beverly, he had probably never experienced a real, unconditional love.

With stunned recognition, I realized I wanted to be that for him.

But I wasn't sure it was in the cards.

Chapter Seventeen

Aspen

My car sputtered as I pulled in next to Owen's fancy sports car. He tried to explain the vehicle to me a dozen times, but it went in one ear and out the other. I left the keys in the cup holder, because I knew not a single soul was going to try to take the rust bucket, and exited the car.

Off in the distance, past the banner proclaiming the area **Owen Ramsey Field**, the man of the hour stood proudly surrounded by a group of boys, all of various heights and ages. I picked out little Roman immediately.

He anxiously swayed back and forth with his bat in one hand as he looked up at his idol. It was the cutest thing I'd ever seen. All the kids and teens hung onto Owen's every word. Reaching into my pocket, I grabbed my phone and snapped a few pictures.

As I slipped my cell back into my pocket, Owen's eyes caught mine, and his grin doubled in size. He mentioned something to the kids, and they scurried off in pairs as he jogged over toward me. Before I could even get a word in, he cupped both of my cheeks while pressing his lips against mine.

"You made it," he said in awe.

Laughing, I replied, "I literally told you thirty minutes ago I was on my way."

He shrugged, but his enthusiasm didn't diminish in the slightest. I wondered how many times growing up he'd been promised something and then it didn't happen.

"How is the camp going?" I asked as he grasped my hand and tugged me into step with him.

"Good. The kids are really eager to learn."

"Have your fans shown up yet?"

Owen chuckled and explained that Coach Rudicell rushed them out of the park, claiming he was going to call the cops since it was a private event.

"I don't have anyone to pair you with, so you're playing with me," he informed me, and he winked as we reached a bag with about ten bats inside.

"Owen. No. I didn't sign up for this. I'm just here to watch."

"Ah, come on," he said with a boyish grin I couldn't say no to. "It'll be fun."

His blue-gray eyes twinkled, and I found myself agreeing but reminded him about my lack of hand-eye coordination.

"This isn't some new competition for you to prove you're better at something else, is it? I am well aware you're better at baseball."

Leaning down, hovering his lips over my ear as he gently slipped a bat into my grasp, he teased, "Maybe I just want to see you handling my big, long stick."

"I have a big stick too!" an innocent voice called out, and Owen and I jumped apart to find Roman standing close by. Thankfully, it was clear the young boy was referring to his actual baseball bat.

"Hey, kiddo. What's up? Shouldn't you be over there with Johnny, practicing your hits?"

"Yeah, but I wanted to come say hi to Miss Aspen." He turned to face me. "Hi!"

"Hi, Roman. When your mom picks you up, please tell her I said hi to her too."

"Okay." He looked back and forth between me and Owen before he scurried off to his partner.

"All right, we probably only have a few minutes before we're interrupted again."

I tried to assure Owen that I was more than content watching him coach for the afternoon, but he wasn't hearing any of it. He set up an area away from the kids for their own safety. Stepping behind me, he pressed his hips against my backside as he adjusted my grip around the bat and then directed me on my stance. I felt ridiculous as I stood there in the grass, watching Owen walk away while he grabbed a ball from his cargo shorts.

"Just try to hit it, okay?" he called out as he positioned himself across from me.

Nodding, I narrowed my stare, hoping it would help me focus. Owen threw the ball much slower than I'd seen in person or on TV. I forced my eyes to stay open, fighting every intuition to close them. Even though I had no idea what I was doing, the ball made contact with my bat with just enough force to bounce it back toward Owen.

"I did it!"

"Great job, baby!" he exclaimed as he collected the ball. "Let's see if we can get one more." He called over one of the older kids to pitch, while Owen came and stood behind me again. The ridge of his cock was pressed against my ass again, and I could barely concentrate.

"You're going to make me miss it with you standing behind me like this," I told him.

"Naw. We got it."

Owen adjusted his grip on the bat around my hands. The moment our hands touched, I felt… powerful. Like I could actually get a grand slam.

"You're controlling it. I'm just the added muscle."

The pitcher wound up and then released the ball. Taking a deep breath, I swung the bat with every ounce of strength I had. Not expecting to hit anything, the *thunk* of the bat hitting the ball startled me. A flash of white soared through the sky, landing on the other side of the park.

"Oh my gosh! We did it!" I dropped the bat as I twisted around and jumped into Owen's arms.

"*You* did it. I just gave you a little extra strength."

"Wow. That was… so cool."

"It is pretty cool."

I peered over Owen's shoulder and saw his camp had formed a little crowd, watching us. "I think you're wanted over there. I'm going to go sit by the lake and watch. Okay?"

"All right," he said, then pressed a chaste kiss to my lips.

The remainder of the camp lasted another two hours. I spent my time listening to music on my phone and watching the kids play. A couple of young families came and went on the playground while the town's walking group made a few laps around the lake.

It was the most relaxing day I'd ever had.

When camp was over, Owen and I agreed to meet back up at his house. He needed to run back by the school to drop off the equipment, and I was tasked with grabbing dinner from the local Chinese restaurant.

We arrived at the rental around the same time, and he helped me carry in the bags of food.

"What all did you get?" he joked as I sorted through the five bags on the kitchen counter.

"I wasn't sure what you wanted. I got beef and vegetables, pork fried rice, General Tso's chicken, shrimp lo mein, egg rolls, and crab ragoon."

"We will never eat all of this."

He underestimated my love of Chinese food.

We sat on the couch, watching a movie that was already playing. It was an action flick I wasn't overly interested in, but with Owen's thigh pressed against mine, I don't think even *Hidden in Plain Sight* could have kept my attention.

"Everything okay? You seem a bit quiet."

"Yeah. Just thinking about something Andrew said this morning." The lie slipped out of my mouth with ease. I'd been thinking about Owen and my pesky virginity.

"Oh. Anything important?"

"No. Just work stuff. Speaking of, how is the therapist?"

"Good. She thinks my shoulder will be good as new before the season. Coach says he'll need me back before long, so she's going to transfer all the documentation to the team's official therapist."

"Are you…? I mean…," I stuttered, unsure how to voice what I was feeling. Owen reached over, took my plate from my hands, and set it on the table.

"Hey, I wish I could stay longer. At first, when I came back, I was dreading having to be here for five or six months. Now, the thought of going back after just two kills me. If it wasn't my job, I'd tell him where he could shove his sponsorships."

"It's okay. I understand."

Owen leaned forward, capturing my lips with his. These were not the soft kisses from earlier in the day. These were demanding, punishing, addictive. Our tongues dueled and danced while our hands explored. Gently, Owen guided me down onto the couch. The soft material felt like heaven against my heated skin.

Within his large hand, Owen gathered my wrists and pinned them above my head and against the arm of the sofa while his mouth assaulted my neck.

"I love your skin, cricket. It's so soft."

"Owen," I whimpered, squirming underneath him. His strong hips nestled between my legs, pinning my hips in place.

"What do you need, sweet girl?"

"I… I need your mouth on my breasts… and your hand between my legs."

Before I could blink, Owen had ripped down the skin-tight athletic pants, leaving me bare before him and the material ruined.

"Take off the top," he commanded, while his feral gaze stayed glued to my aching center. He placed his hands on my thighs, holding my legs apart as I sat up to remove my top.

My breasts bounced as they popped free of the sports bra and crop top. I tossed the material carelessly onto the floor.

Owen's eyes darted up from my pussy to my breasts, triggering a growl from deep in his chest.

"Fuck. Baby, I'm so hungry for you. I… I can't promise I'll be gentle with you."

Lifting my hand, I softly ran my fingers through his brown hair. Like a kingly feline, he purred at the contact.

"I don't want gentle, Owen."

With his eyes closed, he mumbled, "Yeah, but you deserve it. Lay back, baby."

Swiftly, I followed his command and watched as he opened his eyes and ran a steady gaze over my body.

"Shit, I don't deserve you," he confessed as he bent forward and latched onto a nipple while one of his hands slipped between my legs.

Quickly, my body went up in flames as he paid special attention to my most sensitive areas. I'd never given much thought to the skin behind my knees, but as he nipped and sucked, the sensation sent a spark right between my legs. I was growing needier with each passing second. His name was an unrecognizable groan from my lips.

His mouth climbed up my thigh toward my sex as I quivered against his lips.

"I'm aching, Owen."

"What do you need?"

"I… I…." It was a struggle to get the words out.

Owen sat up and rested back on his heels. Those strong hands that wrapped around my legs now held my ankles, and his thumbs brushed small circles along my ankles. The motion was soothing. Immediately, my thumping heart slowed to a steady beat.

"Tell me what you're thinking."

"I've been thinking… I mean, I know what I want. I just…."

"Come on, cricket. You can tell me."

"I want to have sex."

Owen's eyes darkened as his hands tightened around my feet.

"I know you probably have more experience and know what you're doing, but I—"

"It's okay, baby," he inserted softly, and I had to remind myself this couldn't be anything more than it was. Owen wasn't ever going to stay here, and I was going to have to move on eventually.

"This is just sex, Owen. No feelings."

The corners of his eyes creased, and his lips pursed.

"No promises, cricket. You've already branded me."

"What does that even mean?"

"I'll tell you later. Now, be a good girl and let me make you come."

Worried he took my claims of inexperience as nothing more than having one or two partners, I reached for his wrist.

"I'm a virgin, Owen. I don't know how to do any of th—"

Before I could finish speaking, Owen crawled over my body, reached a hand under my neck, and sealed my mouth with a kiss. My body craved more when he pulled back.

"You're perfect, Aspen. You'll be perfect." He lingered over me, and we locked eyes. A softness replaced the lustful gaze from earlier, one a man would have toward someone he loved.

My stomach clenched at the thought.

"Are you sure you want to do this?"

Without hesitation, I nodded, because I knew without a doubt that I wanted Owen to be my first. I wondered what sixteen-year-old me would think of this revelation.

Owen slipped off the couch and hoisted me into his arms, carrying me to the bedroom. With an unfamiliar gentleness, he laid me on the bed. His clothes fell in a heap on the floor while I laid in my birthday suit, watching in awe. I didn't think I'd ever grow tired of looking at his body. It was a work of art.

"You keep looking at me like that and this will be over too fast."

I chuckled as I leaned up on my elbows while he moved around the bed. The frame creaked as he climbed in beside me. Reaching over, Owen slid his hand through my long hair, resting his palm on the back of my head and lightly pulling my face toward his.

Our kisses grew frenzied and hands wildly stroked bare skin. It was both too much and not enough at the same time.

Owen rested on his back, tugging me on top of him. Something about the position made what I was about to do all too real, and my body began to shake.

Immediately, he sensed that something shifted. "Nervous?"

"A little."

"You'll be okay, cricket. I'll take care of you. But you know we don't have to do anything, right? I'm happy just being here with you."

"But what if I do it wrong?"

"I can tell you with 100-percent certainty that there is nothing you could do wrong. Plus, right now, I just want you to focus on you. Let me *finally* make you come."

Owen slipped his hand between my legs, running his finger back and forth along my wet slit. It was already coated in my arousal but grew wetter with each pass.

My breaths became pants as he continued on, swirling around my clit until I was a quivering mess. Against his lips, I cried out as I jerked, my orgasm crashing over me like a tidal wave.

"God, you're gorgeous when you come," he said as I bit my bottom lip to hold back my whimper when he pulled his hand free.

I may have been sensitive, but I wanted more. Yearned for it.

Softly, Owen rolled us on the mattress until I was on my back and his face was between my legs. He lapped at the wetness, murmuring to himself how much he enjoyed feasting on me. I could just be listening to his deep voice as he read a restaurant menu, and I'd still probably soak my panties.

Lost in my own thoughts, I hadn't noticed Owen pull back and slip a condom onto his cock. The large erection pointed toward me like a locked-in missile as he leaned over me.

My body tensed, feeling the tip of his dick poised at my entrance, but instead of pressing inside, he rocked against my pussy, spreading my wetness over his shaft.

"You're beautiful, Aspen," Owen whispered in my ear as he reached down and adjusted his rod. "It'll hurt at first, but I promise to make it go away."

Instinctively, I reached my hands around his back, holding him close. The mushroom head pushed inside my channel, and Owen came to a stop.

"You're so fucking tight, cricket." His words were clipped, as if he was hanging on by the thinnest of threads. The fullness I felt escaped as Owen rocked back. "I'm so fucking sorry."

I wondered what he meant, but then as he thrust inside, all my thoughts evaporated as I felt the first stinging pinch of pain.

Tears pooled along my lids, with a few escaping the corners of my eyes. I'm not sure what I'd been expecting, but the overwhelming bite nearing agony wasn't it.

Why did people do this to themselves?

Without moving an inch, Owen rested on his elbows by my head and swiped at my fallen tears.

"Are you okay? Do you want me to stop?" he asked so tenderly I almost started crying again.

I shook my head and told him I was fine. The agony had already subsided and was now just bordering on uncomfortable, especially as he kissed and nuzzled every inch of my skin his lips could reach without moving a single bustle below our waists. Within a couple of minutes, it was me who started wiggling beneath him, craving something I couldn't name where we were connected.

Feeling my movements, Owen pressed his lips against mine, rocked his hips back, and then surged into me. I expected the pain again, but with each thrust, I was met with more and more pleasure than the one before it.

"Oh!" I cried out in surprise as his cockhead ran across a spot I didn't know actually existed. The overfullness I felt was nothing compared to the dash of pleasure.

Raising one of my bent legs, he glided his cock over the sensitive spot again.

"Owen," I whispered, clawing at his back.

"Fuck, baby, I can feel you clenching around me. You're so fucking tight. I'm not going to last much longer." He nearly growled as I shifted a hand between my legs. Now that the bite of pain was gone, all I craved was the hit of a release. "That's it. Touch yourself. Make yourself come."

As he sat up on his knees to give me more room to work my fingers, he plunged in and out of my tight sheath, beads of sweat running down the sides of his face and his chiseled chest.

"Shit, sweet girl. I can feel you," he panted as I rocked my hips against him. "Take what you need."

Suddenly, flashes of pleasure rocked through my core, and my back arched from such a powerful release. I'd never experienced one that ricocheted from the tips of my toes to the top of my head.

"Yes." Owen's moan only dragged out my orgasm further. Something about his naturally deep voice had its own way of sending me over the edge as my pleasure continued.

After a few more pumps, he grunted with his own orgasm, joining me in a well-sated heap on the bed.

I knew I was going to owe my sister a new set of sheets, as the evidence of my lost virginity was now staining these, but I didn't care in that moment, as Owen rolled my body alongside his, tucking my head against his chest.

"I'm going to draw you a bath, but I need a minute."

"You don't need to do that, Owen."

"Shh," he said as he kissed me sweetly. "I want to. Let me take care of you."

From years of school with Owen, I knew there was no point in arguing with him. Instead, I cuddled closer, listening to his heartbeat slow down. If he hadn't been running his callused fingers back and forth across my arm, I'd have thought he'd fallen asleep.

"I'll be back."

Lying in bed contemplating everything I just did and what it meant for me in the future, I watched Owen stroll in and out of the bathroom multiple times.

"Okay. It's ready," he announced with his hands on his hips in a superhero stance and a wide grin.

My first attempt at rolling off the bed left me wincing as the soreness between my legs traveled throughout my body. Owen rushed over and lifted me in his arms again, carrying me to the bathroom. I glanced up at him as I gasped.

The tub was filled, and a bowl of ice cream waited on the wooden tray set across the edges of the bathtub. When he flipped off the overhead light, that's when I saw he'd lit several candles he placed around the room.

"You did all this?"

Setting me down on my feet, he nodded.

"Thank you, Owen."

"You're welcome. I found some Epsom salts. Those will help with any pain. I use it in my therapy soaks."

Unable to help myself, I wrapped my arms around Owen's trim waist. "Aw… does superstar Owen Ramsey like wittle bitty baby baths?" I cooed at him.

"Shut up and get in the tub, cricket."

I giggled as he playfully swatted my naked butt. Taking my hand, he helped me step inside the large standalone tub, then surprised me as he slipped in behind me.

"From here on out, I'm sure I'll only truly enjoy baths that include you," he murmured as he adjusted his legs on either side of mine, making my heart flutter. "Now, hand me that ice cream."

"Maybe I don't want to share," I said sternly as I noticed Owen stocked the same black-cherry ice cream I liked so much. "This is my favorite."

"I know," he replied, reaching around me for the bowl and successfully pulling it out of my hands. "That's why I'm feeding it to you."

"Oh."

"Yeah. Oh. Now, open up," he commanded, and I dutifully followed.

"You're being awfully sweet," I mentioned around the second bite of the creamy goodness. My muscles were already loosening from the salts and hot water.

"I've always been sweet. You just preferred to argue with me and I love that about you."

"I did not," I claimed, earning a chuckle from the man leaning over my back. "Fine. Maybe I did. I liked that you challenged me. Where everyone else seemed to ignore me unless we were causing trouble, I liked that I had your attention. Even though you annoyed and beat me at everything. Everyone else just catered to me all the time, because I was an Easterly. You never seemed to care about that."

"Your attention was all I wanted."

The word "love" lingered in the air, but I wasn't sure Owen even knew that he used it.

Slip of the tongue, I told myself as I finished off the ice cream. We lingered in the cooling water for only a short time longer before we got out.

Owen dried every inch of my body with a towel, which only left me panting.

"I want you again, Owen."

"You're sore, cricket," he replied, tucking a damp strand of my hair behind my ear.

Slipping my arms around his neck, I silenced him with a heated kiss that quickly turned us into a tangled mess of limbs on the bed.

Owen and I only caught spurts of sleep between my greediness to feel the pleasure only he could provide and his unquenchable desire to feast on every part of my body.

By the time the sun began to rise, I'd had the best night of my life. Not a single spec of my mind went to the farm or to the fact that I should have been there hours ago. My sole thought was of Owen and how we seemed to fit perfectly together.

How quickly things change.

Chapter Eighteen

Owen

Waking up with Aspen in my arms wasn't something I'd ever get tired of. Something about holding her tiny body against mine was a soothing talisman keeping the nightmares of my past at bay.

Aspen wasn't a quiet sleeper, constantly moaning, groaning, whispering, but not in a way I found annoying. If anything, the sounds made her even more adorable.

The moonlight shimmered on her skin, the reflection in the mirror casting a blue hue across the room. My fingers ran back and forth along her bare back, drawing different shapes on her skin.

I was going to miss this when I left. A call from my coach yesterday changed how long I was able to stay. The advertising company for the sports drink I contracted with wanted to begin shooting photos and a commercial in two weeks.

And worse, I knew it was going to break my mom's heart. We'd been working on our strained relationship, and it seemed things were getting better.

"Mmm. What are you doing awake?" a sleep-filled voice asked from beside me.

"Nothing, cricket. I just got a lot on my mind."

"Anything I can help with?" Her finger swirled over my chest, and it left a trail of fire in its wake.

"Well, there is one thing," I said in jest, surprised when Aspen crawled under the sheets and placed my cock in her warm, eager mouth.

We woke later when the sun was high in the sky. A quick glance at my phone and I realized it was approaching noon. In all the days I'd been back in Ashfield, I hadn't slept in, and I was sure Aspen hadn't either. Beside me, she stretched out her body. The sheet slipped off her chest, showcasing some love marks I'd left on her breasts.

"Morning," she said with a smile.

Chuckling, I replied, "Afternoon."

"Really?" She grinned as she sat up and gathered the sheets around her chest.

"Yeah. It's lunchtime. You feel rested?"

"Surprisingly."

My phone pinged with a message from a number I didn't recognize asking if I'd seen Aspen.

"Hey, I think someone is looking for you," I told her as I showed her the screen.

"That's Andrew. Um… where's my phone?" She looked around, finding it nowhere. "Oh, it's probably still in my pants pocket."

Offering to grab the device, I rolled off the bed and headed toward the living room.

With a quick glance, I noticed she had eighteen missed messages and six calls. All within the last three hours. Her sated smile slid off her face as she inspected the notifications.

"Oh no. Oh no. Oh no. Oh no," she mumbled repeatedly, tears welling up in her eyes. Aspen's face had taken on a pasty hue as she moved off the bed, spinning around in circles as she searched for her clothes.

"Aspen," I called out, but she ignored me as she frantically tugged on her pants.

Reaching out, I gripped her arm and garnered her attention. "Aspen, tell me what's going on."

Sniffling, she shook her head.

"Please. Let me help."

"There's nothing you can do. I... I should have been home. This is all my fault."

Her top got caught on her arm while attempting to put it on, and I reached out to right the material. Swatting at me, she connected with my chin in a weak effort to push me away.

"Cricket, stop. Let me help you."

Thankfully, she let me adjust her shirt, and when I pulled it into place, she collapsed into a heap against my body. Waves of tears spilled onto my chest, and all I could do was hold her close.

I felt helpless, and it was the absolute worst feeling.

After five full minutes, the blonde beauty lifted her tear-soaked face toward mine. "I... I should have been home."

"What happened, baby?"

"My dad. He had a heart attack surveying the fields this morning. That's normally my job. I should have been there."

Placing both hands on her cheeks, I ran my thumbs back and forth under her eyes.

"None of this is your fault. These things happen, and it could have happened anywhere."

She nodded, but I knew she didn't believe me. Her eyes held that hint of skepticism.

"I need to go to him. They flew him to Knoxville."

"We'll take my car. It will get us there faster."

She tried to argue, but there was absolutely no way in hell I was allowing her to drive. Not when she couldn't stop breaking down into tears.

Thankfully, she had spare clothes in her car, and I convinced her to change before we left. She called her mom, and they spoke about the incident. Apparently, Nash Easterly had been suffering from a clogged artery that hadn't been treated yet. He'd hoped a diet change would help, but clearly, it hadn't been enough.

Thankfully, Marisol assured Aspen that her father was all right and would make a full recovery.

Aspen wouldn't believe any of it until she saw her dad herself. She nearly tucked and rolled out of the car in her attempt to get inside the hospital faster. I dropped her off at the front of the hospital and went to park.

Since I was alone and not a family member, it took some finagling with the receptionist at the front desk to get the info for Nash's room. I promised to sign a bunch of Coyotes swag to send to her grandson.

As the elevator ascended toward the ICU, my heart sped up. What mood was I going to find Aspen in? In the car, she'd been pulling away. One-word answers to my questions. Shrugs whenever I tried to make conversation.

I sensed she blamed me for her absence. And that killed me.

It took a couple of tries down different halls, but I finally found the room with the crowd of people standing outside. I recognized a few of the farmhands but kept my distance until Colton spotted me. A security guard asked to see my ID, surprise blossoming on his face when he realized who I was.

"The whole family is inside," Colton explained, while I leaned against the wall next to him. I had a feeling we were too big of a group to be in the room and hall, but no one was going to tell us to leave. We wouldn't have listened anyway.

I was here for Aspen, but I was also here for myself. Nash had been both a neighbor and a friend, and I was worried. The man seemed invincible.

Suddenly, a blonde head popped out the door and looked around until her eyes landed on Nate. His twin girls weren't around, so I hoped they were staying with someone. Being in a hospital traumatized me as a kid, with all the times my mom and I made visits to the ER. I didn't want that for them.

As she waved Nate and Colton inside, Alex sighed and waved me in behind them. Instead of searching out my girl, I pulled Alex aside.

"How is he?"

"He's… stable. It scared us all, but he'll be okay." I was surprised at her honesty. It didn't seem she liked me very much, but I appreciated her willingness to try.

"And Aspen? How is she?"

Alex exhaled a deep breath like she'd been carrying the weight of the world. "She's a mess. I've never seen her like this."

"She blames herself," I whispered. "For not being there."

"It's not anyone's fault."

"Yeah, I tried telling her that. She's stubborn. Just… keep an eye on her, please?"

"Owen, I know Aspen and I haven't always gotten along. I don't even remember why. We're just like oil and water, I guess, but I love her."

"That's good," I said with a sigh of relief, unable to turn around and look deeper into the room with the gathered family.

"Why does it sound like you're leaving?"

"Because I am, eventually."

"Hm. She know that?"

"She does," I replied as her husband came over and asked if everything was okay. She smiled up at him like he hung the moon, and his expression mimicked hers.

Slowly, I approached the bed where Aspen held onto her father's hand like if she let go, he'd slip away into oblivion.

"Hi, Nash." My voice cracked with emotion as my eyes connected with the older man's. He wore a bandage around his head. Someone mentioned he'd hit his head on the side of the UTV when he fell from the seat.

"Owen, my boy!" the man greeted with an enthusiasm no one else in the room felt. "How are you, kid?"

The way he spoke, as if nothing happened, broke something inside me. Like a piece of splintered wood leaving bits and pieces deeply imbedded in my skin. That's what my heart felt like at that moment.

"I've been better, sir. What are you doing in here? Was this your way of getting us all together for your birthday?" I asked with a cheerfulness I didn't feel in the slightest, knowing the Easterly patriarch almost didn't live to see his sixty-third birthday next week.

"Ah, you caught me red-handed. I took this prank too far, huh?"

"Probably not the best idea," I replied as silence fell across the room.

Marisol chose that moment to step inside the room, carrying a cup of coffee. Her face was makeup-free, but she was still a beautiful woman. I could see bits of her in each of her daughters.

"Ah, there's the love of my life," Nash said with a certainty I hoped to feel about someone someday. I was fooled into thinking I felt something similar for Vanessa.

The longer we'd been apart, the more I realized I didn't know her at all. She even tried breaking into my house while I'd been gone. Thank goodness for top-notch security. I'd have to deal with her when I got back to LA, and I wasn't looking forward to it, but it was a necessary evil.

Marisol took a spot next to me, closest to her husband, and gripped his other hand, being mindful of the wires and cords poking out of her husband's arm. It was a side of Aspen's mom I hadn't seen before. She looked as if she weathered a storm and barely made it out alive.

Slowly, I stepped back, wanting to give the two some privacy as they exchanged soft-spoken words. Colton, Nate, and Talon did the same, and we huddled near the windows for the family to have a moment. They were only interrupted when the doctor walked in and explained they were going to keep Nash overnight and that he was scheduled for surgery in the morning to remove the blockage. He was going to be out of commission for a few weeks.

I wasn't sure what that meant for the farm, but I knew exactly what it meant for Aspen. She was going to run herself into the ground, trying to fill her dad's large shoes.

Within my pocket, I felt my phone buzz with a message from Kelsey. She heard through the very thorough Ashfield grapevine what happened with Nash and was canceling our session for the day. She'd been working hard on strengthening my throwing arm and shoulder. Her techniques differed from our team therapist's, some new-age methods she learned in school.

Just as I was closing out the messaging app, I noticed an email from the team's marketing assistant with the schedule for the upcoming promotional contracts. The off-season was when most players worked with the team sponsors, and this year, apparently, they all wanted me. I had a record season, and I was the team's top scorer.

Glancing over the list, I even had a meet-and-greet scheduled at a local brewery.

That one could be fun, I thought to myself and wished I'd have the opportunity to take Aspen with me.

Syncing the list with my calendar, I noticed the few blank spaces around holidays and a few random weekends. If I could convince Aspen to keep things going between us, then I'd be able to fly home during those times for a day or two.

"Hey," a shaky voice said beside me. Aspen's eyelids drooped, and the corners of her mouth tipped toward the floor. She reminded me of the guys when we lost the world championships. Except this wasn't a silly game. This was her father lying in a hospital bed, looking so much smaller than I remembered.

"Hey, cricket. You doing okay?" I asked, wrapping my arm around her shoulders. When she returned the embrace, I felt the sigh of relief leave my lungs. At least she wasn't pushing me away, which was my fear the entire drive to the hospital.

"Yeah, I guess. I... um... need to get back to the farm. Do you think you could take me?"

Despite the circumstances, I was itching to leave the building. Everything—the scent, the colors, the layout—was causing my skin to feel as if it was burning from the inside out.

"Of course," I readily agreed and reached down for her hand that felt tiny in mine.

We said goodbye to her family, her father arguing with her the entire time. He knew, just as I did, that Aspen was going to take too much on. Whatever progress she and I had made in giving her any sort of social life was about to wither away to nothing.

I could even sense the apprehension in Andrew as he hugged his sister goodbye. He knew now that this wasn't the life Aspen wanted for herself, but she was going to run herself ragged trying to prove to everyone she could handle it.

I was afraid it was going to cost her more than just her free time. There was always the chance she could be the one lying in that bed.

Our drive back to the ranch was quiet. Only the sound of the radio and the purr of the car engine could be heard. When we arrived at the farm, Aspen nearly jumped out of my car in an attempt to get away from me. Something had changed during the long drive.

She was pushing me away, and I refused to allow our last bit of time together to end like this.

"Aspen!" I shouted as I flew from my car, running to catch up with her. For someone so short, she was incredibly fast. I repeated her name again, but from a quick glance over her shoulder, I noticed the tears on her cheeks, shimmering in the sunshine.

"Baby, wait."

Her steps didn't falter as she made her way toward the barn, where the Easterlys stored their equipment.

"Come on, cricket. Don't do this."

Finally, she turned around. Her cheeks were ruddy and wet, but she was still one of the most beautiful women I'd ever seen.

"Owen, I can't."

"Can't what?" I asked as I stepped closer.

"I... I don't know. I just can't be anything but what my family needs right now. I'm it. I need to run the farm while my dad heals." Her breath hitched as she spoke of her father.

"They don't expect you to do everything all at once, Aspen."

"But they do. They're all relying on me. Not just my family, but the workers, the town, all the contracted companies. They all need me. I'm… I'm sorry. I need to see what needs to be done today."

"Can I see you tonight?"

"I don't think that's—"

"Please. I need to talk to you about something."

Aspen's eyes grew heavy with the weight of my words. We both knew the time was coming, but now that I had an actual date, it made it all the more real.

"Okay. I… um… need to grab my car anyway."

She turned on her heel, and I reached out for her wrist in an attempt to stop her.

"I'll be waiting for you, Aspen. Please try not to overdo it."

The moment I released her arm, she walked away, and my heart thundered in my chest. I wondered what she'd do if I told her I loved her.

It didn't take a rocket scientist to figure out I'd probably been in love with Aspen Easterly since the day I met her when we were kids. But it wasn't until I saw her dad lying in that hospital bed that it hit me like a ton of bricks. I wouldn't want anyone at my bedside but her.

Back at my rental, I tossed around a baseball in a makeshift booth I set up in the backyard. The netting kept the pitches from soaring into the neighbor's yard.

A cool breeze brushed across my sweat soaked back, and I shivered. I imagined Aspen riding around the property, with the devil cow, Carrie, chasing after her. Wounding herself in the process… again. I shook out my arms, trying to rid myself of the memory of Aspen all cut up and bleeding.

In my pocket, my phone buzzed, and I found a thousand unread messages from Vanessa and a new one from Marc. I considered changing my number, but I knew Vanessa would somehow figure it out. Either through my lawyer, who was still working to remove her items from my house, or from my agent. Vanessa had a way of getting what she wanted.

Marc
> She's at it again. Check her socials.

My best friend had been playing private investigator for me while I was gone and keeping me updated on Vanessa's shenanigans.

Pulling up the various social media pages Vanessa owned, I rolled my eyes. Pictures of us from our rehearsal dinner plagued her pages, with a post stating that we were happily planning our nuptials in a new location.

Taking a few screenshots, I forwarded the images to my lawyer and asked him to nip it in the bud. I was growing tired of Vanessa and her clingy nature. I was really not looking forward to possibly dealing with her when I returned to LA.

Taking that thought into consideration, I messaged my lawyer again and asked him to have her stuff removed from my place before the end of the week. Then messaged Marc to see if he could get the locks on my house changed. Thankfully, I lived in a gated neighborhood and had spoken to security about the ongoing Vanessa issues. Their team escorted her to my house whenever she needed something.

A few hours later, I sat on the couch with a beer in hand and dinner staying warm in the oven. Aspen texted an hour ago that Jenna was bringing her to the house, even though I offered to pick her up. Jenna had been at Aspen's house to check in and claimed it was easier.

She was probably right, since I'd spent the better part of my afternoon towing Aspen's car to the mechanic, only to find that it wasn't worth salvaging. I'd already known that much, but having it verified made me feel better about the new SUV I bought for her and had delivered to my rental. It was waiting outside in all its shiny red glory.

Sighing, I moved from the couch to the front porch and leaned my arms against the railing, my beer bottle dangling from my fingers as I waited.

Cricket
> 5 minutes away

Smiling down at my screen, I replied quickly and shoved my phone back into my pocket. I'd spent most of the day worried Aspen wouldn't show tonight. I was seeing her one way or another though, and I planned to go to her house if she tried to avoid me.

Off in the distance, I noticed Jenna's car turn into the neighborhood. Aspen had let it slip a couple of nights ago that Jenna and Derek were still going strong. I was happy for them and jealous at the same time. Some people had it so easy.

Finally, the car came to a stop in front of the house, and I smiled as Aspen stepped out with narrowed eyes.

Jenna was in on the car purchase and immediately drove off once Aspen was safely out the door.

"What's that? Where's my car?" Aspen asked as she approached the luxury SUV.

"That's your car."

"No."

I shrugged as I stepped off the porch and moved toward my girlfriend. I felt like I was approaching a wild animal that was ready to strike at a moment's notice.

"I took your car to the mechanic to get it fixed, and Earl said it wasn't salvageable. He was surprised you were still able to drive it at all. So, I left the car with him, made a few phone calls, and here we are."

"I don't want you spending your money on me."

I couldn't fight the smirk that grew on my lips. Vanessa was the opposite of her in every way. My ex begged me for a car when we'd only been dating for a month, and Aspen wanted nothing to do with my money.

Standing in front of Aspen, I tucked a piece of hair that had fallen from her ponytail behind her ear. "And that's one of the things I love about you."

By the way her breath hitched, I could tell my words surprised her.

"You… I…," she stammered.

"You're welcome, cricket. Now, come inside with me."

"Okay," she whispered, glancing over her shoulder at the SUV one last time before I clasped her hand in mine.

"So, you said you had some things to talk to me about?"

We crossed the threshold, and I closed the door behind us. "Yeah. Why don't we go ahead and sit down?"

I followed her to the couch and shifted to face her, one leg bent and propped on the cushion.

"I'm not sure how to say this, but instead of the two months I thought I had left, I actually have to leave sooner."

Her head gently cocked to the side. "How soon?"

"Two weeks."

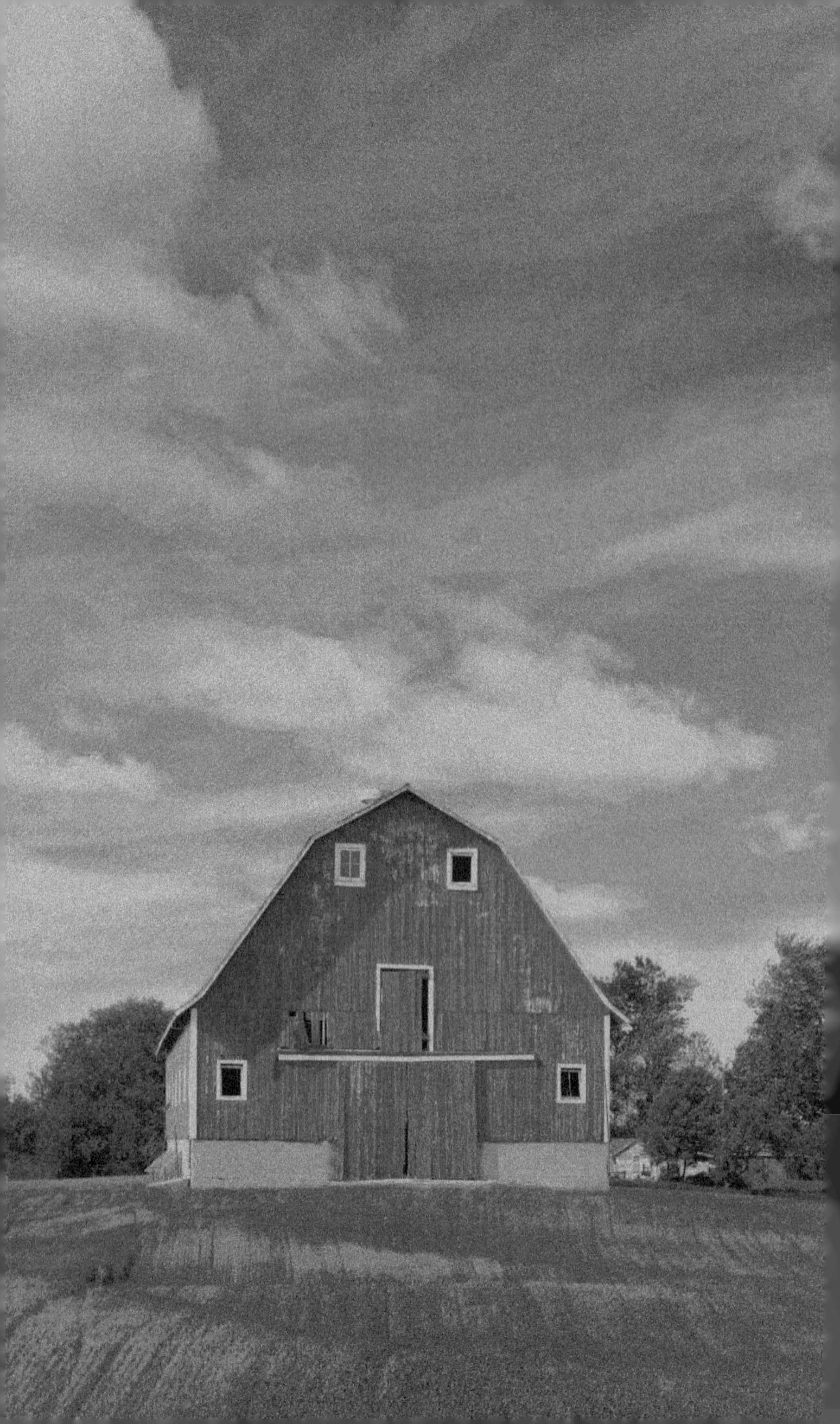

Chapter Nineteen

Aspen

The bomb Owen dropped while sitting across from me took my mind off the enormous vehicle he bought for me parked in his driveway *and* the fact that my dad was undergoing surgery tomorrow morning to put a stint in his artery.

Did I expect to break into tears? Not in the slightest. But that's exactly what happened when the news sank in.

It was too much. His leaving, my life, everything. I was spiraling out of control in a tornado of emotion I couldn't end.

"Baby, come here," he murmured as he tugged me toward his lap and cradled me against him. "I'm so sorry. I wish I could stay or take you with me."

I couldn't understand my gibberish as I blubbered against Owen.

"Fuck. Cricket, what can I do? How can I make it better? Tell me what to do."

Instead of words, I gripped him tighter. My arms clenched around his neck as I tucked my face against the dip between his shoulder and neck and drenched him with my tears.

Time slipped by as I released all my feelings from the steel cage they'd been trapped in. By the time I sniffed back my last sob, the sun had long fallen behind the mountain range.

"Better?" Owen asked, gently stroking my back.

"Um… yeah." My throat was parched, leaving my voice hoarse and scratchy. "I… I don't know what happened."

"It's okay. You have a lot going on. Can I get you anything? Have you eaten?"

I hadn't. And after shaking my head, Owen set me on the couch and jumped up, heading toward the kitchen. In a few short minutes, he returned with a steaming bowl of mac and cheese. After taking the first bite, I knew it was exactly what I needed.

"Thank you," I mumbled around my second spoonful.

While I ate, Owen asked about my dad, the surgery, and the farm. It was nice to speak candidly about everything. With my family, I felt like I had to tiptoe around my fears or insecurities.

As I finished my last bite of pasta, I remembered something one of our lead ranch hands mentioned when he returned to the farm. "Oh, they let me know today that your house is scheduled to be demolished next Wednesday. With it being condemned, it was up to the town to decide the date. Did you and your mom want to go by before or anything?"

I was worried about Owen's reaction, but as he smiled softly, I knew I shouldn't have been. He'd been through so much in that house. His family nearly crumbled at the hands of his despicable father within the walls of the building.

"I'll ask my mom, but I think we're both ready to move on now."

"I worried if things were still rough between you two, but she mentioned you guys have been chatting more frequently."

"Yeah," he said, rubbing the back of his neck with his hand as he perched against the wall. "It's a work in progress, but things are getting better. I… held a lot of resentment toward her, when it was never her fault for what happened to me. I can't imagine the horror she lived through. That bastard is *still* interrupting things in her life."

As he continued to talk, I noticed he began rubbing an area of his arm covered in tattoos. It was something I noticed him do before, but I thought little about it until now. It happened whenever he spoke about his father.

Curiosity got the best of me as I yawned. "Why do you do that?"

"Do what?" he asked, stopping the movement with his hand still wrapped around his forearm.

"Rub your arm. I… um… noticed you do it when you talk about your father."

Owen's gaze traveled out the window for a moment, then returned to me. Holding out his hand, he asked me to join him. "Come with me."

He seemed both distracted and wary as he grasped my hand and guided me toward the bathroom. Wordlessly, he started the shower and began stripping off his clothes. I didn't think I'd see a more gorgeous man for the rest of eternity.

He stepped into the shower and closed the door behind himself, leaving me standing there fully dressed as the billows of steam started pouring from the top of the shower door. "Owen? Is everything okay?"

"Join me."

I'd taken a quick shower before leaving the farm, wanting to rid myself of the smells and sweat, but I didn't hesitate to yank my clothes off and step into the spray.

Owen's body arced in the mist, only his head falling forward into the water as his arms stretched out, his hands braced on the tiled walls. His massive back filled the space, and as I stepped up behind him, I wrapped my arms around his trim waist.

"Talk to me," I urged quietly. I wanted to be that comfort for him like he had been for me.

He turned around and lifted me over to the bench, where he settled me on his lap, raising his intricately tattooed arm up for my inspection.

"Touch it," he whispered, his eyes locked on mine, but I sensed he was mentally elsewhere.

Hesitantly, I ran my index finger across the mountain ranges and shaded trees. There were colorful birds and orange trees that stood out against the darkness on his skin. But beneath it all, I felt what he'd been hiding. Rigid scars marred his skin.

"Those were from my dad. He threw me against the coffee table when I was twelve, and the glass top shattered. That was the first time mom had to stitch me up herself, because he refused to let us go to the hospital." Owen guffawed. "That was the same year he decided to start making wine. The idiot thought he'd have the fixings that year. When they sprouted nothing, he took it out on me."

"Owen," I whispered, running my fingers along the jagged marks, landing on a beautiful set of orange-leaved trees.

"Do you know what those are?" he asked me.

I leaned closer, but they weren't like anything I recognized. "No, I don't."

With two fingers, Owen lifted my chin until my gaze was back on his. He leaned forward, our lips brushing in the softest caress. My nipples pebbled as his hand slid down my neck and between my breasts. Owen grazed his fingertip against the hardened peak, and I jolted in his lap at the contact.

"It's an aspen tree. In Greek, it means shield."

Dazed from his kisses, I pulled back and looked down at his arm. "It's…. You got a tree with my name?"

"I got it because it was a way to keep you with me, always."

"I… don't understand. I thought…."

Owen placed both hands on either side of my neck, rubbing small circles with his thumbs.

"You were the only peace I ever found in this town. Not baseball. Not school. Not my mom. You. Anytime I was around you, everything else went silent inside me."

"Then why were you always trying to one-up me in everything? The fairs, school, the farm, all of it. It was like a never-ending battle we had."

"Because it kept your attention on me. I didn't care what I had to do to get it; I just needed it."

I rested my hands on his chest, just above his battering heart. "I thought you hated me."

"Oh, cricket. I've probably loved you from the moment you stole my box of crayons in first grade."

"I did not!" I exclaimed. "Those were mine, and you know it."

His chuckle echoed in the stall, sounding like a thousand Owens surrounding me.

"I just told you that I love you, and you're arguing with me about crayons."

"I was not. I was just pointing out the fa—"

He silenced me with a brutal kiss that left me panting.

"Aspen Easterly, I love you so much that I tattooed you on my skin so I could keep you with me, always."

Smiling, I wrapped my arms around his neck and pressed my lips in continuous kisses along his jawline.

"Owen Ramsey, I love you so much that I don't want to date anyone else when you leave. I want to try to figure out how to make this work." Pulling back, I added, "Even if it's for a couple of months a year that I get to see you, I want to try."

"Me too, cricket. Me too."

His hand slipped between my spread thighs and rubbed along my slick sex. "Christ, you're so wet for me."

Closing my eyes, I titled my head back, my ponytail capturing droplets of water from the shower. "Hearing you tell me you love me just… does something to me."

His other hand grasped my heavy breast and lifted it toward his waiting mouth. His tongue swirled around the nipple while his hand between my legs pistoned a finger in and out of me.

"I love you. I love you. I love you," he repeated, and I felt myself coating his fingers in all my desire.

He latched onto my breast, sucking on the bud and areola. Around my tight, puckered hole, I felt him run a slick finger back and forth. The sensation combined with his warm mouth as he finger-fucked my pussy left me writhing on his lap. I was feeling everything, everywhere… until I exploded in a myriad of pleasure.

"Oh fuck," I whispered as I fell over the cliff, riding Owen's hand like I was at a derby.

"That's it, cricket. Ride my hand. God… damn," he uttered.

As I came back to reality, he wrapped an arm around my waist and stood. I felt his cock align with my center, and my pussy practically begged for him to climb inside. But he gently swapped our positions, so that I was resting on the bench, and he was standing in front of me.

Owen licked his lips as he kneeled on the hard tiles and pushed my legs apart. My pussy was on full display for him as he skimmed his hands up my thighs until his thumbs brushed against the swollen folds. He flicked a finger up toward my clit, brushing the overly sensitive bundle of nerves, and I twitched, calling out his name.

"Bend your legs and put your feet on my shoulders," he commanded, eyes pinned on my sex.

I followed his directive until I was fully exposed to him.

"Christ, what did I do to deserve you?" he asked rhetorically. "I'm going to fucking devour you, baby."

Owen slipped a finger into my channel as he bent forward, sucking my clit into his mouth. The onslaught was powerful and overwhelming, but as I squirmed against his face, I felt myself pressing closer to him.

His tongue flicked wildly along my clit before he moved down toward my slit. Just when I thought he was going to fuck me with it, he moved past.

He couldn't possibly want to put his mouth on my...

His tongue pressed against my asshole and began moving up and down.

"Oh my God," I cried out, resting my head back against the cool tile. One hand inadvertently reached for his head, gripping his wet hair. Was I trying to push him away or hold him closer? I had no idea, but whatever he was doing, I didn't want him to stop.

While feasting on my rim, he swirled his hand around my clit until my legs began quivering. My toes curled as he moved, his fingers back on my pussy and he lapped at the swollen bundle.

Soon, I was crying out his name again as I clawed at the tiled bench. My legs skated down his arms and fell at his waist. I could barely open my eyes the release was so powerful. It took me a minute to catch my breath, and when I settled, I gazed up to find Owen washing his face.

"What are you doing?" I questioned as I tried to right my body but found myself unsuccessful.

"Well, I plan on kissing you, baby. And as much as I enjoyed eating you until you coated my face with your juices, I didn't think that was on your dessert menu tonight."

My cheeks flamed as I quickly shook my head.

"Can you stand?" he asked, holding out a hand toward me.

It took a couple tries, but I finally managed to pull myself upright.

"Good," he smirked with that sexy grin I fell for every time. Paired with his gray eyes, there was nothing Owen couldn't ask me to do. "Think you can give me one more?"

"More what?" I asked as I shivered and moved under the still-warm spray. Whatever water heater Rory had installed did a great job.

"Orgasm. I want to fuck you, baby."

"Um… yeah, I think so," I replied demurely.

"Thank Christ." Owen wrapped my arms around his neck and lifted me so that I wrapped my legs around his waist again. My overly sensitive folds rubbed against the head of his cock, and I felt an aftershock run through my system.

He held me in place with one strong arm wrapped around my back, while the other guided his cock into my entrance. Inch by glorious inch, I sank farther down until his shaft was buried in my channel.

"Owen," I moaned. "I… feel… so full."

"Is it too much?" he asked, not letting my body move an inch. He sounded as if he was holding on by a thread. I shook my head as I clung to him.

"Good," he growled as he lifted my body slightly, then dropped me back down.

We groaned simultaneously as he repeated the motion. After a few pulses, he pressed my back against the tile. The coolness was welcome against my heated skin. With the new surface to support us, Owen held me in place while he rocked back, then thrusted his erection inside me. I saw stars at the new angle and clenched my thighs tighter around his hips.

"God, baby. I can feel you milking my cock already. Your pussy is so hungry for my dick. I'm going to feed her until she's so full of my cum that I drip out of you for the next week."

I'd never realized how turned on dirty talk would make me. Maybe it was because it was Owen, but I felt myself tremble with yearning as he pounded into me.

"Yes," I whimpered as I clawed at his shoulders.

Thank goodness he'd been doing therapy with Kelsey, because I almost—*almost*—worried I would hurt his shoulder. But I was so lost in climbing to the pinnacle of my release that I didn't care.

"Come for me, cricket. I want to feel you."

Shifting his hold around my waist, he used his free hand to slide under my thighs and rub the puckered hole at my backside.

As he dipped just the tip of his finger inside, my body detonated.

"Oh my gosh," I repeated an unknown number of times as he pumped into me, seeking and finding his own release as I spasmed around him.

"Fuck, how does it get better every time?" he murmured as he turned off the water, still holding my limp body in his arms.

"I don't know, but it's amazing, Owen. I had no idea."

He wrapped us in one oversized towel, with my legs still wrapped around his waist, and carried us to the bed. After tugging back the sheet, he set me down and then slipped in behind me. I turned around and nudged one of my legs between his as I cuddled closer to his chest.

"You know, I've never been much of a cuddler," I told him as I nuzzled my nose against his chest. Owen had a distinct scent that was all him. I even asked recently what cologne he wore, so I could buy some to keep on hand when he left, but he didn't. The man used generic soap. Somehow, he had this naturally intoxicating fragrance that sent the butterflies in my stomach into a tailspin.

"I wasn't either. Not until you," he added as he stroked my bare back. "Can you stay the night, or do you need to get back?"

I thought about it, considered my options. My duty to my family, or my duty to the man I'd fallen in love with. One would be by my side for the rest of my life, the other was leaving next week. Our time was fleeting.

"I'd like to stay," I answered truthfully, and the smile Owen sent my way was one I'd dedicate to memory. I didn't think I'd ever seen him smile with such sincere happiness before. "I should probably grab my phone though. In case my family needs to reach me."

Without another word, Owen rolled out of bed and returned a minute later with my bag in hand. I reached inside and grabbed my cell, noticing a few texts from Jenna. I swiped them open to find screenshots from Owen's ex's social media pages.

Giggling, I set the phone on the nightstand. "Seems like your ex-fiancée is still convinced you're getting married."

My bag dropped to the floor with a thump as he rolled his eyes. "That woman is driving me nuts. Thankfully, my lawyer and security are handling it."

When he slid back into bed with me, I trailed a finger across his chest, asking a question that had been on my mind since our fake relationship turned real. "Do you think she'll be a problem when you go back to California?"

"I can't make the promise that she won't, but I'm doing everything I can to keep that from happening."

I wasn't the jealous type, but something about Vanessa rubbed me the wrong way. But I had to trust Owen if we were going to make this work. And I wanted nothing more than to have this work.

"You can trust me, cricket. You're all I see. You're all I've ever seen."

"I know. I'm not worried. I do wonder what made you want to be with her though."

"Clearly, I had no idea who she really was. Up until the wedding, she was mostly amenable, just pushy about the things she wanted. I suspected most women like her were like that. Honestly, I think I was just blinded by the fact that I wanted to settle down, and she was there."

"Did you love her?"

Owen took a second before responding, his hand stroking my bare shoulder. "I think, at the time, I thought I did. But when I caught her and her best friend together, I felt... nothing. I wasn't angry. I wasn't sad. I wasn't ecstatic. I was just.... I don't know. It didn't affect me at all. So, knowing that, I don't think I ever really loved her. I loved the idea of being married."

"I get it. You *love* love. You're a hopeless romantic, Owen Ramsey."

He shrugged as if he didn't care. "Maybe. I just think, in the end, I knew she wasn't the one for me. I didn't feel the desire to brand her on my skin like I did with the little cricket I had back home."

"As much as I hate that nickname, that's a good answer."

"Now, your turn," he schemed as he rolled me onto my back, his hips pressed between my legs.

"I don't have any relationship history, a scorned fiancé, nor a love life to speak about."

"Ex-fiancée," he corrected. "No, what I want to know is why you've stayed single all these years. I've never heard of you with a boyfriend."

"No time. I've been busy since I was ten and could reach the pedals on the riding lawnmower."

"That's not the real reason. I know that's what you use as your excuse to everyone else, but I'm not them. I want to know why you held yourself back from having a romantic relationship."

Squirming beneath his steely gaze, I ran through a list of lies to tell him, but instead, I chose the truth. If he could share, then I could too.

"I was scared. Scared of making myself vulnerable to someone. Scared of having my heart broken. Scared of never finding my person. Scared of never having what my parents have. Scared of love in general. It was easier to close myself off than to put myself out there. But I promised Jenna I'd try… and now, here we are."

"Here we are," he repeated as he pressed his lips against mine. "And thank you," he added as he brushed a kiss along my cheek and then nose.

"For what?"

"For telling me the truth and for giving me a chance."

I started giggling, which earned me a cocked eyebrow from Owen. "I guess I should thank Vanessa for screwing up and being late to the altar. Otherwise, you may have never returned home."

He rocked his hips against me, instantly silencing my laughter. "Yeah, I'll make sure to send her a bouquet of dead flowers."

"Yeah, you do that." I gasped as his velvety cock glided across my mound.

"Are you sore?" he asked, his voice laced with concern.

"A little, but please don't stop," I begged. "I want you to make love to me, Owen."

"We didn't use anything in the shower. I'm clean. I get tested by the team, and I had a test done after the Vanessa fiasco."

"I'm on the pill. I want to feel you bare again."

Owen coated his cock in slick heat before guiding himself slowly inside my pussy. This time, his touches were tender, his pace slow. But as I hitched my leg higher on his hip, Owen's stride grew crazed. I met him thrust for thrust. Until he spilled inside me and we fell into a heap of sweaty bodies.

"Fuck, I love you," he mumbled next to my head as he yawned.

"I love you too," I replied.

Owen planted a quick kiss on my forehead and rose from the bed to retrieve a washcloth to clean up between my legs.

"Get some sleep, beautiful." He tucked my body up against his, and I drifted away, listening to the steady thumping of his heartbeat.

Tomorrow was going to be a new day with all new responsibilities and what ifs, but for right now, I was exactly where I wanted to be.

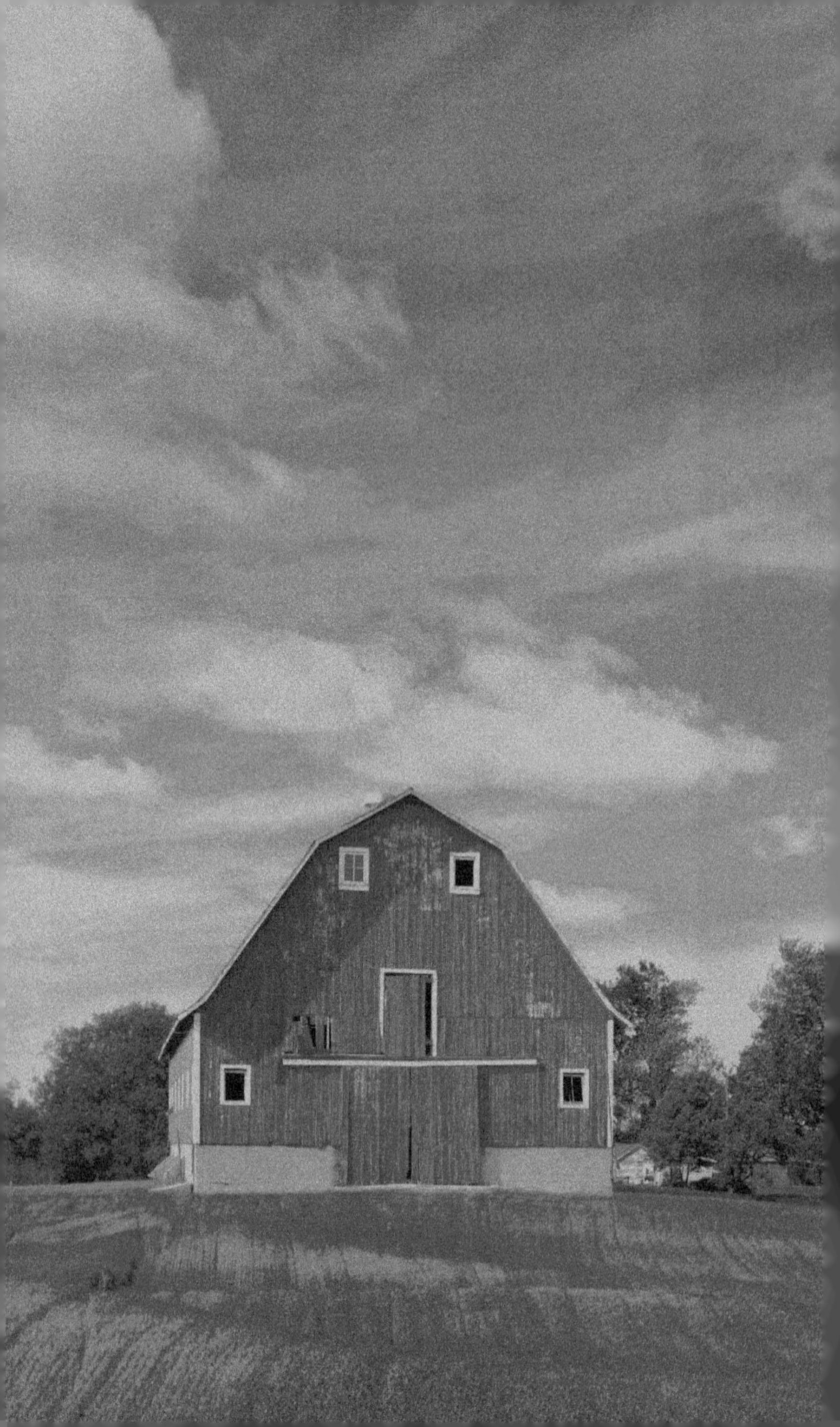

Chapter Twenty

Owen

Dad loomed over me with one of my new baseball bats. I'd begged him for one of the fancy aluminum ones all the other kids used at games, but he said I was only good enough for a wooden one. He'd prefer it if I used a stick.

Coach Rudicell saw I hadn't come to practice with the type required by the school. I lied the first few times and told him I'd forgotten, but then, in my locker, I found a brand-new bat waiting for me. It had been my favorite colors too—blue and green.

Coach didn't have to say anything. I knew it had come from him.

"My own fucking kid can't even appreciate all the hard work I put in. You've gotta go and beg your coach for a new fancy bat? You suck his cock to get this, boy?"

"Dad, no. I didn't do anything. I swear." At fourteen, I was catching up to my dad in size, but he was still larger, especially in the darkened room where I cowered like a five-year-old against my headboard.

"Don't lie to me, boy. I bet you told that old man that I refused to buy it for ya, huh? I bet you told him how horrible of a father I am. Well, you know what? I'm gonna show you how horrible I can really be."

The first smack of the bat landed on my thigh. The next, my ribs. Then everything went black just as I heard my mother scream my name.

"Owen. Owen." My name was a distant cry melded with an earthquake-force shake. "Owen, please. It's Aspen. Please wake up."

Aspen? My Aspen?

I gasped for air as I pulled myself from the despair and blackness of my dream. No amount of medicine prescribed by the team doctor could rid me of the memories that plagued me when I least expected it.

But since being back in Ashfield and sharing a bed with Aspen these last couple of months, I'd been dream-free.

Until today. And I knew exactly why. I was headed back to California on the first flight out of Nashville.

"Sorry, cricket," I groaned as I reached an arm around her stiff body.

"Are you okay? You scared me. I kept hearing you scream 'no' over and over again." Her lithe body was shaking, and I hated that I caused any sort of fear in her. These were demons *I* needed to battle. She didn't need to play a part.

"I'm fine. I promise. Just a dream I have every now and then. Go back to sleep, cricket. It's the middle of the night."

My little minx nodded and curled her body against mine. I waited as her breaths evened out before shutting my own eyes.

***

"Do you have everything?" Aspen asked for the tenth time as she loaded my bags into the back of her SUV that she thanked me for no less than four times a day. Sometimes, she used words. Other times, she used her mouth around my cock. I didn't have a preference on whichever way she wanted to show her gratitude.

"I do. Thank you for letting my mom tag along." I invited my mom to the airport to send me off, and she arrived with both excitement and sadness. It was in the way she hugged and the way she asked if I was going to be home for Thanksgiving.

Last week, we'd gone together to watch my childhood home be demolished. I thought the process would affect me more than it did. I found myself sad for the good parts of my childhood being lost, but Aspen reminded me that all those good memories were still here. The place didn't hold them; I did.

My mom had a harder time watching the house crumble to the ground. I wrapped a soothing arm around her shoulders as she cried. We never talked about it, but I wondered if maybe some of those tears were happy one. She was finally ridding herself of that last lingering piece of my father. I'd never ask her though. Just like me, she had her own demons.

After the demolition, Aspen and I went on one final public date in town. We made sure to have Jenna and my friend Chris post it all over their socials when a group of us went to play paintball. An entire outdoor facility had been created since I graduated high school, and I was eager to play. So was Aspen. It was clear she had a lot of aggression to let out, because the woman was lethal with the paintball gun.

We hoped Vanessa got the final message when I posted on my not-frequently-used social media pages. It was a picture of Aspen and me sharing a kiss while covered in various colors of paint from the game, goggles pushed up to rest on top of our heads. I'd finally taken the leap and blocked her number, consequences be damned. So, if she was trying to reach out to me, she was going to have to go through my agent.

"You're going to be late," Beverly called out from the open window of the back seat.

"Mom, we still have four hours before my flight takes off. I have plenty of time."

Mom harrumphed before ducking back inside the running car.

At the Easterly Sunday dinner, I handed Andrew the keys to the McClaren to use while I was gone. It was the first dinner since Nash's return home, and I would be lying if I said he looked good. The man looked like he'd been to hell and back. I guess, in a sense, he had. But he'd been in good spirits and made me promise to take him for a ride in the exotic car the next time I was in town.

Whenever that would be. Until then, I kept my rental lease open with Rory and asked Alex to stop by periodically to make sure the place was in order. It was on her way to her cake shop.

She had finally started coming around to the thought of me and Aspen being an item, though it was clear she didn't fully trust me yet. I had a feeling trust didn't come easily for her. Either way, she made the best damn desserts, and I planned on ordering her pistachio cake at least once a week while I was gone.

"You're staring off into space again," Aspen said with a not-so-gentle tap on my shoulder.

"Sorry. Just going through a mental checklist," I lied.

"Not sure why. You can buy whatever you need when you arrive in LA."

Stepping forward, I wrapped both my arms around her waist. "Yeah, but I can't buy a cricket, sooo… there is that."

"True. But you could get one tattooed on you somewhere."

"Not the same," I mumbled as I brushed my lips against hers. As I pulled back, she checked her watch for the third time since we stepped out in the driveway. "Everything all right?"

"Yeah, sorry. I have the wood for the fences on your property arriving today. I'm just anxious to get it started."

With a quick peck on her nose, I added, "It's *your* property, baby. Remember that."

"All right, Casanova, let's get you on the road." Her voice wobbled on the last word, and I knew my leaving was affecting her as much as it was me. I'd tried to pull every favor I could to extend my stay, but my contracts with the team and marketing were iron clad. When they wanted me to do something, I was required to be there if I wanted to keep playing for the salary I earned.

It was too bad that contracts didn't change when your dreams for the future did.

***

California was exactly like I'd left it. Warm, sunny, and lonely. While I loved the people I met since I started playing for the Coyotes, the city of stars was one of the most isolated places I'd ever visited.

A waiting town car ushered me from the airport to my house, then over to the main offices of the Coyotes. I'd only had enough time to change into one of my tailor-made suits before I was expected to show my face in front of the general manager and the team owners. Per my coach, they both wanted to congratulate me on my previous season.

The minute I threw on the bespoke suit, I missed the jeans and flannels I'd been wearing around Sunny Brook Farms. I'd done my best to help Aspen around the farm—something I found myself enjoying—as she tried to fill her dad's shoes. But I could see the work was already taking a toll on her. The weight of the farm and fulfilling her family's legacy was all on her. I couldn't fathom why no one else seemed to notice the strain she was under. Most of all, her mother and brother.

But I knew it wasn't my place to speak up. All I could do during that time, and now, was support her and her decision.

On the plane, I thought about how Aspen wanted to travel but had never even been on a flight. My chest ached thinking about all her sacrifices that seemed to go overlooked.

"Welcome back," my coach said as he waited for me in the lobby of the massive building.

"Thanks."

"How'd the work go with that therapist? Your arm up to speed?"

"Kelsey did a great job. Seriously. I feel better than when I started last season."

"Good to hear, kid," he said with a jovial slap on my back. "Now, it's the head honchos up in that room," he added as we boarded the elevator. "I know you've been down this route a few times, but remember, they're in it for the current and potential sponsorships."

Yeah, I remembered my first meeting when I was twenty and nearly shit my pants while I was speaking with the general manager. He was the one who signed my paychecks, after all. At that time, I didn't know I still held the power to say no. Now, I knew better, although they could overrule me at any time. It was why I tried to stay on my best behavior.

As Coach and I stepped out of the elevator and into the conference area, I had a sudden fear that the Vanessa issue was causing trouble for me and the team. Sports players relied on more than their stats to draw in new fans. We were also celebrities in our own right and had a certain image to portray. The leaked footage of my ex's cheating scandals during our relationship could tarnish the appearance I tried to keep up.

As I stepped inside one of the glass-walled rooms, I analyzed the faces of the GM and team owners. They smiled, but it was forced as they congratulated me on a great season. The corners of their eyes didn't wrinkle in the same way they had in the past.

Just as we collectively sat down, the public relations director, Rebecca, stepped into the room with a stack of papers and a laptop. Quietly and efficiently, she plugged in the device, and an image popped up on the projection screen.

I immediately recognized the woman in the picture. Vanessa, wearing one of her slinky red dresses, was standing outside the training area dressed to the nines. The next image showed one of our newest recruits stepping over to her and pressing a kiss to her cheek.

She may have been done with me, finally, but she was trying to sink her claws into another unsuspecting male.

"Mr. Ramsey, do you know the woman in these photographs?" the general manager asked, and I replied truthfully and explained we hadn't been together since the non-wedding.

"It seems she's been causing a problem with our players."

"Well, she's signed with Venture Models. You could let them know how she's behaving. Her job means everything to her."

"But you're serious about her not being a problem?"

"Not for me. She's history."

The slideshow flickered to another image, and I felt the tips of my ears redden as a shot of me with Aspen appeared. It was one of our afternoon dates at The Purple Goat, and I kissed her outside under the awning as it poured all around us. The rain had come from all different directions, and we were soaked just by stepping outside.

"And her?" he asked, tilting his head as I smiled.

"She's… everything."

"And will she be a problem like the last?"

"Not at all."

One of the team owners chose that moment to chime in and ask where the new woman was and why she wasn't with me.

Chuckling, I leaned back in my chair, at ease for the first time since I walked into the room.

"Her family owns a farm in my hometown. Aspen is slated to take it over once her dad officially retires."

"Farmer? That's some hard work there."

Another owner in the room added, "Is she going to be a distraction at all?"

"No, sir. She's been in my life since I was six years old."

The man nodded and flipped through the stack of papers resting on the table in front of him.

"Aspen?" Rebecca asked, and I confirmed her name. "That's the tattoo. On your arm, I mean. It's an aspen tree."

"Yeah. How'd you know that?" I questioned as I rubbed the area.

"I grew up in Alaska and recognized it." She shrugged and clicked a few keys on her laptop. "From a PR perspective, I don't think she'll be an issue either. People love a childhood-friends-to-lovers romance."

"Oh, we were definitely not friends growing up. We practically hated each other."

"Really?" Rebecca asked, the screen switching to another picture of me and Aspen standing in line at Chuck's grocery store. She was leaning against me, her back to my chest, and I had my arms wrapped around her shoulders with her favorite candy bar dangling from my hand.

"It's the truth. Ask anyone from our town. It took six weeks of us dating before they stopped running in the opposite direction whenever they saw us together."

All conversations in the room halted as the group looked at me with wide, wary eyes.

"There was an incident in the chemistry lab in high school. I'll leave it at that." I chuckled.

The PR director paused with her mouth agape, before she continued, "Well, we'll spin it as a Hallmark-esque romance then. Either way, when the public learns more about your new girl, they're going to go a little nuts, since your last relationship ended with you being stood up at the altar."

"I wasn't stood up. She was just late to the nuptials, and I happened to stumble upon what had her running behind," I replied diplomatically. "Is my personal life really that interesting?"

"For most sports players, no." I narrowed my eyes and waited for Rebecca to resume her point. "But you've been listed as one of the World's Most Eligible Bachelors and the World's Sexiest Men multiple times. The public is interested. Believe me."

Turning back toward the screen, she shows a bar graph that illustrates searches of my name against other players in internet browsers. I surpassed everyone on the team and only fell short behind some of the most famous players in recent years. I'd never realized how well-known I'd become.

"Oh."

"So, when the public asks about your new relationship, we'll have something prepared. We should probably consider a soft-launch of sorts. Maybe a charity event." Rebecca went on and on about ways to spin the coupling to help with team recognition and boost the overall public view.

"Rebecca," I chimed in. "I hate to burst your bubble, but Aspen won't be attending any of those things. She works seven days a week, for at least fourteen hours a day. Her life is busy all the time."

"So, how do you expect to make the relationship work?" she asked, but my coach immediately interrupted and asked about the sponsorships that required my attention. Since they had been the reason I needed to return to LA early.

But through the rest of the two-hour meeting, in which they droned on about team and individual sponsorships and promotions, things that didn't require my attention, I couldn't help but think about when I'd get a chance to see Aspen again. Outside of daily calls, I had no idea. I was even scheduled to be present for parades around the holidays, leaving me little opportunity to travel home.

And it wasn't only Aspen I wanted to devote time to. My mom and I were finally patching up our relationship. I didn't want to put a strain on that so soon.

As the meeting came to a close, I pulled Coach Hampton and Rebecca aside.

"Thanks for the meeting, and I look forward to helping the team in any way I can, but moving forward, please limit my sponsorships, charity work, and promotional events to five or less during the off season," I said professionally, but to my own ears, I sounded like a whiny child.

I was surprised when Coach smirked and nodded. Rebecca, on the other hand, wrinkled her nose.

"I thought you said the girl wouldn't be an issue."

"It's not the girl, Rebecca. It's called downtime for a reason. I need time to train and prepare for the next season as well as rest. And on top of that, I just started making amends with my mother. I'd like to be able to visit with her when I'm not playing."

"Well, I…. You're our most popular player, Owen. The fans expect—"

"The fans expect to see me play and play well. I can't do that if I'm exhausted when the season starts. You have plenty of good-looking up-and-coming players. I'm certain any of them could fill those spots just as good as I could. I'm not asking you to move things around this year. I've made the commitment. But please keep it in mind when the season starts."

With little argument, she nodded and scooted down the hall. Suddenly, a heavy hand landed on my shoulder. Tom Sung, the general manager and hall-of-famer, stood at the doorway looking pleased.

"Glad to see you making your life a priority, Owen. This game can be a brutal one with long seasons. Family should always come first."

"Thanks, Mr. Sung."

"Now, what do you say to a midday drink? After sitting in that meeting for the last two hours, I can't feel my ass any longer."

Chuckling, I agreed, as did Coach Hampton. I knew better than to decline the chance to talk ball with a player immortalized in the MLB Hall of Fame. Even if he could sign me away at a moment's notice. I liked to think we had a good relationship. He's the one who took a chance on me when I was just a little asshole in college.

A few nights later, I was lying in my newly delivered bed watching *John Wick* for the umpteenth time. I'd spent the majority of the week purchasing all new furniture for the house. Vanessa had decorated it from top to bottom when she moved in, all in her glamorous style. I didn't have a need for a pink velvet couch or a fur rug under my bed.

There was also a lingering scent of her perfume that had always made my nose tingle with an incoming sneeze. It was now gone thanks to a diffuser of miracle-working essential oils. I hired an interior designer that Marc knew, and she helped me make my house feel more like a home. Before Vanessa, I filled the space with everything needed for a bachelor pad. Lots of leather and metal. But the new space reminded me of Aspen's and Rory's homes. A little mix of mid-century and a bit eclectic. Sure, it probably came off a bit feminine, but it felt like being back in Ashfield.

Beside me, my phone buzzed, and I glanced over to find Aspen calling. We'd made it a routine to speak every night, even when she was exhausted or I was in the middle of training. We both made the time. That had been our agreement.

Pressing the Answer button, I saw her face pop up on the screen. She was on a video chat, so I immediately turned on my camera.

"Hey, cricket."

"Hey," she said warmly. Aspen was outside, somewhere among trees. Her backdrop was filled with yellows, greens, and oranges. The fall in Ashfield was one of those things I missed most when I moved away.

"Where are you?" I asked. I couldn't quite determine the location, but I knew it was somewhere high in the mountains. She panned out the camera and flipped it around. Aspen sat on a rock ledge overlooking the town. It reminded me of those postcards people pick up of picturesque getaways.

"Wow, that's a view," I said when she turned the camera and herself so that it showed both her and the view over the ledge.

"It's my favorite spot. I come here when I need a breather, you know?"

"Everything okay?"

"Yeah. Not much is happening on the farm today. Mr. Frener is moving his cattle onto the new fields. Andrew is overlooking it."

"Ah, so you get some time away. That's good, cricket."

"Andrew has been helping out more, and we're looking at hiring some people. I'm just not sure how I feel about it."

We'd spoken on this a few times since I left. Aspen didn't think it was right for someone else to run the family farm. I kept trying to convince her she could still oversee Sunny Brook Farms but could hire others to manage the property.

"I know. But I don't think it'll hurt to hear him out."

Off in the distance, I heard a popping sound, and Aspen held up a soda into view as she took a sip.

"What did you get into this morning?" Sometimes I forgot we had a two-hour time difference. It was midafternoon where she was and early lunchtime here.

"I had a call with my agent and Vanessa's."

"Oh, really? What about?" Aspen asked eagerly.

"She has agreed to stay away from me and all Coyotes players. Essentially, the general manager enacted a client restraining order of sorts. We wouldn't use her agency for any models, whether for promotions, advertising, or things like that, so long as she was linked with one of the players."

"Is that even legal?"

"No idea, but it worked. Last I heard, Venture Models was only keeping her on because she tends to land exclusive runway shows and editorials."

"Well, I'm glad you're rid of her."

Chuckling, I replied, "I'm sure you are."

"What happened between her and her best friend?"

"Not sure. I don't really care, to be honest. Her agent let it slip that she was looking for apartments in New York, so hopefully we'll never run into her here."

"We?"

"Well, I was kind of hoping I could get you out to a game or two once your dad is back on his feet. How is he doing, by the way?"

Aspen's giggle sounded like it echoed across the mountain range and valley. "Same as yesterday and the day before that."

The alarm on my phone sounded, and I knew my call was going to be cut short.

"Hey, cricket, I have to go hop in the shower. I'm due to take some pictures for a sports drink this afternoon."

"Ooo, in your underwear?"

"No." I laughed. "At least I don't think so. They usually like us in our uniforms."

"Fine. But if you *do* have to get half naked, please have someone send me pictures."

"You got it, babe. And don't worry—everything will all work out. I love you."

She sighed in the same way she did when she'd snuggle up against me in bed right before falling asleep. "I love you too."

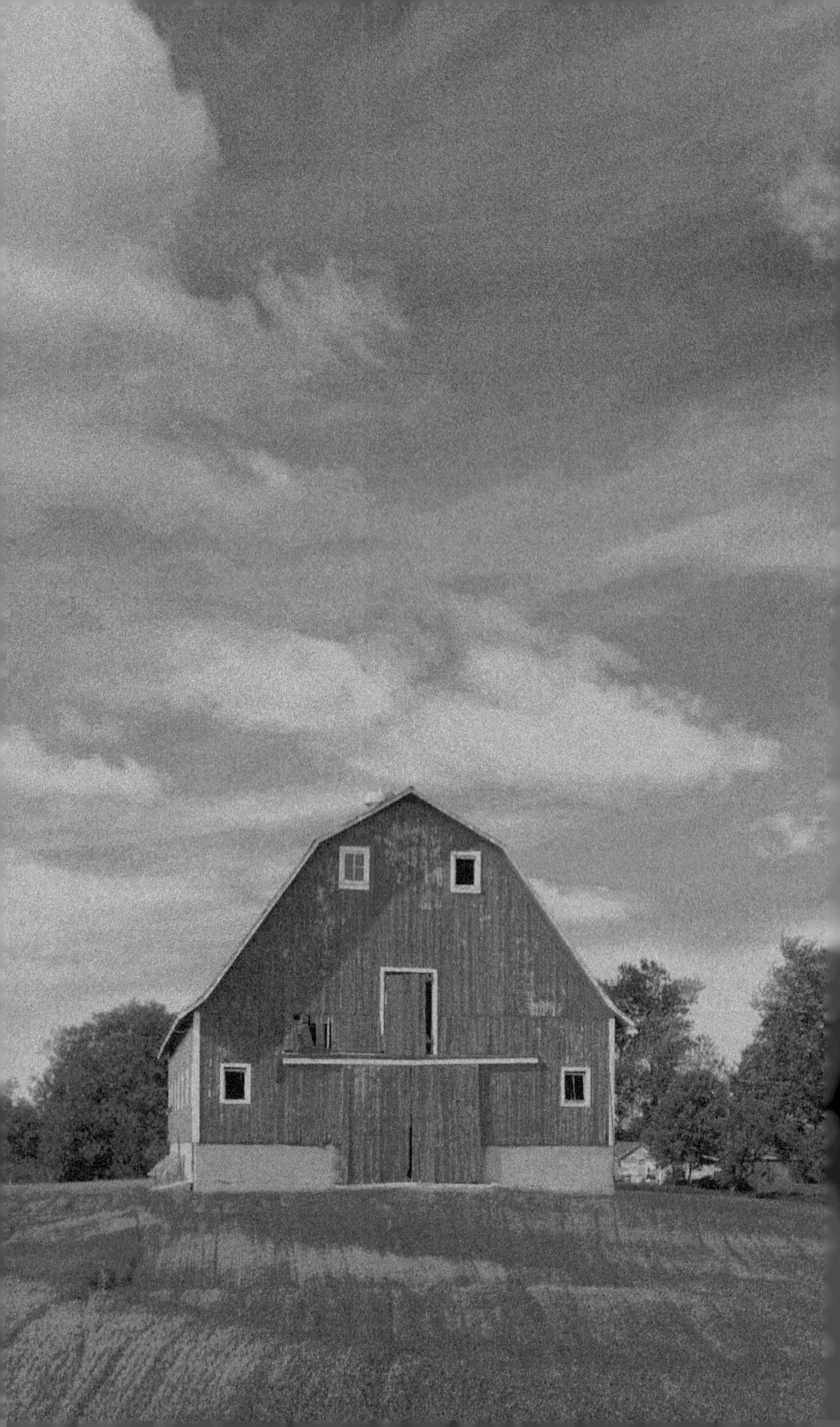

Chapter Twenty-One

Aspen

Staring up at the cloud-covered sky, I listened to the birds chirping as they made their plans to head south for the winter and the leaves rustling. Autumn in Ashfield had always been one of my favorites.

It had been a family joke that since my sisters and I were all named after something to do with the seasons that I would love winter, Autumn the fall, Aurora the spring, and Alexandra the summer. The latter, I wasn't quite sure how they were related, but my mother insisted. And one thing I learned at a young age was to never argue with a southern woman.

Owen had been gone almost a month now, and I would be lying if I didn't say it was a struggle. Despite the gifts, calls, and random messages, it wasn't the same as having him close. I had no idea how anyone with loved ones in the military got through it. My mother had at one point, but we were still walking on eggshells around her, so I hadn't had it in me to ask for her advice. Since my father's heart attack, she'd been a bit more withdrawn than usual. Of course, we all understood. She'd lost her first husband at war, and now her second nearly lost his life as well.

Now that it had started growing colder and the sky was darkening far earlier than I liked, I refrained from heading to my ledge to think unless it was the middle of the day. Soon, the small creek that crossed through the path would freeze, and I wouldn't be able to go at all until the spring.

Instead, I usually drove one of the UTVs over to the property, where a fence used to separate the Ramsey farm from our own. We had the natural waterway on our side of the property, and Mom had set up a gazebo just under an old oak tree. When I was little, it was one of my favorite places to play, even though it would always scare her when she couldn't find me.

I used to lie across the bench and watch Owen play baseball in his backyard. I envied how he could play sports and use his free time to be a kid. I rarely got the luxury. My sisters had all attended dance classes, or art, something to keep them busy, but my only hobby had been tending the garden.

Funny thinking back to how I coveted Owen's freedom, when all along he'd been in a worse prison than me. Mine was of duty; his was his father.

I jumped as my phone rang, and I found myself giddy with anticipation, my hands shaking as I pulled it free of my jacket, only to sigh in disappointment when I saw it was my eldest sister calling.

"Hi, what's up?"

"Well, I was kind of hoping you could run by the bed-and-breakfast and grab my hospital bags."

"Why?" It felt like Autumn had been pregnant forever. Thankfully, she was due anytime now.

That's when it all hit me.

"Oh my gosh, are you in labor?" I jumped from the gazebo and ran toward the UTV parked close by.

"I think so, but my doctor said it could take a while for the first baby. So, I'm in no rush to head to the hospital, but I'm over at Alex's cake shop with the twins right now. You're probably the closest."

"Sure. Where can I bring them? Did you want me to drop them off at your house? Where's Colton?" I asked frantically. As the father, shouldn't he be the one running around in circles, getting everything together, and—like in all the funny movies—forgetting the most important part: his wife? Instead, I could barely get the keys to the UTV into the ignition, dropping them three times before I was successful.

"Colton is with Nate right now. They were practicing with the rec hockey team. He's on his way, but he needs to shower and everything."

"Why is he not panicking? Why aren't *you* panicking? Why am I the only one panicking?" I questioned as I pressed my foot to the accelerator and flew across the field.

"No need to panic, Aspen. We have plenty of time. Mom labored for forty-three hours with Andrew. I'll meet you at the B&B and take a nice relaxing bath until I think I need to go to the hospital."

"All right. I'm on my way. Thirty minutes tops."

Autumn chuckled as she ended the call, and I soared across the farm. To the workers, I probably appeared like a madwoman. My loose hair looked like a blonde cape as it flapped behind me in the wind. The UTV caught air as it hit a particularly high bump in the dirt path.

"Fuck," I muttered as she landed back on the ground with a *thunk*. I was certain something broke underneath, but I didn't have time to waste.

I got to the barn faster than ever before, dropped off the UTV, and ran to my house for my car keys. Before leaving, I glanced down and noticed I was still wearing my dingy jeans and jacket. Quickly, I stripped down to my bra and panties and grabbed a clean pair of jeans and a black long- sleeve shirt from my dryer. Tugging on my trusty boots, I was out the door in record time.

Moments like this, when my car started immediately, made me thankful Owen bought me the SUV. My old car would have sputtered for a solid fifteen minutes before she decided if she wanted to start or not. In that amount of time, I was already halfway to Colton and Autumn's house.

I used my copy of their key and let myself inside the house, then headed toward the nursery. She'd sent me a text while I was driving, letting me know that room was where I'd find the two bags and a special pillow.

Moving at a speed to rival Marvel's Quicksilver, I tossed the bags in the far back of the vehicle and headed toward the bed-and-breakfast. It was a twenty-minute drive on a normal occasion, but as I arrived, I felt oddly proud that I made it in thirteen.

Bags in hand and pillow tucked under my arm, I used the tips of my fingers to open the back door to the bed-and-breakfast, cutting through the side deck where I joined Owen and his mom for lunch what seemed so long ago.

"I'm here!"

Beverly came around the corner and greeted me first. "Oh, there you are, sweetie." She kindly helped me set the bags down.

"Is Autumn here yet?"

"Yes, she just arrived."

Weird, I hadn't seen her car anywhere, although maybe she parked out front. I tended to use the staff parking area in the back.

"Okay, great. Is she feeling okay?" I asked as we walked toward the main living space. I wasn't paying any attention as we turned the corner, until I came face-to-face with the majority of my family. The only people missing were Rory's husband Talon and my twin nieces. Talon was down in Miami with his grandmother Gigi—arguably one of my favorite people on the planet.

They stood in a semicircle together like we were in a freaking intervention.

"What's going on?" I asked the room collectively, then set my eyes on my eldest sister, who stood with a gentle hand on her belly as if she hadn't told me she was in labor. "I'm sorry. Aren't you supposed to be having contractions or something?"

With an air of confidence I'd never felt myself, she waved a hand in the air. "They're bearable."

"So, what's everyone doing here? What in the hell is going on?" I felt like the kid in the school play who had suddenly been given a role they never prepared for. The spotlight was on me, and all I felt was stage fright.

From behind me, a gentle but familiar hand landed on my shoulder. "Why don't you have a seat, and we can chat? Okay?"

Turning to face my father, my eyes narrowed. Though he'd been feeling better, it was clear he was still trying to keep from overdoing it.

"Okay."

He gestured to the couch, and he and my mom followed me over to it. The rest of my siblings, their spouses, and Beverly found chairs of their own that seemed to be brought in from random rooms of the house. A couple of the rocking chairs from outside were parked beside a dining chair.

And everyone stared at *me*.

"I feel like I'm inside a fishbowl, and y'all are just waiting for your chance to tap the glass but haven't decided who gets to go first."

"Well, I'll take that honor," my dad said, much to the relief of my siblings, who all sighed and relaxed into their chairs.

My dad reached toward me and placed his hand gently on my knee. It was something he'd always done when he wanted to make sure he had my or my siblings' full attention.

"I can never thank you enough for all you do around here, Aspen. You may have thought it went unnoticed, but *I* saw. I witnessed you sacrificing your personal life to carry this place, and that was never fair to you. I'm afraid I put too much pressure on you from the start, and you never got the chance to grow your own wings. Instead, you stayed in our safe cocoon, waiting."

"Dad, I—" I tried to interrupt, but he gave me that fatherly glare that had my lips sealing together.

"All I want to say is… I'm sorry you felt like you had no choice but to take over."

Mom quickly chimed in. "And I'm sorry you felt like you couldn't talk to one of us about how burned out you were, when none of this was what you wanted in the first place."

"But I love the farm, and I'm happy to take over."

"Sweetheart, we're not the only ones who've observed the amount of time and effort you put into this place. You're doing the job of five people. You can't sustain a life like that."

"Dad did it every day."

"I did," my father said. "And look where it landed me." He gestured to his chest.

Across the room, Alex surprisingly spoke up. "We want you to have a life too, Aspen. Owen let it slip that you want to travel and write about the places you go. We had no idea. We're all sorry we never saw… you."

Any hope of suppressing the tears that threatened to spill over was lost. They fell onto my flushed cheeks as I sniffled.

From over in the corner, I made eyes with Beverly. "Did Owen have something to do with *this*?"

"Not at all, sweetie. Though he might have been given a hint that it was going to happen."

"So, what do you want me to do? I'm confused. I have a business degree but nothing else I can do with it."

"We'd love if you still wanted to work on the farm, but we want you to take a step back. See if this is really the kind of life you want. Ask for help. Hire help. You have great ideas for ways to utilize the land when we're not in harvest. But don't make this your life, or you'll regret it when the time comes to an end," my father said.

"I'm also *really* thinking about moving back soon, if that helps at all?" Andrew added casually as he rested back in a recliner.

"Really?" I prompted. We talked about it before, but he hadn't mentioned it since then, so I didn't think he was seriously considering it still.

My brother hadn't lived in Ashfield since he graduated high school. He immediately moved away for college, then Knoxville. He visited on the weekends, but that was it. We had a feeling an incident with his ex was the source of his departure.

"Maybe we can talk about some changes? All of us?" I asked the room. Whether they worked here or not, Sunny Brook Farms was our family legacy. Someday, one of their children might take over, and they deserved a say in everything that took place.

"Now that's what I like to hear. Anywho, if we're done here, I should probably make my way to the hospital."

I glanced over to Autumn, who had a distinct line of sweat beading along her forehead.

"Beverly, I owe you a new chair," she added as she pushed herself up, using the armrests. "My water broke about five minutes ago."

Pandemonium broke out in the blink of an eye. Siblings rushed around the room, trying to figure out who was doing what, while my parents sat quietly on the couch. Me? I quickly made my way over to Autumn and helped guide her to my SUV out back. Beverly followed with her bags I brought inside earlier.

"Beverly, can you run tell Colton I'm heading out with her now? I think he should follow in his car, since that's where they installed the car seat for the baby."

"Yes, dear. Good luck, Autumn. Please keep me up to date," she replied as she hurried back inside.

I carefully helped my sister into the passenger seat as her husband rushed out to take over the task, speaking to her in a soft, loving tone. I did my best not to overhear, but neither of them seemed to care that I was next to them, buckling myself into the driver seat.

The journey to the hospital was uneventful except for a tractor trailer accident that brought out the demon buried deep inside my sister's soul. But the moment we broke free of the traffic, she calmed right down.

Colton must have called ahead, because once I parked the SUV and helped Autumn inside, they already had a room prepped for her. Since we were alone, I got to go into the room with her and watched as they poked and prodded her. I felt myself squirming, but the smile never dropped from her face.

"He'll be here soon," I said calmly as she squeezed my hand through a contraction. Autumn had every intention of getting drugs for the birth, but she wanted to go as long as she could without them, forsaking my fingers in the process.

"I'm not worried. I have my incredible baby sister with me."

"Stop, you'll make me cry." She shrugged and mumbled something like "better you than me," but I could barely hear her over the incessant beeping in the room.

"So, are we going to talk about why you're here and not with your boyfriend?"

"Did y'all have a family meeting about this?"

"Maybe, but I want to hear it from you."

I pried my fingers loose from her grip and tucked them into my pocket while staring out the window. "You know… we weren't actually dating. Not in the beginning, at least."

I glanced down to witness her eyes widening, but then she wiped away the expression in the blink of an eye. "But it turned real?"

"It did."

"And you love him?"

"Yeah."

I went on to tell her about his tattoo, the reason we started fake-dating, and even why he antagonized me so much in school. Autumn nearly swooned her way off the bed as she clapped and giggled.

"What are you still doing in Ashfield, Aspen?"

"He… never actually invited me to join him."

"Do you think he wants you there?"

"Maybe. I don't know. We always just talked about the time we'd have together during his off season. Five months is enough time. It has to be," I whispered at the end.

Regardless of what my family thought, I didn't *want* to give up my place at the farm. It was all I knew up until this point. Leaving it all behind would be a giant leap of faith I wasn't sure I was ready for. Or if I ever would be.

Thankfully, Colton arrived, and I moved to the waiting room, where the rest of my family gathered. I messaged Owen to let him know what was going on, and five minutes later, he sent me a screenshot of a receipt for flowers and chocolates he had sent to her room.

It was around 10:00 p.m. when I walked out of the waiting area in search of coffee. I knew it wasn't going to be great, but it was better than nothing at the moment. Colton had popped into the room a few times to let us know the baby had turned over and they were working to get the little troublemaker back into position. Then he updated us when Autumn got her epidural and was finally sleeping.

I watched enough medical dramas that I knew we could be here for the rest of the night and the next day. Mom and Dad already ushered most of our crew to a hotel close by to get some sleep. I was hopeful they'd do the same soon too, but as for me, I was invested in this birth at this point. As the person who got the honor of being the official escort, I was staying.

"Hey, getting a coffee?" Andrew called out as he exited the restroom.

"Yeah. I think the cafeteria is open for another hour or so."

"Great. I'll join you."

We boarded the elevator and headed toward the cafeteria on the third floor. Thankfully, they had a twenty-four-hour coffee shop, so I didn't have to settle for the nasty stuff out of a tap.

I grabbed a tea for Mom while Andrew dressed a decaf coffee for Dad. He'd been laying off the caffeine since his heart attack.

"So, I was serious about helping more with the farm."

"Really? I thought you decided against it when you never mentioned it again, after we talked a couple of months ago. I figured you didn't have any interest in it."

"No, I mean, I've always been interested. I just found another passion for a while. But I'm not twenty anymore and need to look toward my future."

"Is that why you're moving back home?"

"Partly."

"Can I ask why you've always been so… I don't know… distant, when it comes to talk about the farm? If anyone should have taken it over, it should've probably been you and your kids."

"Yes, you can ask," he joked.

"Andrew—"

"It's hard to take over a family birthright, when you never felt like you truly belonged. Nash isn't my father, Aspen, and the farm belonged to *his* family. It felt…"

As we stepped into the elevator to return to the labor-and-delivery floor, I wrapped my arms around my brother's waist.

"You are just as much a part of this family as any of us. You're my brother, and Dad has always viewed you as his own flesh and blood. And don't you ever forget it." I poked his chest as I pulled back in mock anger.

"Yeah, okay, squirt. Calm down now."

"But anyway, I would appreciate your help. It might be nice to have some sort of social life. I'm sure Jenna would *really* love it." My best friend had a massive crush on Andrew when she was younger and made sure he knew about it back then. Thankfully she was very happy with her new beau, Derek.

Back in the waiting area, we handed off the extra drinks to our thankful parents just as the nurse popped her head in and told me we were nearing the end. It seemed a little bit of drugs relaxed my sister enough that the baby was making its entrance into the world.

At 1:30 a.m. my nephew, Elijah Henry Crawford, was born. He was the most precious baby boy I'd ever seen, and I wasn't just thinking that because I was destined to be his favorite aunt, but because he truly was. Even the nurses were talking about how cute he was while gossiping in the hallway. Thankfully, security for Colton had arrived a few hours before the birth to keep the tabloid photographers at bay, but that didn't mean a couple of shots hadn't been taken of us all waiting inside the hospital.

As my siblings returned and took their turns holding the precious baby, I nestled onto the bed next to my sister, who was a rockstar by all accounts.

"How are you holding up?" I asked her. She had this glow about her, even with the tired eyes and sweat-drenched hair. Autumn had never looked more beautiful.

"I'm good. Really good."

"I'm happy for you, Fall."

"Thanks, Winter." We smiled, using our childhood nicknames for each other.

Colton strolled over with the tiny bundle in his arms. He was a massive man who usually had to bend a bit to enter doorways, and with Elijah, it looked like he was holding a small melon or something.

"Ready for your turn, Aunt Aspen?"

"Really? You want me to hold him? What if I drop him? I've never held a baby," I asked as I stood and put my arms into a certain position I thought would help.

"You won't," he assured me as he placed the small human in my arms.

"Oh my gosh, he's so precious," I murmured through my tears. It was one thing to look at him in my sister's arms, but it was an entirely other thing to hold him close to my heart.

"Quick, take a picture," I gestured to Rory, who was closest, poking out my hip for her to snag my phone from my back pocket. As she positioned the camera, I smiled down at my nephew, and a deep yearning built in my chest. It was a feeling I never imagined having, and suddenly I knew it was something I wanted for myself one day.

"Here," Rory said, and I took the phone from her.

It was late, and I was sure Owen was asleep, but I maneuvered my thumb over the screen and tapped his number without waking the baby. I was a pro already.

I was surprised when he answered the video call. The dim light on his nightstand cast glorious shadows across his bare chest as I held the screen up.

"Wowza," Autumn cooed from her bed, ignoring Colton's eye roll.

"Sorry to wake you," I said, "but I wanted to introduce you to my nephew, Elijah. Eli for short."

I held the phone just far enough away so that Eli and I were on the screen together and you could make out his chubby cheeks and button nose.

"He's beautiful. Congratulations, Autumn and Colton. I can't wait to meet him in person."

"Hold on," I said to Owen as I carefully handed Eli to my sister. I stepped toward the door of the room while the rest of the family continued their excited chatter.

"Sorry, I know it's late, but I had to call."

Owen stretched his long limbs, and I found myself hoping the sheet around his waist would fall just a few inches lower. Since he'd taken my virginity and the couple of weeks I got to enjoy afterward, I'd been missing our intimate moments together. I'd made good friends with the vibrator he purchased for me a week after he left. The only stipulation was that I could only use it if I filmed it for him or while we video-chatted. Those were some of my favorite nights, but it still wasn't the same as having him with me.

"I'm glad you called, cricket. I'm always happy when I can talk to you."

"How's training going?" His coach had asked him to host a workshop for a few of the new players, and Owen seemed to be excited about it. The first sessions started yesterday. It wasn't just about how to play the game but how to present yourself to the public amidst the fame and fortune. He'd also brought in a financial advisor to set the new guys up with a team, so they didn't spend their million-dollar contracts right away.

"It's good. We have some real potential this year to make it to the championships again, and the guys are really open to listening to my advice. For whatever reason."

"Because you're their idol, baseball star."

We laughed together, and then a comfortable silence blossomed.

"I miss you."

"I miss you too, cricket. I'm sorry about the holidays. It's just easier to fly my mom out."

I'd been hopeful he'd make it home to Ashfield for Thanksgiving or Christmas, but he was recruited to host a charity marathon on Thanksgiving—a Turkey Trek. And on Christmas, he'd be participating in a local food drive with a guest spot on the televised New Year's

Countdown. It was less than ideal, but at least I'd get to see his pretty mug on TV.

Beverly was ecstatic to join her son for the holidays. They'd really made headway in healing the rift caused by Owen's father. It took a while for Owen to understand that his mom had his best interests at heart, but I knew it would happen eventually.

"It's okay. I understand." I yawned uncontrollably and felt my jaw ache when my mouth closed.

"You should get home and rest. Seems like you've had a big day."

"You're probably right. I'll call you tomorrow."

"Text me when you get home or I won't be able to sleep."

"We're staying at a hotel across the street. Dad insisted."

"Good. I love you."

"I love you too, Owen."

With my hand on the door handle, I glanced at my sister and her husband curled over their newborn son, looking like they were in the most blissful dream. My family stood by watching, and it was in that moment I knew something I wasn't ready to admit yet. Not to myself or anyone else.

And my chest ached as I made a decision.

Chapter Twenty-Two

Owen

The breeze whipped around my cap, cooling off my face in the midday California sun. I'd been gearing up for this day for the last two months, since we started our physical training schedule. It was the end of February and the first day of spring training.

Most of the players on the field were first years, with just a few of us veterans scattered throughout. It was where the coach and general manager could get a good feel for the team as a whole.

It always reminded me of the scrimmages we used to play in gym class. The games didn't matter, but they were played as if they did.

Today, though, was special in that we were playing the Nashville Bears. The same team that loaned us one of their physical therapists to help me with my shoulder in the off season.

We were only two innings deep, and I could tell a few of the players would need more field time. The others we would pair with a veteran player to tailor their training regime. But overall, the team was solid, and I thought we'd have a good chance at the championship.

The score read two to one, Coyotes.

The inning ended with a walk for the other team, and we headed toward the dugout.

Coach Hampton pulled me aside as I descended the steps.

"You're doing great tonight, Owen. I'm putting you up on the batting roster for the third. Knock one out for us."

"Sure thing, Coach." He glanced down at his phone for a moment and then smirked before walking away.

While I waited for my turn, I leaned against the railing and glanced toward the crowd. Spring training wasn't always full, but most of the seats were occupied. A group of ball chasers catcalled from the far end, hoping to get a picture, signature, or a hotel key. They called my name, but I sent them a quick wave and descended back into the dugout. That was a fire I definitely didn't want to play with.

The first two Coyotes players struck out. I watched from my stance as I swung my bat in practice. I hated watching anyone miss their hits, but the pitcher for the Bears had a great arm. I couldn't deny it. He was going to be one I'd have to look out for during the regular season.

Walking up to the plate was like coming home. I felt a sense of peace and belonging as I scuffed my foot along the dirt and took my position.

The first pitch flew by my face, and I felt myself sneer as the umpire called out a strike. Adjusting my legs, I crouched down a bit lower. Suddenly, an image of me standing behind Aspen came to mind when I helped her at the camp in Ashfield. Before the next pitch launched, I took a step out of the box to collect my thoughts. I'd never broken out of my mental block during a game. I was always focused. Always absorbed in the role I needed to play.

Not until Aspen.

"You've got this, Ramsey," someone called off in the distance, and I stepped back onto the plate and took my stance.

The pitch was too low to swing, and the umpire called a ball. I set up for the third pitch and adjusted my grip on the bat.

"Let's bring it home, Owen!" There was something oddly familiar about the voice, but I couldn't afford the distraction.

I watched as the pitcher wound up and adjusted his hand. I knew in an instant that this was going to be the same fastball he'd thrown at me first. With a clench of my grip on the bat, I swung at just the right mark, sending the ball flying through the air.

"Yes!" the crowd screamed, and the voice from earlier was louder than the rest. I launched my bat behind me as I ran toward first base, my eye on the ball the entire time. When it was clear it was going to soar past the outfielders and over the wall, I slowed my pace as I approached second. The guys on the other team held out hands for me to smack as I jogged across second and third base. It wasn't until then that I noticed my entire team standing outside of the dugout, pointing toward the crowd.

I looked up and nearly toppled over my own feet. Aspen stood in the stands behind home plate, wearing the purple dress I bought her.

Holy fuck. What is she doing here?

I sprinted toward home, then backtracked toward the dugout, only to climb over the railings and into the seats.

Aspen and I collided in the kind of embrace you only saw in movies. Our teeth clanked as we kissed, and I dove my hands into her silky hair.

Pulling back a tad, I asked, "What are you doing here?"

"We came to watch you play."

"We?"

She pointed over my shoulder, and I noticed the rows of empty seats behind the dugout were now filled with most of Aspen's family *and* my mother.

"I promised Roman I'll send your mom back with a souvenir for him."

"Owen!" the coach called, and I saluted him, then turned back toward Aspen.

"Fuck, I have a game to play."

She smiled in that sweet way that left my balls tightening in my pants.

"I know, superstar. I'll be waiting for you."

It was the longest fucking game of my life. There were no extra innings, but it felt like the game was never-ending. I stripped off everything and showered in record time. Thankfully, I'd spent time signing things and taking pictures for the guests before the game, so I was able to leave right after I dressed, while some of the players were still out on the field, meeting with the fans.

Checking my phone, I noticed no messages from Aspen, but as I exited the locker room, I found her waiting alone.

"Cricket," I called out and watched as she rolled her eyes before approaching me.

"Somehow, I'll get you to stop calling me that."

"Nope, never," I joked as I wrapped her in my arms. The players whistled and teased me as they exited the locker room behind me, but I didn't care.

"You ever going to tell me what it means?" she asked just before she pressed her lips against mine for a quick peck. No matter how many times I kissed this woman, it was like I found a new addiction every time.

"You're telling me all this time you haven't figured it out?" I asked her as I guided her out of the stadium and toward my car.

"I just assumed it had to do with the crickets you put in my backpack."

Opening the passenger door for her, I held her hand as she dipped inside. I was reluctant to let go in fear of her slipping away. As I jogged around the car, I breathed a sigh of relief when I got in and she was still there, not a figment of my imagination.

"Naw, that was just a lucky happenstance."

"Of course it was."

"Come on, cricket. Think harder."

"Owen, I have no idea. Believe me."

As I turned on the car and pulled out of the stadium parking lot, I thought about why I'd given her the nickname all those years ago.

"You're my good-luck charm, Aspen. Ever since I stepped foot into that first-grade classroom and Mrs. Epperly sat me in the chair next to you, I knew you were going to be special to me. There is a superstition that crickets represent good luck. So, that's how I came up with your nickname."

She was silent as she watched the LA skyline as we zipped down the highway.

"I'm your good luck charm?" she finally asked.

"Yep. I even have a small cricket in the bark of your tree on my arm. I didn't point it out that night you said I should get one tattooed. Thought it might freak you out, since I'd just gotten done telling you about the Aspen tree."

I knew she didn't quite understand the deeper meaning of what I was saying. She had no idea that during the beatings, during tryouts, during tests... all I had to do was think about her, and I felt a sense of peace. She was going to have to take my word for it.

After a twenty-minute drive, I pulled up to my place. It was a modern house with craftsman elements. It was much larger than one person needed, something I learned when I rented Rory's house, but it was of my first big purchases when I signed my contract with the Coyotes, so it was special.

Outside, the landscaper installed lights to shine on the house when it grew dark. The stonework along the base of the columns shimmered in the glow.

"Wow. Owen, this is beautiful."

"Thanks. I hope you like it."

I exited the car and jogged around the car to get her door. I still couldn't believe she wore the dress that nearly brought me to my knees when she first wore it.

"Baby, I'm not sure I'll be able to give you a tour tonight. I've missed you for too long."

"That's okay," she added as we stepped over the threshold. "The only thing I expect tonight is to be with you."

I brushed my lips across hers as I slammed the front door closed behind me. "That can definitely be arranged."

My hands worked quickly at peeling her dress off, though finding the zipper was a challenge. Just as it fell into a pool of material at her feet, her stomach rumbled.

"Did you eat? Are you hungry? Let me feed you."

I started to pull away, but Aspen reached out and gripped my wrist like a vice. "Don't you dare move, Owen Ramsey. I did not fly across the country to surprise you and have you feed me rather than make love to your girlfriend."

"Well, now. What is it you'd like me to do?"

"Carry me up to your bedroom, and make sure I can't walk for the rest of the week."

"Jesus," I murmured as I lifted her into my arms and carried her down the hall to the master suite.

"See? Good-luck charm," I said, showing her the tattoo when she peeled my shirt over my head after I set her on my bed. And then she launched herself at me, and

I made her come four different times before the clock struck midnight.

In the early-morning California sun, I sat at the small kitchen table, watching as Aspen cooked up some eggs and bacon, wearing nothing more than my baseball jersey. I'd already taken a dozen pictures I was sure would have her swapping my shampoo for glue if she ever found out, but she was the sexiest thing I'd ever seen.

"What's your family up to today?" I was still amazed almost her entire family traveled to LA for the week and that my mother had plotted with my coach to get Aspen to the game.

"I think they're going to do some touristy things. See the Hollywood sign. Do a celebrity bus tour. Things like that. Nate is playing tour guide."

I knew her brother-in-law lived in California before moving to Ashfield, but he didn't come across as the tour-guide type. When I mentioned it, Aspen agreed and said Alex had a backup on speed dial in the form of one of her dancer friends from school.

"And what are you doing today?" I asked as she spun around with two plates of food. She sashayed toward me, and instead of taking the seat across from me, she planted herself right on my lap, exactly where I wanted her.

"I plan on watching my boyfriend play baseball."

"Good answer," I mumbled around a delicious piece of bacon. "I could get used to this."

Watching her move around my kitchen was something I'd only fantasized about.

"I know it's probably a touchy subject, but who is watching the farm?"

"Well, funny you should ask that." Aspen set her fork down on her plate with a clink and spun around until her legs were on either side of my hips as she faced me. "Andrew is watching the farm while I'm gone."

"Well, that's nice of him."

"He's actually moving back to Ashfield to help more. And we've hired two more managers for Sunny Brook Farms."

"Okay." Her tone was suspicious. Almost like there was a "but" coming, yet not exactly.

"And I made a decision. If you're up for it."

I tried not to get my hopes up, but my heart was beating so erratically in my chest that it sounded like a marching band was playing outside my door. "What's that, cricket?"

"I was hoping that maybe I could move *here*... with you."

I swallowed, trying to keep my voice calm, even though my insides were jumping around like a cheerleader. "Really? Is that what you want?"

Her fingers twirled the lower part of my hair around my neckline as I slid my hands up and down her bare thighs.

"I want to be with you. And during our time together, you taught me to have more confidence and courage. I'm taking the leap."

"*I* didn't do that, cricket. *You* did it. I just gave you a little extra strength. Remember?"

It was the same thing I'd said to her when I helped her during the camp. Aspen always had the strength; she just needed that extra push from someone who believed in her.

"That doesn't answer my question, Owen. I don't want to overstep or anything."

"Baby, I'd move your stuff in *today*. I'll pay for a moving company to bring it all by the weekend."

She laughed so lightheartedly, with her head tilted backward, that I couldn't help but press a kiss against her exposed neck.

This woman was giving me everything I ever wanted. A friend. A companion. Love.

"So, we're doing this?" she asked as she took a few calming breaths.

"Abso-fucking-lutely. I can't wait to have my good-luck charm with me all the time."

"Maybe this time you'll actually win the championship."

She bolted off my lap as I stared at her in shock. "How dare you! You *know* we've won two already."

"A little extra luck couldn't hurt," she joked as she grabbed a piece of bacon and made her way toward the living room.

I stood up quickly and chased after her, toppling us over the back of the couch as I tackled her. Our laughs intermingled until she settled against my body, tucking her face in my neck.

"I can't believe you're really here with me and moving in."

"Believe it, superstar, I'm exactly where I want to be. With you."

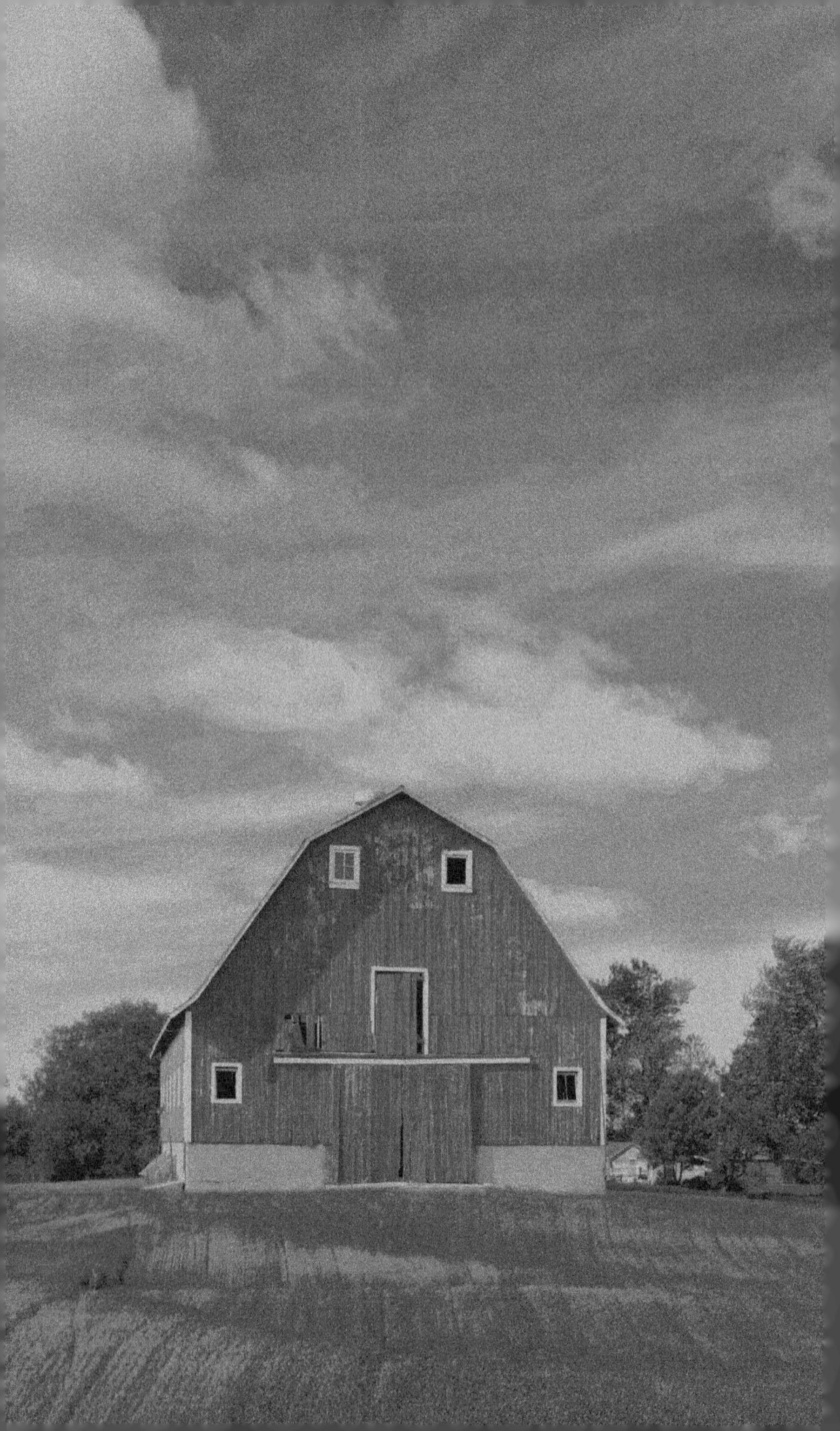

Epilogue

Aspen

Two Years Later

"Are you sure about this?" I asked for the dozenth time while hovering over Owen, who's seated at the desk in our hotel room. Beverly was on the sofa across from us.

We were in Miami for a charity event, a first for me, and I was busy writing a blog post about my ventures so far, when Owen popped into the room with a call from the general manager. The Nashville Bears were interested in a trade.

I knew he adored playing for Coach Hampton and the Coyotes. Most of the players had been at our wedding last year. And Owen had taken his team to the championships twice, winning both.

But he wanted to be closer to his mom, and with the changes about to come our way, he wanted me home with my family.

A popular travel show had taken notice of my blog and wanted to commission me for a series. I was scheduled to film two episodes as a pilot in the next month.

I worried Colton, our Food Channel Star, had something to do with it, but he assured me he didn't. His connections, however, did make it easier to convince the studio I could film anywhere. Thankfully, they agreed. Only, in my mind, I had planned to film in the guest house out back behind our home in California. Not in Tennessee.

Owen rested a reassuring hand on mine, running his finger across my wedding band and the gorgeous diamond engagement ring. It had been his grandmother's on his mom's side, and I loved that Beverly passed it down to me.

"I'm positive," he said.

We hadn't shared the news yet that we were expecting. It was still early, and I was trying to navigate the television series options available while being pregnant. I convinced Owen that we needed to wait until I was through the first trimester before telling anyone, though I was certain he let it slip to our friend, Marc. A three-foot teddy bear had been delivered to the house last week, and I had the damnedest time trying to talk my way out of that one when my mom saw it during our daily video chat.

"Please don't do this for *me*, Owen. I know how much you love the Coyotes."

"I do, and I'm thankful for everything they've done for my career. But things change. And, cricket, we—" He dropped his eyes to my stomach. "—will always come first."

"Okay," I whispered, unable to pull my gaze away as he signed his name on the trade agreement.

"And it's done!"

I giggled as he stood quickly, the chair falling backward onto the floor as he wrapped his arms around me.

"Thank you," I whispered behind my unshed tears. Though I enjoyed all the places Owen and I visited, and I adored our house, it wasn't Ashfield. I had a major case of homesickness. And being pregnant only intensified that feeling. There really was no place like home.

"I can't believe you're finally moving back," Beverly said from the couch as she swiped at the tears falling in a steady stream.

"I'm not sure if it will be Nashville or Ashfield, but either would be fine by me," I said.

"I'm thinking that plot of land your dad spoke to me about when I asked for your hand would be perfect. I don't mind a drive, cricket. So long as I have you to come home to."

I placed my hands on either side of my husband's cheeks, the diamond sparkling in the sunrays coming from the window.

"Guess I really am your good-luck charm."

"Always have been and always will be."

Stay in Touch

Newsletter: http://bit.ly/2WokAjS

Author Page: www.facebook.com/authorreneeharless

Reader Group: http://bit.ly/31AGa3B

Instagram: www.instagram.com/renee_harless

Bookbub: www.bookbub.com/authors/renee-harless

Goodreads: http://bit.ly/2TDagOn

Amazon: http://bit.ly/2WsHhPq

Website: www.reneeharless.com

Acknowledgements

This romance was so fun to bring to life. I loved the antics between Owen and Aspen when they were younger. I was giggling the entire time. I hope you enjoyed them as much as I did.

Kayla Robichaux, your ability to make my words shine deserves so much more than just my thanks. I couldn't have finished this one without you.

Patricia Rohrs, you literally are the best and I owe you so much for all the late night reading you have to do.

Crystal Burnette, for believing in me and loving this story as much as I did.

Lisa Hemming, Sally Sutherland, Kelli Harper, for being some of the sweetest and brightest beta team I've ever had.

Carolina Leon, for keeping me in line when I'd rather be doing anything else.

And to all the readers that read this book and loved it. Thank you for taking a chance on Owen and Aspen

About the Author

Renee Harless is a *USA TODAY* bestselling romance writer with an affinity for wine and a passion for telling a good story.

Renee Harless, her husband, and children live in Blue Ridge Mountains of Virginia. She studied Communication, specifically Public Relations, at Radford University.

Growing up, Renee always found a way to pursue her creativity. It began by watching endless runs of White Christmas- yes even in the summer – and learning every word and dance from the movie. She could still sing "Sister Sister" if requested. In high school, she joined the show choir and a community theatre group, The Troubadours. After marrying the man of her dreams and moving from her hometown she sought out a different artistic outlet – writing.

To say that Renee is a romance addict would be an understatement. When she isn't chasing her kids around the house, working her day job, or writing, she jumps head first into a romance novel.